GREYSTONE SECRETS

THE MESSENGERS

GREYSTONE SECRETS
THE MESSENGERS

MARGARET
PETERSON HADDIX

ART BY ANNE LAMBELET

 KATHERINE TEGEN BOOKS
An Imprint of HarperCollins Publishers

Katherine Tegen Books is an imprint of HarperCollins Publishers.

Greystone Secrets #3: The Messengers

Library of Congress Cataloging-in-Publication Data

Names: Haddix, Margaret Peterson, author.
Title: The messengers / by Margaret Peterson Haddix.
Description: First edition. | New York : Katherine Tegen Books, an imprint
   of HarperCollins Publishers, [2021] | Series: Greystone secrets ; #3 |
   Audience: Ages 8-12. | Audience: Grades 4-6. | Summary: Told from
   separate viewpoints, as evil forces from the parallel world invade their
   home, the Greystones, their doubles, and friends must return to the
   alternate dimension to save both worlds.
Identifiers: LCCN 2020023308 | ISBN 9780062838438 (hardcover)
Subjects: CYAC: Brothers and sisters—Fiction. | Family life—Fiction. |
   Brainwashing—Fiction. | Good and evil—Fiction. | Supernatural—Fiction.
Classification: LCC PZ7.H1164 Me 2021 | DDC [Fic]—dc23
LC record available at https://lccn.loc.gov/2020023308

Typography by Aurora Parlagreco
21 22 23 24 25   PC/LSCH   10 9 8 7 6 5 4 3 2 1
❖
First Edition

For truth tellers everywhere

ONE

FINN

Mom inched the car into the garage. The Greystones were finally home.

But nobody moved until Mom said, "Quick. Grab whatever you need from the house, and let's get out of here."

Finn's older sister and brother, Emma and Chess, sprang out of the car and dashed for the door into the kitchen. But Finn shook his head.

"I don't need anything." He dived into the front seat of the car, grabbed Mom's hand, and held on tight. "I'll help *you.*"

"Oh, Finn," Mom said. She drew up the corners of her

mouth into a shaky smile. "You can take your favorite toys. Or games. There's room. It might be a while before we come back here again. Or . . ." She looked down at Finn's hand in hers and whispered, "It might be forever."

A month ago, Mom wouldn't have said that. She would have pretended everything was fine. She *had* pretended everything was fine, actually—back then, she hadn't told Finn or Emma or even Chess how much danger she was in. She'd just left, and pretended it was an ordinary "business trip."

A month ago, she'd probably treated Finn and Emma and Chess as though they were younger than eight and ten and twelve.

Now it felt like they'd all grown up.

And *Mom* was the one *they* needed to protect.

"Toys and games?" Finn said, like those were unfamiliar words. The corners of Mom's mouth quivered. He tried again. "We're going to stay at Ms. Morales's house for now, right? She's got all the old toys and games Natalie outgrew. We could probably play forever and never get to them all." He leaned close and whispered, "They're really rich. You know?"

Mom's smile almost looked real now.

"And generous," she murmured.

"Come on," Finn said.

He reached past her to open Mom's car door. Together,

they walked into the house. Chess was coming up from the basement.

"All clear," he reported. "Emma checked upstairs and I checked downstairs. There's nobody here."

Mom put her hand over her mouth. Her already-pale face turned completely white.

"*I* should have checked," she said. "I should have left you three kids in the car until I knew for sure it was safe. . . ."

Chess might as well have had his thoughts written on his face: *Nowhere's safe.* But he patted Mom on the arm and repeated, "Nobody's here."

Chess was at that age when it seemed like he could grow three inches taller overnight. That must have happened last night, because he towered over Mom now. His arms and legs looked even spindlier and more stretched out than ever, as though his whole body were made of Silly Putty and someone had pulled it too far.

"But anybody could show up, anytime," Mom muttered. "If they've been using our house as a crossing point . . ."

She meant the bad guys. Finn, Emma, and Chess had known nothing about it until a month ago, but all four of the Greystones had escaped from a bad place when Finn was only a baby. The bad place was a completely different world—Finn had started thinking of it as almost a mirror image of the world he'd known most of his life. Duplicated versions of lots of people existed in both worlds, but they were sadder and meaner—or at least more desperate—in the other world.

Even some of the people who were actually nice in the other world had to *pretend* to be mean, just to survive.

Finn liked to think of it as though his entire family had escaped from the bad world when he was only a baby, but he knew that wasn't completely true.

His father had died in the other world. He'd been *killed*.

And could you really say that his family had escaped, when the bad people had found a way to follow them?

And when Finn, Emma, and Chess—and their friend Natalie—had had to go back to the other world again and again, and they still hadn't ended all the danger?

"We're going to fix everything," Finn said now. "We're going to make it so the bad guys never bother us again. We'll make it so they never bother anyone again! Even in the other world!"

Mom ruffled Finn's hair. She always did that. If he'd wanted to, Finn could have closed his eyes and imagined that the last month of his life hadn't happened, and he was still just a goofy little kid whose worst problems were that his hair stuck up whether anyone mussed it or not, and he had trouble remembering not to talk all the time in class.

But Finn kept his eyes open, and fixed on Mom's face.

"You're . . . so brave," she whispered. "My little Finn. Who knew?" She turned to Chess. "And you and Emma . . ."

"Mom, we really shouldn't stay here long," Chess said gently. "I just need one box from upstairs, and then I'll be ready. I don't think Emma wanted much more than that."

Mom squared her shoulders.

"Then Finn and I will get everything I need from the Boring Room," she said.

The Boring Room was what the Greystone kids had always called their mother's basement office. It had turned out not to be so boring, after all. Finn hoped neither Mom nor Chess noticed how hard he had to work to quell a shiver of fear as he started walking toward the stairs.

Halfway down the steps, Mom sniffed, made a face, and laughed.

"I guess you were all too busy rescuing me to clean Rocket's kitty litter, huh?" she asked.

"It wasn't my turn," Finn said. "Honest!"

And just for a moment, this felt normal and right, to argue over chores. But the Greystones' pet cat, Rocket, was still at Natalie's dad's house, and there was no telling when they'd be reunited.

And when Finn reached the bottom of the stairs, the first thing he saw was a pile of Hot Wheels cars. Emma had dumped them on the floor a week ago when she and Chess had received an unpleasant surprise.

We won't have any surprises today, Finn told himself. *See? This is just our normal basement rec room, and that's just Mom's normal Boring Room over there. . . .*

He trailed Mom into the Boring Room with its empty desk and vacant bookshelves. And then Finn couldn't pretend anything was normal, because the secret door to the hidden space behind the Boring Room hung wide open. Mom turned on the light and ducked through the secret doorway to peer around at the shelves holding canned food and boxes of cash. The shelves at the back of the secret room were cracked and sagging. But that was the only sign that a tunnel had once lain behind those shelves, leading into the other world.

Mom picked up a can of tuna fish and absentmindedly rolled it back and forth in her hands.

"I thought I was so well prepared," she muttered.

Finn grabbed one of the boxes.

"We should take the cash," he said, because anybody could have figured *that* out.

He opened the box—it was empty.

"The police already took it as evidence," Mom said. "Mr. Mayhew explained all about that." Mr. Mayhew was Natalie's dad. "I'll have to go down to the police station and claim it and . . . I just haven't felt up to doing that yet. You know. I may have to lie."

"Because the police don't know about the other world," Finn said. "They don't know you were trapped there. Because they *can't* know about the other world."

This made Mom snort and nearly giggle, and it was like having Normal-Mom back, Before-Everything-Happened-Mom back.

"Can you imagine telling them the truth?" she asked. "They'd never believe me!"

"Honest, Officer!" Finn said, as though she'd asked him to act it out. "You *really* don't want to meet your evil twin!"

Mom's smile faded.

"Finn . . . remember, *we're* from the other world," she murmured, still rolling the tuna can back and forth in her hands. "You can't assume one world's all good and the other's all evil. I have to believe that everyone in the other world still has the capacity to—"

She broke off as chimes pealed through the house. It was the doorbell.

"Mom?" Chess called from above. "I don't know who . . ."

Mom took off running for the stairs. Finn was right on her heels.

Then Finn heard Emma cry from even farther away: "No, Mom, I see who it is! Stay hidden!"

TWO

EMMA, A FEW MINUTES EARLIER

Emma had just picked up the book *Codes and Ciphers for Kids* when she heard a car drive by outside. Her heart thumping, she raced to her bedroom window.

A rust-colored SUV was pulling into the driveway next door.

And . . . it was just their neighbors, the Hans, bringing their son Ian home from a soccer game. He had a smear of mud across his face, and his green uniform looked sweaty.

Perfectly normal, Emma thought. *Nothing out of the ordinary.*

She was pretty sure Ian had soccer games every Saturday. Still, it took a moment for her heart rate to return to normal.

This is . . . not very scientific of me, Emma thought.

If she made a pie chart showing her entire life, she could label almost all of it "Normal" or "Ordinary." Or maybe "Happy and Fun." Maybe that was the label she really wanted. Only a tiny sliver—the past month—would need the label "Weird and Scary."

So didn't it stand to reason that most of what she saw around her now would continue to be ordinary and normal?

Oops, she thought. *I forgot about the first two years of my life, when we all lived in the other world. That was weird and scary, too. I just didn't know it.*

And, really, hadn't her entire ten years of life always had weird stuff going on in the background? She'd just *thought* everything was ordinary and normal because she didn't know about the other world or the secrets Mom had been keeping until about a month ago.

Anyhow, the labels shouldn't be "Happy and Fun" vs. "Weird and Scary," she told herself. *Those aren't opposites.*

The happiest moment of her life had been rescuing her mom from the other world. And even though she'd been worried and scared, she'd had fun figuring out the codes that Mom had left behind. On their trips to the other world, those codes had helped the Greystone kids and their friend Natalie to rescue not only Mom, but also Natalie's mom, a man named Joe Deweese, and three kids who were the closest thing this world had to doubles of Emma, Chess, and Finn. Those three—the Gustano kids—had been kidnapped by people from the other world who thought the Gustano kids belonged to Mom. The Gustanos' mom *was* this world's version of Mom, but their father wasn't like the Greystones' dad. So the kids weren't exact duplicates like their mothers were.

And the Gustanos belonged in this world, where everything was normal and ordinary and sane. While the Greystones were . . . were . . .

Caught in between?

Emma decided it was too messy to try to figure out the right description—or a pie chart of her life. She liked it better when math and science gave her clear-cut, logical answers.

She liked it when life made sense.

She looked down at the book in her hand, *Codes and Ciphers for Kids.* She'd had the idea that maybe she should take the book with her to Ms. Morales's house. Just in case there were more codes to crack as the Greystones and Natalie's family decided what to do next. But after everything Emma had been through, the book looked babyish now. Nobody was going to slip her a message written in lemon juice. Nobody was going to send her codes as easy to decipher as pig latin.

She put the book back on her shelf. There really wasn't anything she needed from her room. During the past month, the three Greystone kids had been living with first Natalie's mom and then Natalie's dad, so Emma already had all the clothes she wanted.

But Emma still slid open her closet door and dug past boxes of Legos and crumpled-up diagrams of inventions she might make someday. At the back of the closet, she found a little plastic safe that she'd begged for at Christmas one year. She spun the combination lock forward and back and forward again, and the door swung open.

The only things she kept inside were an old-fashioned calculator that had belonged to Mom when she was a little girl, and a piece of paper with columns of numbers scrawled from top to bottom. As far as Emma knew, the numbers were just scribblings, a scratch pad of notes. Gibberish. But her father had written those numbers. And even though Emma had been only two when he died, she could remember clutching this paper and saying to Mom, "Daddy did? Daddy did?"

And Mom would always say, "Yes, that's your father's math."

Was that the only nudge Emma needed to fall in love with math, even as a two-year-old?

Emma heard another car puttering a little too slowly down the street. She tensed, listening hard.

Stop it! she told herself. *It's a public street. All sorts of vehicles drive by all the time. This has nothing to do with my family. Or the other world* . . .

She shoved her thick, dark, curly hair away from her face and forced herself to go back to staring at the page full of numbers. With everything else they had to worry about, wasn't it just silly and sentimental to want to take this paper with her?

Outside, the car shut off its engine. It sounded . . . close.

Emma stomped her feet with impatience, because she *couldn't* stop straining to listen to what was happening outdoors. She tried to force herself to study her shoes instead: her favorite red sneakers. Emma could remember her joy at finding these shoes on a shopping trip with Mom a few months ago. It felt like Emma had been a totally different person then—someone who had no trouble concentrating on numbers. Someone who knew nothing about other worlds or danger.

Someone who thought happiness was as simple as a pair of red shoes.

Thud. Thud. Those were definitely car doors closing outside. Emma couldn't help analyzing the sounds. Had a third or fourth door shut at the same time? Was each *thud* doubled?

Emma gave up and went back to the window.

A tan car sat in the Greystones' driveway. It wasn't one Emma recognized. But that didn't mean anything, because ever since Mom had gotten back from the other world, people kept calling and stopping by to bring them casseroles and congratulations, celebratory cards and gifts. The Greystones' friends didn't even know the whole story, but they were so relieved that everything had turned out okay and the family's long ordeal was over.

(At least, most of their friends thought the ordeal was over. Natalie's family and Joe Deweese knew better.)

Emma heard footsteps. The tan car was close to the garage, and Emma had taken too long getting to the window. So whoever had been in the car was already on the sidewalk leading to the front porch. And Emma couldn't see that sidewalk because the porch roof blocked her view. She had to yank her window open and poke her head out.

And she'd delayed a little too long doing that, too. She caught only a quick glimpse of the last person to step onto the porch.

No, it was too fast even to be called a glimpse. It was more like an impression—the *idea* of the person, not the actual view.

And still Emma recognized the person exactly: her stance, her bearing, the way she swung her arms when she walked, the way she clenched her jaw to brace herself for some unpleasant task or chore. Emma had never met this person before in her life, but she knew exactly who it was:

Mom's double from this world. Mrs. Gustano.

Oh no. Oh no . . .

They'd all been so worried about dangerous people from the other world showing up again. Why hadn't any of them thought about how certain people from this world were huge threats, too?

Emma jerked her head back into the house, slammed the window shut, and took off racing for the stairs.

THREE

CHESS

Chess opened the front door.

Somebody had to do it, and Emma was too busy rushing for the basement and yelling to Mom, "Stay down there! Don't come out!" And Chess always wanted to protect Finn. As for Mom . . .

Now I have to protect her, too.

So Chess stood alone, clutching the front door, as he regarded the woman and three kids huddled together on the Greystones' front porch.

It was like seeing ghosts.

The last time Chess had viewed Rocky, Emma, and Finn

Gustano, the three of them had been laughing and crying all at once, and screaming, "We escaped from the kidnappers! We're free!" They'd had what appeared to be an entire police force clustered jubilantly around them, tucking blankets around their shoulders and handing them Styrofoam cups of hot chocolate.

And high-fiving them. The cops had high-fived the Gustanos *a lot*.

Now the three Gustano kids stood silent and wary on the Greystones' porch. You might even say they looked surly. It was disorienting for Chess, especially when the three kids looked so much like Chess and his siblings. They weren't identical matches—it wasn't like with Chess's friend Natalie and her exact duplicate from the other world, Other-Natalie. The Gustanos had slightly different hair colors and slightly different heights than the Greystones; they had a slightly bigger nose here, a slightly smaller mouth there, as if someone had played around with altering pictures on some phone app. But the three Gustanos could easily have been cousins of the three Greystones—cousins whose mothers were identical twins, maybe. Finn Gustano's shoulders sagged just like Finn Greystone's shoulders did when he was sad or worried (which had almost never happened before a month ago). Emma Gustano had her jaw thrust up into the air the same way Emma Greystone did when she was

16

observing everything around her and thinking hard.

And then there was Rocky Gustano—who also carried the given name "Rochester" but had a different nickname than Chess. Rocky had his arms cradled protectively around his younger siblings in a way that Chess recognized instantly.

No, no, no! Chess wanted to yell at the family clustered before him. *You all got the happy ending! The* completely *happy ending! While we're still . . . floundering. Why did you come back? Why risk getting messed up in our lives again?*

But all he said was a faint, "Yes?"

Rocky took a step forward, neatly tucking his brother and sister behind him. He kept his arms protectively on their shoulders.

"We need to know the truth, Chess," Rocky said. "You told us what to say to the cops so we could just go home. That was all we wanted three weeks ago. But now, but now . . . we have to know why we were kidnapped. Why *us*. Why we ended up in a basement in Ohio, when we'd barely been out of Arizona before. Why everything was so strange. Why . . ."

"Please?"

This came from Mrs. Gustano. Somehow Chess had managed not to look at her until now. Because she was Mom exactly, but she *wasn't* Mom. Mrs. Gustano's face was tanner and more weathered—not surprising for someone who lived

17

in Arizona. Mrs. Gustano's hair was cut short and pixie-like; Mom usually kept her hair pulled back into a messy ponytail. Mom tended to make haircut appointments and then cancel them at the last minute because "something came up."

For the first time ever, it occurred to Chess that maybe the "something" that so often came up was related to the other world. Maybe Mom had been dropping clues about the other world all along, and Chess, Emma, and Finn just hadn't known it.

Chess threw a glance back over his shoulder. Mom, Emma, and Finn were still down in the basement. Out of sight.

Good.

"I understand why you think you want to know the truth," Chess said carefully. He pulled the door closer against his shoulders, so none of the Gustanos could see past him if someone came running up the stairs. No—if *Mom* came running up the stairs.

There was no way Chess could let the Gustanos see how much Mom and Mrs. Gustano looked alike.

"It's not just something we *think* we want," Emma Gustano said, tossing her head in a way that made her look even more like Chess's sister.

"We all have to go see counselors now, and social workers, and people like that," Finn Gustano piped up. "And they all say we need to understand what happened to us so we can 'heal.' I guess it's kind of like needing a Band-Aid."

"Or ripping off a Band-Aid," Rocky said.

Was he the Gustano who was least like any of the Greystones? Rocky seemed like the kind of kid who would rip off Band-Aids all at once, as quickly as possible.

Chess preferred the gradual approach, exposing barely a millimeter of skin to pain at a time.

"Okay," Chess said weakly. "But sometimes knowing the truth . . . sometimes it's not enough. Sometimes it just leads to more questions. And . . . more danger."

Mrs. Gustano pulled her kids closer, like a mother hen gathering chicks in under her wings. This too was a gesture Chess recognized.

"We can't stay ignorant, Chess," she said, her voice a dead ringer for Mom's. "Not when the police are saying now that my husband was involved in the kidnapping. Not when they say they have *proof*."

Chess felt the door being yanked from his grasp. And then Mom was there beside him, drilling her gaze into Mrs. Gustano's. Chess heard all three of the Gustano kids gasp.

"What did you just say?" Mom demanded of Mrs. Gustano. "Proof? That can't be true!"

FOUR

FINN

Finn tucked himself between Mom's leg and the doorframe. He, Emma, and Mom had crept up the basement stairs and hidden in the kitchen, listening intently. *He'd* thought they were going to stay there until Chess sent the Gustanos away.

But the word "proof" sent Mom running for the front door.

Of course Finn and Emma had to follow her. Emma kept hissing, "Stop! Mom, no—this isn't a good idea. . . . She'll see you. . . ."

Finn was pretty much fine with anything Mom wanted to do, as long as he could stay glued to her side.

Now the two sets of moms and kids just stood there on opposite sides of the doorway, staring at each other.

"Kate Greystone," Mrs. Gustano said, in a way that made Finn think of a sheriff in some old Western movie challenging, "This town ain't big enough for the two of us."

"I'm sorry," Mom whispered. "I'm so sorry for everything that happened to you."

Mrs. Gustano gave a ragged laugh.

"The police said you and I looked a lot alike, but I thought they were exaggerating," she murmured. "I thought they had too much imagination, because they were just looking at fuzzy photos of you from when you . . . went missing. I thought they'd messed up when they said our fingerprints were virtually identical. Even identical twins don't have identical fingerprints! But standing here now, seeing you directly . . . how is this even possible?"

The other Finn tugged on his mom's arm and said in a tone he probably thought was a whisper, "If that lady put on a wig and a little makeup, she'd look *exactly* like you, Mom. *Is* she a twin you never knew you had?"

Mom cast a glance far past the Gustanos. It was like she was scanning for dangers on their quiet street. Far down the block, three girls were jumping rope together while a smaller boy made chalk drawings on the sidewalk. A man in one yard was mowing his grass; a woman in another yard was spreading mulch. Finn knew all the kids—Harper, Paisley, Emilia, and Sebastian—and he was pretty sure Mom knew the grown-ups.

Still, when Mom looked back at Mrs. Gustano, she spoke in a hushed way, as if she feared being overheard: "Perhaps you should all step inside, so we can talk privately." She held the door open wide, and drew Chess, Emma, and Finn to the side to make room for the Gustanos.

"Perhaps you can understand. No one in my family wants to walk back into a house where my kids were held prisoner," Mrs. Gustano said. "No offense."

She had the same look on her face that Mom always got when she told Finn he couldn't push his bedtime back anymore, he couldn't have a second serving of ice cream, and he really had to start doing his homework *right now*. And then the way she said, "No offense," made it sound like she was waving a sword.

It was like she was really saying, *I will defend my kids no matter what. I will make sure no one hurts them or frightens them ever again. And I don't care how that makes anyone else feel.*

That was exactly how Mom sounded, talking about protecting Chess, Emma, and Finn.

But Mrs. Gustano was *wrong*.

"You think your kids were held prisoner here?" Finn exploded. He was almost eye to eye with the other Finn, so he addressed him directly: "I know you couldn't tell the cops everything, but didn't you guys tell your *mom* what really happened? That this was just where we brought you when we *rescued* you, and the kidnappers were never *here*?"

Other-Finn kicked his sneaker against the strip of wood at the bottom of the doorway.

"All the grown-ups say we're just confused about what really happened," he muttered. "Because you told us to *lie* starting out, they don't believe anything we say now."

"Finn, honey, that's not exactly . . . it's not that Daddy and I think you three are still lying." Mrs. Gustano patted the other boy's back in such a familiar way. "It's just . . . being kidnapped had to have been so traumatic. Sometimes people's minds—kids' *and* grown-ups' minds—when something awful happens to you, your mind doesn't store memories the same way it would if things were . . . normal." She went back to glaring at Mom. "My kids and I are not walking into any small, confined space where we could be trapped with strangers. I'm sure you can understand. We don't do anything anymore if we're not sure it's *safe*."

"But you came here," Emma said, as if presenting scientific evidence. "*You* rang *our* doorbell. You took that risk."

"Yes, well . . ." And now Mrs. Gustano sounded even more like Mom. She seemed just as vague and lost and worried as Mom had been for the past week.

"I don't like small, confined spaces anymore, either," Mom said. Finn remembered that she'd been in prison in the other world; she'd had weeks of being trapped, desperate, and alone.

"So we talk outside, in a public place," Mrs. Gustano said. "Somewhere either of us can walk away any time we want. A park, maybe?"

"No," Mom said. "Anyone could spy on us there. Anyone could eavesdrop."

Now it was like the two moms were having a staring contest, each one silently daring the other to blink.

The silence stretched on and on.

Grown-ups could be so ridiculous.

Finn looked straight at Other-Finn.

"Are you hungry?" he asked. "There's this restaurant in our town, the Cuckoo Clock, where they have really good cheeseburgers. And they have these rooms where people have birthday parties sometimes. We could go there, the moms could talk, and you and me, we could eat as much as we want!"

"I *am* hungry," Other-Finn said, starting to grin back at him. "I'm always hungry."

"That . . . could actually work," Mom said.

Mrs. Gustano nodded.

Finn wanted to jump up and down and laugh at how

easy that had been. That made him think other things might be easier than the grown-ups thought, too. He tilted his head back to peer up at Mrs. Gustano.

"I bet that 'proof' the police say they have about Mr. Gustano being involved in the kidnapping is just a big mistake," Finn told her. "I bet it's nothing to worry about at all!"

Mrs. Gustano raised an eyebrow at Finn, and now it didn't matter that Mrs. Gustano had shorter hair and tanner skin than Mom. This was *exactly* Mom's "Oh, yeah? We'll see about *that*" look.

"The police say my husband's fingerprints were found in your family's basement," Mrs. Gustano said. "My husband insists he was never there. But I *don't* think it's a mistake. I think someone planted evidence. And I'm going to clear my husband's name if it's the last thing I do. The kids and I— we're going to prove him innocent!"

FIVE

EMMA

"I'm sure your husband *is* innocent," Emma told Mrs. Gustano. "Any fingerprints the police found, those had to belong to his double from—"

"Emma," Mom said sternly, pulling her so close that Emma had to stop talking or else she would have ended up with a mouthful of Mom's T-shirt. "Not here. Let's wait to tell the Gustanos everything at the Cuckoo Clock."

Emma pulled back and peered up at Mom. *Would* Mom tell the Gustanos the whole story? Or would she gloss over the truth and reveal only enough to stop the Gustanos' questions?

Emma sneaked a glance at the other Emma. She was waggling her eyebrows up and down and muttering, "Doubles? How could Dad have a double? He isn't a twin, and anyhow, a twin wouldn't have the same fingerprints. And besides . . ."

Emma was pretty sure the ideas were exploding in the other girl's head just as fast and frantically as in Emma's. Emma knew a lot about the other world—and she'd seen doubles there of people she knew in this world—but she still had a million questions.

Why was the other-world version of Mr. Gustano in our basement? Could he have been one of the bad people from the other world creeping in and out through our house? Why were they doing that?

Emma's heart started beating too rapidly again.

"So, the Cuckoo Clock," Mrs. Gustano repeated, pulling out her cell phone and beginning to type. "I'll put that in my GPS and—"

Mom reached out and shoved Mrs. Gustano's phone back toward her purse. It was the rudest thing Emma had ever seen her mother do.

"*Don't* use GPS," Mom said. "I'll give you directions. And turn off the location tracker—no, turn the whole phone off. That would be safest."

Emma waited for Mrs. Gustano to refuse. After all, Mrs. Gustano had more reasons to suspect Mom than to trust her. Wouldn't she think keeping her phone on could help prevent another kidnapping?

But Mrs. Gustano's eyes met Mom's, and she slowly nodded.

"I see," she said.

The two women were almost smiling at each other.

Weird, Emma thought.

It was like how their friend Natalie and her double, Other-Natalie, had seemed so much in sync in the other world. They'd finished each other's sentences; they'd acted like they'd known each other their whole lives even though they'd just met. Finn had claimed that they were even more alike than identical twins.

Do all duplicate people just . . . match . . . when they're together? Emma wondered.

Maybe that would happen with all the exact duplicates of people from both worlds, if they encountered one another. But the two worlds existed because people had made different choices, creating different outcomes. Could a duplicate from one world control her double from the other?

Which world's people were more powerful?

Emma remembered that people from the bad world had poisoned Natalie's grandmother.

But we're from the bad world, too, and we want to do good things, and . . .

Maybe Emma should just stick to figuring out similarities

and differences between the Greystones and the Gustanos.

Emma tried to peer at Other-Emma as intently as Mom was staring at Mrs. Gustano. The other girl didn't just have a slightly rounder face and softer features than Emma. It also looked like she'd combed her hair more carefully than Emma ever did hers; it looked like her eyes were wider and she was even more dazed than Emma was by the weird turns their lives had taken in the past month.

The other Emma also did not seem to feel Emma's gaze on her. She didn't immediately turn to stare back at Emma—it wasn't anything like how Natalie and Other-Natalie behaved together, or how Mom and Mrs. Gustano acted.

That's got to be evidence of . . . something, Emma thought. She and Other-Emma were only near-duplicates; they weren't exact genetic matches. Apparently the mind-meld factor only worked for total duplicates like their mothers.

"Okay, we'll meet there in fifteen minutes," Mrs. Gustano said, turning to go. Emma realized she'd missed hearing the rest of the logistics the two mothers had worked out.

Mom shut the front door and Emma saw through the front window that the Gustanos went back to their car. Emma trailed Mom and her brothers back to the garage. Belatedly, Emma realized she was still carrying the little plastic safe and the paper holding her father's handwriting. As she got into the car, she stuffed the paper back into the safe, spun the combination lock, and tucked the safe under the front seat of the car. It clunked into a hard, oblong object in a thick fabric case meant for carrying baseball bats. Emma clutched the case and could instantly tell: The object inside had nothing to do with baseball.

"Mom, you brought the lever?" she gasped. "You've been carrying it around with us all along?"

The lever was their key to traveling between the worlds. The Greystone kids had first found it on the wall of the secret room in their own basement. They'd ripped it off the wall to close the tunnel when police officers and guards from the other world were chasing them. They'd lost two weeks before figuring out that the lever could be used in other locations as well.

Mom bit her lip and sagged against the open car door.

"I shouldn't . . . have left it in the car," she murmured. "I should have strapped it to my back, kept it with me every minute. . . ."

"Because you think we might need to use it at any minute?" Chess asked. He sounded every bit as distraught as Mom.

"*No*," Mom said. "Don't worry about *that*. I just don't want any of our . . . opponents . . . to find it. And I can't think of anywhere safe to leave it. . . ."

Mom got into the car along with Emma, Chess, and

Finn. Mom hit the release to open the garage door, which made Emma remember that Chess had been the one who'd thought to close it in the first place.

Mom is . . . rattled, Emma thought. *We really do need to watch out for her.*

Mom turned the car on and backed out of the driveway. The Gustanos' car was idling on the street, waiting. Apparently they were just going to follow Mom.

None of the Greystones said anything as Mom drove them toward the center of town. Somehow the familiar scenery around them made Emma feel better, though. It was a lovely spring day, and flowers bloomed in their neighbors' yards. When they got to the streets filled with shops and restaurants, all the friendly signs around them—"Welcome!" "Celebrating thirty-five years of being your neighborhood hardware store!" "Come sample our new ice cream flavors!"—made Emma think about how different everything had felt in the other world. There, all the houses were hidden behind fences or walls or forbidding thick hedges. Beyond the neighborhoods where people lived, all the buildings were cold steel and glass, with blue-and-orange banners everywhere. Emma had never even understood what the banners stood for; they just made her feel scared.

They reached the Cuckoo Clock parking lot, and all the Greystones got out. Mom picked up the baseball-bat carrier with the lever inside and slipped it onto her shoulder.

"Mom, I'll carry that," Chess said. "I can pretend I've got a game later today, or something like that."

"Don't you think I could be in an adult softball league?" Mom challenged, with an attempt at a grin.

Either way, it looks weird to carry that into the restaurant, Emma thought.

But she didn't say it aloud.

They walked into the Cuckoo Clock, and the Gustanos joined them.

"Oooh," Finn Gustano gasped, and Emma couldn't help smiling. People always reacted that way, seeing this restaurant for the first time. The entire back wall—two stories' worth—*was* a cuckoo clock, with clock hands that were taller than Chess.

"Just wait until that door opens and the cuckoo comes out," Finn said, pointing to the top of the clock.

"Table for eight in a private room, please," Mom said to the hostess. "Indoors."

"That'll get you to the front of the line," the hostess said. "It's so beautiful today, everybody else wants outdoors."

She led the Greystones and Gustanos to an empty, glassed-in room by the back wall, so close that Emma could make out the cheerful expressions on the enormous carvings at the side of the giant clock. Puppies, kittens, goldfish, turtles, penguins . . . so many happy wooden creatures seemed to tumble joyously past the numbers marking the hours.

Everyone got a menu as they all sat down. As soon as the hostess left the room, Mom turned to Mrs. Gustano.

"You're not wearing a wire to tape everything I say for the police or the FBI, are you?" she asked.

"Of course not!" Mrs. Gustano protested. "Believe me, the police did *not* think it was a good idea for us to come here and meet you in person."

"But you came anyway," Mom murmured. "And . . . you probably let them think that you were following their advice."

It would have been smart for Mrs. Gustano to say, "No! Of course the police know we're here! All sorts of authorities know we're here!" But she just kept staring steadily back at Mom.

"Okay, I get it," Mom said.

It was almost as if they could communicate without talking.

Thinking hard, Emma glanced back at the carved wooden creatures on the clock. She'd been to the Cuckoo Clock plenty of times, but she'd never sat in this particular spot in this particular room before.

So she'd never before noticed that not all of the carved

wooden creatures on the giant clock were animals.

And yet, one of the figures on the clock looked so familiar. . . .

Suddenly Emma realized where she'd seen it before. She jumped up, practically knocking over her chair.

"I've . . . got to go to the bathroom!" she announced. "Chess, Finn—didn't you say in the car that you needed to go to the bathroom, too?"

"Uh, no, I'm fi—" Finn began.

But Chess met Emma's eyes.

"You're right, Emma," he said. "Whether Finn remembers or not, that is a *great* idea, to do that before we order. . . ."

He hauled Finn up out of his chair. Finn blinked twice, but stopped protesting.

And Emma had to quickly turn toward the door to hide her grin.

She, Chess, and Finn definitely weren't duplicates of one another. But sometimes they could read each other's minds, too.

Emma rushed out the door of the private dining room toward the mysterious carvings of the wooden clock. And her brothers were right behind her.

They knew she needed them.

SIX

CHESS

"There," Emma said, pointing at a carved angel on the clock's face, just slightly to the right of the numeral 5. "What does that remind you of?"

Chess instantly felt dizzy, thrown back into frightening memories. He left it to Finn to whisper a reply: "Judge Morales's desk."

Judge Morales was the other-world version of their friend Natalie's mom. For most of the time the Greystone kids and Natalie had spent in the other world, they'd been terrified of the Judge; they'd believed she was one of the most evil people in that horrible place.

They'd believed she was their mother's worst enemy.

Only in their last, desperate moments in the other world had they found out that the Judge was like a double agent—only pretending to be evil, while secretly working behind the scenes to rescue people.

And one of the Judge's behind-the-scenes secrets was that she could sit at her desk in her home office and spy on people in lots of other locations. The little buttons for calling up those spied-upon scenes were hidden in carvings on the underside of her desk—carvings of angels and lambs, not the scary-looking demons and wolves that seemed to dominate all the other carvings the Greystones and Natalie had seen in the other world.

And the angels carved into the underside of the Judge's desk in the other world had been *exactly* like this angel carved into the face of the giant clock.

"This doesn't mean anything," Chess whispered to Emma. "Except, I guess, that the wood carver who made the Judge's desk in the other world has a double in this world who carved this clock."

"No, look closer," Emma insisted. "This angel is carved in a different style than the entire rest of the clock. Look how the cuts are made, how the angel is smiling. . . . It's like this is *art*. Not . . ."

Not cartoonish carvings in a restaurant for little kids' birthday parties, Chess thought.

"So what happens if you press this angel's wing?" Finn asked, reaching out.

"Be careful!" Chess grabbed his brother's hand away, because this seemed dangerous. Pressing the angel's wing in the other world had been a good thing, but the worlds were mirrored—practically mirror-image opposites. So would it be a mistake to press this carved angel wing?

Emma glanced back over her shoulder, as if checking to make sure that Mom and the Gustanos hadn't noticed that the three Greystone kids had stopped before reaching the bathrooms. Or maybe Emma was checking to make sure that no one else was watching them either.

"Chess—we really should try it," she murmured. "Just in case."

"Okay, okay," Chess agreed. "But let me do it."

What if some knife suddenly dropped out of the clock's face and cut him? What if this turned out to be another way to open a tunnel into the other world? What if it made the clock collapse on top of them? Or . . .

Chess shuddered, and told himself to stop being so paranoid. He pressed his finger hard against the angel's wing.

At first, nothing happened. But then the angel's jaw

dropped, and a small, round metal token slipped out.

A coin.

Chess caught it in his hand.

"What is it? Let me see!" Finn cried.

Chess unclenched his hand and held out his palm to the other two. The coin glistened, nestled against his lifeline. It wasn't money—or, at least, not any kind Chess had seen before. The coin's brassy color made it hard to read the letters along its edge.

No, that wasn't the only reason the coin was so hard to read.

"It's code!" Emma breathed reverently. "More code!"

SEVEN

FINN

"But it's not even the alphabet!" Finn complained.

"It's not *our* alphabet," Emma corrected.

And then suddenly she closed her hand over Chess's palm and the coin, and she yanked Chess's arm back down to his side.

"What are you looking at?" a voice asked behind them.

It was Rocky Gustano.

He was a little shorter than Chess, but somehow he seemed to cast more of a shadow. A more *menacing* shadow.

But that's just because you know Chess, and you know he's always nice, Finn told himself. *Maybe Finn and Emma Gustano see Chess and think* he's *scary.*

"We're not looking at anything," Emma said, totally sounding like she was lying.

"Don't you know where the bathrooms are?" Rocky asked. "Or did you get lost?"

"We just stopped to admire . . . the clock," Chess said weakly.

Finn loved his sister and brother more than anyone else in the whole world besides Mom. But they were both terrible actors.

"We have this game, see?" Finn said. "Every time we come here, we pick an animal and count how many times that animal shows up on the clock. Today we're counting monkeys."

Rocky cast a quick glance at the clock.

"Thirty-two," he said.

Emma gasped. "You figured it out that fast?"

Rocky rolled his eyes.

"*No*," he said. He flipped back the dark hair that hung down into his eyes. "I'm just messing with you."

Huh, Finn thought. *Rocky* is *good at lying.*

But then Rocky's face went soft and defenseless. "You guys can still do that?" he asked. "Play silly baby games? Even after everything that happened when we were all . . . in that place?"

Finn tried to decide if he should be offended by the term "silly baby games." But Emma said, "Sometimes we pretend to," and Chess said, "Not very well," and it was clear that they weren't trying to act anymore.

"None of you had to go to the bathroom, did you?" Rocky asked.

"No," Finn said. "We needed to talk."

"Is *your* mom okay?" Chess asked Rocky.

Rocky snorted.

"She's better off than our dad right now," he muttered.

Sometimes it was a jolt for Finn to be reminded that other kids had *two* parents in their lives, two adults who meant everything to them. Or, sometimes, even three or four.

But the feeling was even worse around the Gustanos. With them, his brain kept flipping between *They're so much like us* and *They're totally different.*

It seemed even more unfair with them that they still had their dad, and the Greystone kids didn't.

"Forget going to the bathroom," Emma said. "Let's go back and hear what the moms are saying."

All four kids went back into the room with Mom and the rest of the Gustanos. Finn snuggled against Mom, practically crawling into her lap.

Across the table, Finn Gustano *was* on his mom's lap.

"I *am* trying to help you," Mom was saying. "But there's

certain information . . . certain facts . . . it's hard to know what's safe to tell you. Or what you can bear hearing."

"Look, my kids were kidnapped, and I didn't know where they were for an entire week," Mrs. Gustano said. "And now my husband's been accused of planning the whole thing. I've already had my worst nightmares come to life."

"That's not the worst that could happen," Mom said. It almost sounded like she was choking. Finn peered up at her face. Tears trembled in Mom's eyelashes as she stared directly at Mrs. Gustano. "Your children came home. Your whole family was reunited. Your husband's still alive. Mine . . . isn't."

"Are you threatening my mom?" Rocky asked, scraping his chair back like he was ready to fight. "Threatening my *dad*?"

"*No*," Mom said. "I'm trying to save your whole family. So I'm *warning* you all. I'm trying to be kind."

"What do you want me to do?" Mrs. Gustano asked in a strangled voice. "What would you do if you were me?"

"I'd jump on the offer I'm about to make you," Mom said. "If I were you, I'd take my husband and my kids and run away. I can recommend someone who will help. It'd be like . . . your own private witness protection program. Change your names, move somewhere new, start a new life—that's the only way to make sure you're all safe."

"Wait, what did you just say?" Emma Gustano gulped. "Do you mean—"

"But I *like* my name," Finn Gustano moaned.

Mrs. Gustano patted his arm comfortingly and studied Mom's face like she was memorizing it.

"That's what *you* did, isn't it?" Mrs. Gustano asked Mom. "Ran away? I still don't understand how you and I are connected, or why we look so much alike. Or what you did to offend whoever your enemies are—is it organized crime? Drug dealers? But I'm guessing you took your kids and you ran away . . . did you take part of *my* identity for yourself and your kids? Is that how I got involved?" Mom started to protest, but Mrs. Gustano waved her objections away and kept talking. "Regardless, how's that working out for you? You look just as haunted and exhausted as I feel. Your eight-year-old is cowering in your lap just as desolately as mine is. Your ten- and twelve-year-olds—"

Finn did not wait to hear what she said about Emma and Chess. He scrambled up and shouted at Mrs. Gustano, "This isn't Mom's fault! She didn't just run away—she kept trying to fix the other world! And Emma, Chess, and me—we want to fight against the bad people from the other world, too! And you should help us!"

"Finn . . . ," Mom whispered. "Don't—"

But Rocky bolted upright.

"Other world?" he repeated. "You weren't lying about that before? And there's a way to fix things? To fight back against the people who kidnapped us?" He swiveled toward Finn. "I'm in!"

EIGHT

EMMA

Emma heard Mrs. Gustano gasp, "Rocky, no. You don't even know what you're agreeing to. . . ."

Her voice seemed to come in stereo.

Oh, right, Emma thought. *That's because she and Mom said exactly the same thing at exactly the same time: "Rocky, no . . ." And I'm sitting halfway between them, so I'm hearing it exactly doubled.*

"Are we going to have to deal with the bad guys again and the . . . the bad place . . . to clear Dad's name?" the other Emma asked. She wrinkled her nose. "That's scary. But I'd rather do that than go hide somewhere and pretend I'm someone else. And stay scared forever. So I'm in, too."

"Me, too!" Finn Gustano piped up. Clearly he didn't like to be left out any more than Emma's younger brother did. Then he looked around as if trying to figure out what the others were talking about.

Well, did any of us really know what we were agreeing to, when we said we wanted to fix the other world? Emma wondered.

She thought of the mysterious coin Chess had tucked into his shorts pocket. She thought of all the questions she still hadn't had a chance to ask Mom.

The door to their glassed-in room opened, and all eight of the Gustanos and Greystones jumped.

"Sorry—I wanted to see if you were ready to order. But if I'm interrupting, I can come back later."

It was just the waitress. She was a teenager wearing a googly-eyed headband and the restaurant's official T-shirt, which showed a frantic-looking bird springing out of a clock and proclaiming, "CUCKOO! CUCKOO!" in the midst of lots of weird spirals. That logo always made Emma want to giggle. But today it felt like if she let herself do that, the giggles would turn hysterical.

Mom and Mrs. Gustano both slid back into acting like normal mothers who just wanted to feed their kids.

"No, no—we're ready," Mom told the waitress. "Finn, do you want to go first?"

Emma barely paid attention long enough to ask for fish

sticks. She kept her gaze on the carvings on the clock. Were any of the other wooden figures carved in the same style as the angel? No. But maybe if she went over and pressed other carved figures, they would shoot out other clues.

Was the coin Chess had found truly connected to the other world, or was it just a coincidence that this carved angel looked like the one they'd seen there?

Emma remembered that the restaurant had a few carvings on the outside of the building, too. She was lucky she was sitting at the end of the table, so she just had to shift a little in her chair to be able to peer out toward the parking lot. One section of the restaurant jutted out to the side . . . nope, none of the carvings there were angels. Emma swept her gaze across the parking lot as she craned her neck to try to see a section farther away, back near where Mom had parked.

Then Emma forgot about carvings.

Why was a man standing by the Greystones' car, staring at their license plate?

He was angled away from her, so from the back, Emma could see only that he wore jeans and a dark-colored, athletic-style windbreaker with the hood pulled up. It was a warm, sunny day. Why would anyone wear a jacket with the hood up?

Because he's hiding something, Emma thought.

While she watched, the man backed away from the

car. He inched over to the patio of the restaurant and stood behind a tree, peeking through the branches to gaze at the crowded tables.

That's not a crime, Emma thought. *He could just be meeting someone he doesn't see yet. He could have thought our car was his friend's car, and . . .*

The man slid over to the nearest window of the restaurant and pressed his face against the glass. He held his hands up by the sides of his face. Was he just blocking out the glare of the sun or still trying to hide?

The man moved to the next window.

Emma checked over her shoulder to make sure that the waitress was gone—she was—and then Emma stood up and walked over to the window nearest her.

"Emma?" Chess asked, gazing over at her from the table. "What's wrong?"

"Probably nothing," Emma muttered. "I'm just watching . . ."

"Emma, honey," Mom began. "Are you—"

Emma held up her hand to signal, *Wait.* Then, for good measure, she turned back toward Mom and pressed a finger to her lips. That was because she'd seen the man turn his head to the side and press his ear to the glass as if he was trying to *listen* to something inside.

He was truly acting strange.

Emma could see from Mom's expression that Mom thought Emma was behaving strangely, too. In Emma's normal life before she and her brothers had found out about the other world, that expression would have led Emma to expect a little talk with Mom about not being rude to other people at the table with her at meals. But now Emma could tell Mom was thinking, *Please don't make the Gustanos freak out even more than they already are!*

Emma looked back outside. The man was still stalking through the restaurant's flower beds and bushes, listening at every window. When he got to the bush closest to Emma, Emma couldn't take it anymore. She released the latch to open the window, unhooked the screen, shoved it out onto the ground, and reached out to grab the man's windbreaker.

"What are you doing?" she demanded, shaking the man's shoulders. "Who are you spying on?"

The man froze, then gazed at her in shock. For the first time, she saw his face.

Emma let go.

"Joe?" she asked.

NINE

CHESS

Fearless, Chess thought. *Emma is absolutely fearless.*

He was quaking in his shoes and his stomach churned, and all he was doing was sitting at the table.

Meanwhile, Emma was pulling some strange man in through the open window. No—it wasn't a strange man. It was Joe Deweese, who'd helped them in the other world. Like Mom, Joe had secretly crossed over into this world many years ago, but kept trying to help the people still trapped in the misery of the other world. And then, after the Gustanos were kidnapped, Joe and Mom had both gone back to the other world to try to rescue them, and gotten trapped themselves.

Mom and Joe had had a pact until a month ago, that they stayed away from each other and usually only communicated in secret, coded messages. They'd worked together for years, but most of that time Joe hadn't even known what Mom looked like.

So it was very odd that Joe was here now.

Joe was a tall man, so he took a while unbending his elbows and knees and straightening up. But even then, he kept the hood of his jacket up, mostly hiding his face from the Gustanos.

Still, Chess could see that Joe had beads of sweat running down his brown skin.

It wasn't *that* hot out.

"What's going on?" Emma asked. "Why were you listening to people inside this restaurant? And why didn't you use a bunch of listening devices instead of standing out there where anyone could see you?"

Joe was a genius with electronics.

"Emergency measures," Joe muttered. He darted his gaze toward Mom, but seemed to notice Mrs. Gustano first. "Ooh . . ."

He shrugged and let the hood of his jacket fall back against his shoulders.

"How did you even know we were here?" Mom demanded.

"Hacked into satellite imaging, traced your car's location . . . Kate, it was easy," Joe said.

The blood drained from Mom's face, and she looked like she was about to faint.

"So easy that anybody could do it?" she asked weakly.

She means, even people from the other world could do it, Chess thought.

"Should we get out of here?" he asked, springing to his feet. "And go . . . somewhere else? Without the car?"

He couldn't think of anyplace safe. The image he had in his head was of burrowing down into the ground to hide.

But all their problems before had started underground, with the tunnels connecting the two worlds.

Joe cast a quick glance over his shoulder, back toward the parking lot.

"I think we're safe here," he said. "For now. I took security measures." He peered down at Emma. "I set up *perimeter* listening devices. I'll be alerted if anyone . . . unexpected . . . shows up within a hundred feet of us."

Chess guessed that "unexpected" was code for "from the other world."

"So what's the emergency?" Rocky asked.

Joe winced, and jerked his head to the side. Was that supposed to be some secret signal to Mom?

"Kate, could I have a word with you?" he asked. "Privately?"

Couldn't he see that Mom was about to fall over?

For that matter, Joe himself was swaying a bit.

Chess stepped between Mom and Joe.

"We're all in this together," Chess said. "If there's an emergency, we kids need to know what's going on, too."

"*All* of us kids need to know," Rocky said, stepping up beside Chess. Rocky wasn't like Chess, and Chess wasn't like Rocky, but it felt like they were a team just then.

Joe frowned.

"Well, actually . . . this is about you Gustano kids," he murmured.

Mrs. Gustano hugged Other-Finn so hard he let out a yelp.

"*What* about my kids?" she asked.

Joe leaned back weakly against the wall. His eyes didn't quite meet Mrs. Gustano's. Instead, he stared at Rocky, Other-Emma, and Other-Finn.

"After you were kidnapped," Joe began, "could you tell you were being used in scientific experiments?"

TEN

FINN

"Like guinea pigs, you mean?" Finn asked helpfully, because everybody else seemed frozen, shocked into silence.

"The police assured me nobody hurt my children," Mrs. Gustano said, in a voice that could have turned boiling water into ice cubes. "Rocky, Emma, Finn—you all told me you were fine the whole time you were away. Not in pain, anyway. You were just really, really scared, and—"

"Scared," Emma repeated, as though the word itself was something she could put on a glass slide and slip under a microscope. Emma got like that sometimes. She was probably going to be a scientist when she grew up; she would probably discover everything there was to know.

"Of course they were scared," Chess said. "They'd been kidnapped, and they didn't know where they were or how to escape. *We* were terrified the whole time we were in the other world, and we at least sort of knew what was going on. And *we* were rescuing *them*. We had *some* . . ."

"Power," Rocky finished for him. "Control."

Emma brushed Rocky's fingers with hers. Finn couldn't quite tell if she was trying to high-five him or shake his hand. Either way, it looked like she was welcoming him onto a team.

"You understand," she marveled.

Joe's frown only deepened.

"Do you Gustano kids remember any unusual smells?" he asked.

"Fire," Other-Emma said, gazing thoughtfully toward the ceiling, as if that helped her answer. "But not like fire-in-a-fireplace, where it makes you feel cozy and glad to be indoors. More like burning tires, burning garbage—a smell that made us want to gag."

"*Rotten* burning garbage," Other-Finn added. "And maybe dead rats, too. Dead rats and dead mice and spiders and snakes . . ."

"Yeah!" Finn said. "I know just the smell you're talking about. Yuck!"

"We all smelled that when we were in the Public Hall for Mom's trial," Emma said. "Everybody there was forced to, I don't know, *marinate* in those horrible odors. And it made everyone terrified and angry. But you already knew that, Joe. We talked about it, and you agreed with my theory that the people in charge of the trial were using those smells to control people. Because the leaders of the other world, they don't want anyone thinking for themselves. Or making any decisions for themselves."

"The more we breathed in that bad air, the more we felt weak and helpless and scared," Finn told the Gustanos. "Did you feel that way, too?"

"It's hard to feel *more* of something you're already drowning in," Other-Emma muttered.

"I meant, what do you remember from before you got to the Public Hall?" Joe asked, still studying the Gustanos. He had the same glint in his eye that Emma always got when she talked about scientific experiments—the glint that meant, *My brain is working really hard right now.* "From the time you were kidnapped until they brought you into the Public Hall. Did you smell anything unusual then?"

"Cotton candy," Other-Finn said. "But, like, cotton candy that was left in the heat too long and started to burn."

"The same kind of deodorizer they use at school when someone throws up," Other-Emma said.

"You mean, the stuff that never works right?" Finn asked. "The stuff that just makes the throw-up smell worse?"

"Exactly," Other-Emma said.

"Gym shoes," Rocky said. "You know how, when you get a new pair, at first they smell really good, just because they're new?"

"And then you sweat all over them, and they are *nasty*," Other-Emma finished for him. "And Mom makes you leave them outside on the porch so they don't stink up the whole house."

"Can you blame me?" Mrs. Gustano asked, and for a minute, it felt like they could all be happy if they just stuck to talking about stinky gym shoes and nothing else.

But of course they had lots of other things they *had* to talk about.

"So you're saying the whole time you were with the kidnappers, you smelled all sorts of odors that were good and bad mixed together," Emma said. "Or—good things ruined, and bad things that can't be fixed no matter how much someone tries to mask the odor."

"And those smells were supposed to be *science*?" Other-Finn asked.

"We've intercepted messages, and now we've decoded them," Joe said. "From the government in the bad world. They told the kidnappers to test the Gustano kids' reactions to all sorts of these smells. The Gustano kids in particular, because . . ."

He was back to staring at Mom, as if he didn't want anyone else to hear what he was about to say.

Maybe he'd even started talking in code that only Mom could understand.

Finn wanted to jump up into Mom's lap and put his face in front of Mom's, blocking hers. Maybe that way Joe would go back to talking to everyone at once.

But just then Joe jerked to attention and put his hand up to his ear.

"What's that you say? Slow down!" he hissed.

Joe wasn't talking to Mom anymore. Finn didn't know as much about electronic gizmos as Emma did, but even he could tell: Joe had to be wearing a tiny earpiece and probably an even smaller microphone hidden somewhere in his clothes. And that's what he was talking into now.

"I don't understand what you're saying. Has the perimeter been breached?" Joe seemed to stagger backward. "Are you under attack? Are you in danger?"

Finn couldn't hear an answer. He couldn't tell if Joe heard one, either.

But even as he said the word "danger," Joe jumped through the open window.

And then he took off running across the parking lot.

ELEVEN

EMMA

Of course Emma followed Joe. He might need help with whatever danger he was running toward.

And how could Emma bear not to know what had just happened, that made him run away?

She dived out the open window after him. Joe had gone feet-first, and Emma didn't really think until she was half in, half out of the window that going arms-first meant she would have to roll herself into a somersault once she landed in the mulch outside. She tucked her head under just like she'd learned in gym class and was soon back up on her feet, too.

"Wait!" she yelled after Joe.

"No! Stay—" he called back to her.

But Emma lost track of what he was saying because the shouts of everyone behind her were louder: Chess yelling, "Emma, be careful!" and Finn crying, "Where are you going?" And somewhere in there was Mom's voice calling, "Emma, I'm coming, too—but wait, here's some money so they don't think we just dined and dashed . . . or ordered and dashed. . . ."

And Emma wanted to giggle, because that was so *Mom*, that even as they were running away, she was still trying to be fair to the restaurant.

Joe sprinted across the parking lot, getting farther and farther ahead of Emma because his legs were about twice as long as hers. Still, Emma risked a glance back over her shoulder: Mom, Chess, and Finn were all trailing along behind her. So were all four Gustanos. Mrs. Gustano was still in the process of climbing out the window even as she yelled back to what must have been a startled waitress, "We'll be back for the food in a minute! I think we will, anyway! Regardless, the money's on the table. . . ."

When Emma turned back around to look for Joe, he was already speeding across the street. He ran up to a dark van on the other side. It had windows only at the front.

That's the kind of van kidnappers use, Emma thought. *Because no one can see in the back.* She wanted to shout a warning to Joe, but she and her family and the Gustanos were already making enough of a scene. She shifted to looking at the van's license plate instead.

It was blacked out.

Joe whipped open the doors at the back of the van. Emma reached the street and just barely remembered to look both ways for traffic—fortunately, there wasn't any. She bounded over to Joe.

He was peering into the back section of the van, which was crammed so full of electronics gear that it took Emma a full minute to notice a girl sitting in the midst of it all. The girl wore one set of headphones smashed down onto her hair and had three others dangling along her collarbones like so many necklaces. She was also shouting into a microphone, "I didn't say it was *that* kind of emergency!"

And she had the same wiry frame as Joe; her eyebrows had the same inquisitive arch. . . .

This girl looked so much like Joe she *had* to be related.

Emma remembered the day they'd first met Joe, when he'd explained why he hadn't rushed to help Mom sooner in the other world: *I have kids, too. Kids I was trying to protect.*

Was this Joe's daughter?

The next thing Emma noticed was a wave of stench coming out of the van. The smell was so vile and overpowering that she practically gagged.

"Hold your breath!" she yelled to the girl who was probably Joe's daughter. Then Emma whirled toward Joe. "Do you think this is an attack? Did someone from the other world cross over and . . . Or, no, this smell isn't making me feel hopeless or like giving up, so this is something new, some other unidentified source—"

"I *know* where this smell is coming from!" the girl in the van yelled back at Emma.

She reached down, and Emma braced herself for the girl to lift up a stink bomb, or something equally disgusting. Instead, she lifted up . . .

A baby.

It was actually a rather adorable baby in a lacy yellow dress, with a giant yellow bow wrapped around her dark curls.

But she *really* stank.

"You gave the emergency code word because Kafi has a dirty diaper?" Joe asked in disbelief. "Don't you remember I said to stay inconspicuous? And now I've run across the parking lot with"—he looked back, to where Mrs. Gustano and Other-Finn was just now crossing the street—"eight people chasing me?"

"We're out of fresh diapers. And wipes," the girl said, waving the baby around as if she enjoyed sharing the stink. "So, Dad, if you want to sit in an enclosed space monitoring every movement within a mile while Kafi cries and you hold your breath, be my guest. We can trade places. I'm pretty sure I can deliver bad news as well as you can."

"Bad news?" Emma repeated.

"You mean about the Gustano kids having smells tested on them," Finn piped up. "Joe already told us that. We're done with the bad news now."

The girl holding the baby raised her eyebrows a little higher and peered at Joe.

Then she asked: "You didn't tell them the rest?"

TWELVE

CHESS

Joe darted his gaze around, as if seeing danger everywhere. Then he clenched his jaw and told the girl in the van, "No. The rest is only speculation and reckless theories. We need more data. And a safer place to talk. And . . . you're right. Let's deal with the diaper first, shall we?"

After that, Mom and Mrs. Gustano insisted that all the kids needed to go back into the restaurant and actually eat the food they'd ordered. Joe joined in, saying it was dinnertime for his kids, too. He made hasty introductions: His daughters were Kona, who was eleven, and Kafi, who was just a week shy of her first birthday.

One time when Chess was younger, he'd gone with a friend to a company picnic for his friend's parents. All the grown-ups had made happy chatter: "Who wants more popcorn?" "The relay races are coming up next!" But in the background they'd been muttering about falling stock prices and missed promotions, and none of them seemed truly happy.

Now Mom, Mrs. Gustano, and Joe were acting just like the adults at that picnic. Chess sidled up beside Mom when they got back to the table and wanted to ask, *What's going on? Can't you and Joe talk privately? Or—you and Joe and* me? *After he gets back from buying diapers?* But Mom was dividing up fish sticks and chicken fingers so there'd be some for Kona and Kafi, too; she was telling Mrs. Gustano, "Oh, yes, I asked them to bring ketchup for the fries. . . ."

Finn and Other-Finn kept the whole table entertained biting their chicken fingers into various shapes—no one seemed to mind that Finn's "dinosaur" and Other-Finn's "rocket ship" looked virtually identical. And baby Kafi cracked everyone up by suddenly roaring, "More!" during the one moment of silence. And then, a second later, "Pees?"

In big crowds, Chess often felt himself growing quieter and quieter, and this felt like a big crowd now. He wanted to whisper with Emma about what she might have figured out about the coin that had come from the angel carving—but, no, the coin was still in his own pocket, and since she'd ended up on the other side of the table, he couldn't slip it to her secretly.

He couldn't even catch her eye, because she was staring off into space.

The rest of the evening went like that, too. The grown-ups decided that the Gustanos and Joe and his girls would spend the night at Ms. Morales's house along with the Greystones—Ms. Morales had enough room as long as each set of kids stayed in the same room as their parent. And then there was such a rush of finding sleeping bags and pillows and air mattresses that Chess didn't even have a chance to say anything to Natalie.

Maybe after the younger kids are asleep, Chess thought. *Maybe then . . .*

He pictured some solemn gathering of the grown-ups and him and Natalie—okay, maybe Rocky, too. Maybe then the grown-ups would stop talking about fish sticks and ketchup and say to Chess, Natalie, and Rocky, "You three are old enough to know everything. . . ."

At bedtime, Mom finally whispered something for Chess alone—but all she said was, "I need you to make sure Emma and Finn really do go to sleep instead of trying to sneak out or anything. . . . *Everyone's* going to need sleep if we have any hope of coping with the next few days."

There wasn't even time to tell Mom about the coin they'd found, before Ms. Morales was summoning Mom back into the hallway with a question about Natalie's grandmother, who was still in the hospital.

Only that really isn't Natalie's grandmother; it's Other-Natalie's grandmother from the other world. . . .

Chess watched as Emma fell asleep in the midst of fingering the coin they'd found and muttering theories to explain it. He listened as Finn fell asleep asking how much he and Other-Finn would be alike: Half and half? More? Less? Chess waited long after they both stopped talking, to make sure Emma's and Finn's breathing kept the slow and steady rhythm of sleep. How long should he wait before getting up to search for Mom? Or should he just wait until she came back?

Maybe, even if he didn't exactly sleep, he did zone out for a while. Because he suddenly found himself jerking back to attention. Had there been the softest sound of someone tiptoeing out in the hallway? Or just someone besides Emma and Finn breathing nearby?

Chess sat up and listened. The sound—if there'd even been a sound—was gone now. He could see a digital clock over on the nightstand. It was midnight. And the bed beside the nightstand was still empty.

So Mom hadn't come back yet. It hadn't been her tiptoeing around.

"Emma?" Chess whispered, peering over at the sleeping bags stretched out beside his own. But both Emma and Finn were just lumps in their sleeping bags; neither of them stirred.

Chess sighed and eased out of his sleeping bag. He tiptoed to the door of the bedroom and out into the hall. He hesitated for a second outside Natalie's door, wanting another chance to talk to her. Then he remembered that she'd given her room to the Gustanos. He didn't know where she was sleeping that night.

He headed for the stairs. He didn't know Natalie's house as well as his own, so he wasn't sure which steps here might creak, or which to skip. So he settled for descending very slowly, stopping on every step to listen. The house stayed completely silent and dark. He wasn't sure if it was just a moonless night, or if Ms. Morales had done something to the windows to block out every hint of light from outside.

And then, halfway down the stairs, his bare foot brushed something.

No, someone.

Someone's . . . arm?

Chess opened his mouth to whisper, *Who's there?* But he'd barely puckered his lips for the *Who's . . . ?* before he felt a hand on his face. The hand covered his mouth.

"Don't make any noise!" someone hissed in his ear.

Girl's voice, Chess thought frantically. *Not Emma, not Natalie, not Other-Emma . . .*

It was Joe's daughter. Kona.

Chess shoved her hand aside and whispered back, "Why are you standing in the middle of the stairs in the middle of the night?" His mind put together the sequence of his foot brushing her arm, and then her hand wrapping around his face. "Were you *sitting* in the middle of the stairs? Are you *trying* to trip people?"

Kona tugged on his arm, pulling him down to sit with her.

"We're less visible, sitting," she whispered. "Come on. Keep me company. Sit lookout with me."

"Lookout?" Chess echoed. "Are you kidding? I can't see a thing!"

Kona slipped something over his head. The darkness around him turned greenish and almost eerily illuminated. Now he could make out shapes of furniture in the living room down below. He tilted his head back and could see the chandelier hanging from the ceiling above. He looked back at Kona, who had something like a mask covering her eyes and the top part of her dark hair.

"Oh . . . night-vision goggles," he said. "Are you— what's it called?—'monitoring the perimeter' again? Acting as lookout for your dad?"

"I'm acting as lookout for *myself*," Kona muttered.

Chess wasn't sure what to say to that. It wasn't just because he was sitting in the dark wearing night-vision goggles in the middle of the night with a girl he'd just met. He rarely knew what to say to girls anyhow. It'd taken him two trips to the other world to rescue a total of seven people—or eight, depending on how you counted it—to get to the point where he was comfortable talking to Natalie. And he really, really liked Natalie, and knew her well now.

Kona was a complete mystery.

"You're Chess, right?" Kona whispered beside him. "Not Rocky? The oldest Greystone, not the oldest Gustano?"

"Uh, right," Chess said.

Maybe Kona's night-vision goggles didn't work as well as his—Chess and Rocky were *so* different. Chess was tall and thin and awkward, and Rocky was shorter and more muscular. And Rocky seemed to move through the world like a football player—like someone who could tackle everyone in his way.

Anyone looking at Chess should be able to see that he was the kid more likely to *be* tackled.

But Kona had never met any of the Greystone or Gustano kids before tonight, so maybe it made sense that she would be confused.

"So what are the jokes?" Kona asked.

"Jokes?" Chess repeated uncertainly.

Kona gently bumped his shoulder with hers.

"You know, with your name," Kona said. "I know how it goes. Back in kindergarten, one kid said my last name should be 'ice cream,' so my name would be like 'Cone of Ice Cream.' That was fun. Then in fourth grade, because my last name *is* Deweese, a few mean kids tried to get everyone to start calling me 'Cone of Weasels.' But it didn't catch on. So I like hearing what other kids with unusual names deal with. We've got *solidarity*. We can fight ignorant comments from small-minded people together."

"Oh. Yeah," Chess said. "Got it. I wouldn't ever call you Cone of Weasels. Or let anyone else do that. But . . . I guess I've been lucky. People don't really make fun of my name." Chess almost let himself explain that other kids were more likely to ignore him than make fun of him, but that seemed truly pitiful.

And yet, he didn't actually *mind* being ignored.

Beside him, Kona suddenly stiffened.

"Here," she said. "You should listen to this, too."

Now she pressed something into his ear—an earbud. And then Chess heard Joe saying, "We've got to figure this out!"

"You're spying on your dad," Chess breathed. "Eavesdropping. No—you're spying on all the grown-ups."

He added the last because he heard Mom's voice next,

saying, "Joe, we'll work through this. Maybe we already have all the data we need, and we just need to . . . to *think*."

Or maybe it was Mrs. Gustano saying that. It was so weird how Chess couldn't tell the difference between Mrs. Gustano's voice and his own mother's.

"They all went into that room together," Kona whispered, pointing toward the door to Ms. Morales's office. Her *soundproof* office. "All the adults and that one girl. Ms. Morales's daughter. Natalie?"

Chess remembered imagining the adults and Natalie and *him* conferring together, figuring things out away from the younger kids. Evidently that was happening now—only without Chess.

Natalie, at thirteen, was grouped with the adults. But Chess was being treated just like baby Kafi and eight-year-old Finn and Other-Finn. And, well, ten-year-old Emma and Other-Emma, and eleven-year-old Kona, and twelve-year-old Rocky. But still.

The dividing line between who was and wasn't old enough to know things shouldn't run between him and Natalie.

Chess didn't often get angry, but he was *furious* now.

And he was as mad at Natalie as he was at the grown-ups. Why didn't she stick up for him? Why didn't she say he deserved to know everything, too?

Through the earbud, he heard Natalie say, "I've already told you how I felt in the other world. You should ask Chess or Emma or Finn if you want more information. More *data*."

Oh. Natalie was sticking up for him. And for Emma and Finn.

All Chess's anger ebbed away so quickly that his spine went weak, and he had to catch himself from toppling forward and falling down the steps.

"I'll go knock on that door," Chess told Kona beside him. "You and me both—we should be in there, too. They'll want to hear what I have to say, and you can . . . you can . . ."

Kona put her hand on Chess's arm.

"Wait," she said. "You didn't hear what they said before, about how—"

She broke off, undoubtedly because her dad was talking now.

"We can't tell any of the other kids they're being targeted in particular, until we know how to protect them," Joe said.

"We wouldn't have even let you in, Natalie, if you hadn't forced your way in," Ms. Morales said ruefully.

Oh. Natalie had done exactly what Chess wanted to.

But rather than standing up and stomping toward the office, Chess turned to Kona and repeated weakly, "Targeted in particular?"

Kona shook her head warningly.

In the office, Mom was saying, "We *know* the Gustano kids were taken in the first place because the kidnappers were trying to trap me. Because they thought the Gustano kids were mine. Maybe these 'scientific experiments' you're talking about were just . . . random. Meaningless."

"Our spies told us it was very clear," Joe said. "The kidnappers had control groups and everything. They wanted to know: How did the Gustano kids react to mind control? Was it the same or different than the reactions of kids who'd only ever lived in the other world? The fact that they wanted to know that . . . the fact that the mind control worked on the Gustano kids . . . that means this world isn't a safe place anymore, either. Not for any of our kids. Not for any of *us*."

This world, the other world . . . , Chess thought dizzily.

He leaned toward Kona again and asked, "What about you? Where are you from? Originally, I mean. You're Joe's daughter, so . . ."

"Don't you know you should never ask someone like me 'Where are you from originally?'" Kona said. "Because my dad's Black and my mom's Filipina, and—"

"Oh no!" Chess said. "I'm sorry!" He was horrified that his question had come out sounding so rude. "I didn't mean—"

Kona patted his leg.

"I forgive you," she said. "This time. But it's funny. My

whole life I've known I was both of my parents' races. But I didn't know until we were driving here today that I'm a mix of two *worlds*, too. My dad's from the other world. My mom's completely from this one. So what am I?"

"You're . . . you," Chess said weakly.

He felt an odd pang of jealousy. Ever since he'd found out that he and his family were from the other world—and that it was such an awful place—he'd wanted someone to pop up and say, *Oops! We made a mistake! Just a mix-up . . . We had things backward—it's the Greystones who are from the good world, and the Gustanos who actually belong in the bad one. . . .*

But if she wanted to, Kona could ignore her other-world background and just focus on being from this world, and . . .

And Kona was sitting in a stranger's house in the middle of the night wearing night-vision goggles and an earbud to eavesdrop on her dad and other grown-ups who were in a locked, soundproof room talking about the other world.

Kona couldn't ignore her other-world connections any more than Chess could.

"No, really," Kona said. "I'm like both my parents in a lot of ways. I'm good with gadgets like my dad, and good at sports like Mom. What did I get from each of their worlds? What did *you* get from being from the other world?"

Fear, Chess wanted to say. *Sorrow and grief, because the other world killed my dad. Secrets hanging over me my whole life. Secrets I still don't completely understand.*

But a different word came out when he opened his mouth: "Responsibility."

"Wh-What?" Kona sputtered.

"I mean, I have a duty," Chess said. The words spilled out of him now. He started talking so fast, he could have been mistaken for a chatterbox like Emma and Finn. "A purpose. A meaning for my life. My brother and sister and me—and our mom—we all know we want to fix things in the other world. Natalie and her mom, they feel that, too. We're going to make things right."

Kona turned to stare at him. Through the night-vision goggles, she looked as green as everything else around them.

"Then," she said, "I have that responsibility, too."

THIRTEEN

FINN

Finn woke up first the next morning. This *never* happened—
Finn was usually the best of all the Greystones at sleeping.
But Emma and Chess were still sacked out in their sleeping
bags beside him, both of them looking worried even in their
sleep. And Mom was huddled on the bed, her knees clutched
in tight, as if she'd fallen asleep trying to hide. She moaned
as if she were having a nightmare.

Finn did not like seeing the rest of his family like this.

A month ago, before the first time he'd traveled back to
the other world, he would have immediately shaken all three
of them awake. He would have made Mom assure him she

was *only* having a nightmare; he would have made Emma and Chess play silly games with him to cheer them up.

Today, though . . .

Maybe they just need to sleep. Maybe that's the best thing.

Finn slipped out of his sleeping bag and tiptoed out of the room. All the doors in the hallway were still closed—was everyone else in the whole house still asleep?

Ms. Morales's house was a little creepy like this, so silent and still. Even the bright sunlight streaming in through the window at the top of the stairs didn't help. It just seemed to light up all the ways this house was like Other-Natalie's in the other world.

And in that house, Finn, Emma, Chess, and Natalie had been afraid of everything.

They'd had good reason to be afraid of everything.

Finn rushed downstairs, because the first floor of Ms. Morales's house was less like Other-Natalie's house than the second floor. He didn't try to be quiet, but still, nobody flung open any doors behind him; nobody cried, "Good morning!" or congratulated him, "You're up early! Good for you!"

The first floor seemed as empty as the second. Finn wandered through the vast living room, trying not to think about how shadowy it was with all the first-floor blinds and curtains still drawn.

And then he tripped over a leg. A leg attached to . . .

78

"Mom!" Finn cried, just as he heard Mom say, "Finn!"

Finn whipped his head around to stare at the woman huddled in the corner of the shadowy couch. His brain felt scrambled. *But I just saw Mom asleep upstairs and there wasn't time . . . oh. This is Mrs. Gustano.*

Mrs. Gustano blinked at him in the same confused way he was blinking at her.

"Oh, right," she said. "Finn *Greystone*. Sorry. For a moment I thought you were my Finn. And he *never* gets up this early, so that would be as weird as everything else that's happened."

Mrs. Gustano's eyes looked like they could twinkle just as merrily as Mom's did when Finn said something funny. But they weren't twinkly now. They were sad and worried and had lines around them that Mom's eyes didn't have.

Or . . . maybe Mom's eyes did have lines now. Mom had changed in the past month, too.

"I swear," Mrs. Gustano said. "You walk just like my Finn. You turn your head like he does. I mean, of course I'm looking right at you, and I can tell that your eyes are bigger and your nose is smaller, and of course you're *not* my Finn, but . . ."

"But I was looking at you thinking your hair should be longer," Finn said. "And thinking, did Mom get a haircut overnight?"

In the shadowy light, that was the only way to tell Mrs. Gustano from Mom. If Mom did get her hair cut really short, instead of pulling it back in a ponytail, maybe even Finn wouldn't be able to tell them apart.

Mrs. Gustano touched the little curls at the base of her neck.

"This must be so strange for you kids," she said. "At least you all don't look *exactly* alike. But do you want to know something else that's weird? Ever since I met your mom yesterday, I've been thinking I should grow my hair out. Is she influencing me without even trying?"

Then Mrs. Gustano put her hand to her mouth, as if she shouldn't have told Finn that.

"What do you mean by—?" Finn began, but broke off because just then the doorbell rang.

Mrs. Gustano stiffened, then tiptoed over to peek out one of the blinds. Finn tiptoed right alongside her.

"You can let Ms. Morales come down and decide if she wants to open the door or not," Finn whispered. He wasn't tall enough to see what Mrs. Gustano saw through the gap in the blinds. And . . . he wasn't feeling quite brave enough to pull the blinds back and peek himself. "It's probably just, like, UPS or FedEx or . . ."

"No, I think this caller's here for me," Mrs. Gustano muttered.

She stalked over to the front door and yanked it open.

Without even thinking about it, Finn ducked down behind the nearest couch.

"Yes?" Mrs. Gustano asked, standing in the doorway.

Finn peeked out from behind the couch. A silver-haired police officer stood outside on Ms. Morales's porch. Even though Finn had met lots of the local police when his mother was missing, he didn't recognize this one.

"Good morning, ma'am," the police officer said. "Kate Gustano, correct?"

"How did you know I was here?" Mrs. Gustano asked. "Have you been tracking my movements?"

"You aren't helping your husband's case," the police officer said. "It is my duty to inform you that you are putting yourself and your children in danger, trying to investigate on your own when you should let the proper authorities—"

"You didn't answer my question," Mrs. Gustano snapped. She sounded just like Mom when Finn, Emma, or Chess were in trouble. "I am in no danger in this house. And last time I checked, this is a free country, and I am a free citizen, and my children and I are allowed to go anywhere we choose. Unless . . . are you accusing me, too? Have you found—or contrived—false evidence against me, just like the false evidence against my husband? Should I be calling my lawyer to report improper arrest or police harassment or—"

"Ma'am, ma'am, please," the police officer interrupted. "Calm down."

"It is never a good idea to tell a woman who's being treated unfairly to calm down," Mrs. Gustano said, her voice completely icy now.

This was not going well. What if the police officer did have false evidence against Mrs. Gustano?

Finn thought about the other Finn sleeping upstairs. What if he woke up to find that his mother had been arrested and taken away? How awful would that be?

Finn popped up from behind the couch.

"Oh, hi, Officer!" he chirped. He dodged around the couch to go stand beside Mrs. Gustano. "Mrs. Gustano isn't from our town, so she doesn't know how nice the whole police force was when my mom was missing. Could you say hi to Officer Dutton for me? There was this one day when he brought bags and bags of stuffed animals for my brother and sister and me. And then he and Officer Dao came to visit while Mom was in the hospital, and they brought more flowers than anybody. Could you say hi to Officer Dao for me, too? Do you know them—Amy and Ben? They told us to call them Amy and Ben. . . ."

The silver-haired police officer on the porch looked confused. But at least he and Mrs. Gustano weren't arguing anymore.

Then the officer stiffened his jaw.

"Young man, this doesn't concern you," he said. "As it happens, I do need to take Mrs. Gustano and her children down to the station for questioning."

Mrs. Gustano gasped. "Why?" she asked. "Under what pretense?"

Finn didn't quite catch the officer's answer, because he was distracted by a noise behind him. Footsteps. Was someone running down the stairs?

Finn spun around, and there was Emma, her hair sticking up in full bedhead mode, her feet bare, the oversized math club T-shirt she'd slept in sliding back and forth on her shoulders. Emma raced past Finn to step in front of Mrs. Gustano. She glared at the police officer. Then, oddly, she reached up and tapped his name badge.

"Just as I thought!" Emma exploded. She spread her arms protectively in front of Mrs. Gustano and Finn. "Mrs. Gustano, don't go anywhere with this liar! He's not a police officer from our town! I bet he's not even from this world! I bet he's from—"

Before Emma could finish her sentence, the man turned around and took off running.

FOURTEEN

EMMA

Mrs. Gustano threw her arms around Emma.

"You saved us!" she cried.

"Should we chase him?" Finn asked, as if he were about to take off running himself.

"Oh, no—that wouldn't be safe," Mrs. Gustano said, putting a firm hand on Finn's shoulder.

Emma just ruffled her brother's hair.

"We don't have to," she announced with a grin. "Don't worry. I put a tracker on him. When I touched his name badge. So we'll know everywhere he goes. As long as he doesn't discover it and take it off."

Mrs. Gustano's jaw dropped.

"You're even more of an evil genius than *my* Emma," she said. "I mean, not *really* evil, but the exact opposite in this case."

She was still staring off after the fleeing "police officer." He'd reached his car down at the bottom of Ms. Morales's driveway, scrambled into it, and was now speeding away.

"How'd you know he was fake?" Finn asked, tugging on Emma's arm. Or maybe he was patting it in a congratulatory way. It was a little hard to tell. "You were upstairs! I thought you were still asleep!"

"I woke up just in time," Emma said. She tried to make her smile a little modest, but that wasn't possible. She could feel the corners of her mouth stretching out as far as they would go. "I could see out of the window upstairs and . . . Well, you know how much time we spent talking to cops when Mom was missing. No real cop would park that crookedly and then just amble up to the door. And I heard what he said. He didn't identify himself, which the cops always did unless one of us said their names first. And did you see the . . . what's it called? . . . the font of the writing on his name badge? Totally wrong."

Mrs. Gustano started laughing. At least, Emma thought it was laughter. It sounded a little hysterical.

"You're amazing," she said.

"I just notice things," Emma said, and this time she did

manage to make it sound like she wasn't bragging, but stating a fact.

Mrs. Gustano was maybe holding on to Emma a little too tightly.

"What's going on?"

It was Ms. Morales. She appeared at the top of the stairs, rubbing her eyes and blinking in the sunlight from the upper-story window. She looked like she'd just jumped out of bed—she was still putting her arms into the sleeves of a silky robe.

And then Mom and Chess and Joe and Kona and Natalie crowded in behind Ms. Morales, all of them asking questions, too.

Emma waited for Mrs. Gustano to answer, but she didn't. So Emma pulled away. She shut the door, then spun back to tell the whole crowd, "Everything's fine."

"It's fine *now*," Finn added quietly.

Finally Mrs. Gustano seemed to recover enough to tell the story as the whole crew came pouring down the stairs. Chess slipped in beside Emma and Finn in the midst of the hubbub.

"Good job," he said, sounding like a proud big brother.

But he didn't look like he thought the crisis was past. His eyes seemed huge in his pale face. His hair stuck up all over the place just as badly as Finn's (and likely just as badly as Emma's, too, though she hadn't checked). Only when he glanced toward Natalie on the other side of the room did he reach up to start slicking it down.

Just then, Joe slid an iPad into Emma's hands.

"Want to put in the code for that tracker, so we can see where that guy went?"

"Oh, right," Emma said, typing away. She liked working with Joe—he already had the right website on the screen. Maybe because he knew the Greystone kids had gotten all the same electronic gizmos he'd used in the other world.

A map appeared on the screen, with one flashing light blinking across it.

"He's turning out of this neighborhood . . . ," Joe murmured.

"Here, Dad," Kona said behind them.

Emma turned to see that Kona was holding out two laptops.

"The surveillance footage you wanted," Kona said.

"That's the Cuckoo Clock!" Finn exclaimed, pointing at one of the screens. "Are you checking to see if that fake police guy was there yesterday at the same time as us? Was he watching us then?"

"No, that's the Cuckoo Clock *now*," Emma corrected her brother. "See how empty the parking lot is?" In the grainy surveillance video, the normally cheerful, busy restaurant looked a little forlorn. "But why—"

"I *think* I've figured out a way to locate every spot anyone's ever crossed over between the worlds," Joe said. "For some reason, that restaurant is one of them."

Because of the angel wing carving, Emma thought. *The coin.*

Was now a good time to gather the adults together and tell them about the coin? And show it to them and see if any of them could figure it out?

No—Joe was too fixated on staring back and forth between the two laptops and the iPad.

"So that's the only reason you're watching our house on your other laptop," Finn said, as if this was a huge relief. "Because *we* used it as a crossing point. But Mom took the lever away from there, so—"

"We don't know how many levers are out there, Finn," Emma said, a little too sharply.

She looked back at the flashing light on the iPad and tried to mentally translate the lines of the map into the familiar streets of her own town. The fake police officer's blip was twisting along a curvy stretch now—was that the street that Finn called Roller Coaster Road?

"Oh no," Chess said, sounding as pained as if someone had stabbed him.

"What?" Kona and Joe both asked at once.

"That's . . . that's the route back to our house," Chess mumbled. "What if he's going there?"

"We already knew the bad guys have used our house as a crossing point," Finn said. He sounded like he was trying to be brave, but couldn't keep his voice from shaking. "Other-Natalie's grandma told us that. It won't matter if he goes there or not."

But it does, Emma thought. Because their house wasn't just a house. It wasn't just a *thing*. It was where the Greystones had lived for eight years, the only place Emma remembered living. It was where they'd raced home from school every day, where Mom had tucked them into bed every night, where they'd read books and played games and drawn pictures and created inventions. Where they'd felt safe.

It was home.

Helplessly the three Greystone kids and Kona and Joe watched the flashing light on the iPad wind closer and closer to the Greystones' neighborhood on the map. When the blip of light turned the last corner, Kona put the Cuckoo Clock laptop down on the couch and held out the one showing the Greystones' house.

It only took a few moments for the fake police car to appear in the surveillance footage on that screen. The car pulled up in front of the Greystones' house. The silver-haired fake police officer got out and ambled—no, *sauntered*—up to the front porch. He looked around, and then seemed to look straight up into the surveillance camera.

Joe must have placed it in the porch light.

The silver-haired fake police officer smiled. He ripped off his fake name badge, flung it to the ground, and ground it under his heel.

On the iPad, the blip of light blinked completely out.

"He found the tracker," Emma groaned. "Okay, so what? At least we can still watch and see . . ."

The fake police officer moved to the edge of the porch and crouched down to reach into the mulch in the nearest flower bed. He seemed to be prying up one of the stepping stones the Greystone kids had each made in kindergarten, when they'd pressed their hands in plaster.

"Why does he want my handprint?" Finn whimpered.

"I think that one's mine," Emma said. "Because, see, the edges are decorated with plus and minus signs. But . . ."

The fake police officer raised and lowered the stepping stone, as if he was calculating how much it weighed. Then he reared his arm back—and hurled the stepping stone toward the porch light.

On the laptop screen, Emma's handprint stone seemed to fly closer and closer.

And then suddenly the screen showed nothing but fuzz.

"He broke the surveillance camera!" Emma wailed. "He knew we were watching all along! He did that on purpose!"

FIFTEEN

CHESS

"He's taunting us," Chess said.

"We've got to tell him he can't do that!" Finn stomped his feet. "Let's go! Who's going to drive? Mom? Joe? We'll make him get away from our house. And—I know! The real police should arrest him for breaking our light!"

Chess watched Joe's gaze slide away from the laptop and toward the blind-covered windows framing the front door of Ms. Morales's house.

"No," Joe murmured. "We can't. By the time we'd get there, he'd be back in the other world. And . . ."

And doesn't Joe think we still have an advantage in this world? Chess wondered.

"What was he trying to do?" Emma asked. "Did he really think Mrs. Gustano and her kids would go with him, even into the other world again? Didn't he think we would catch on?"

Joe closed his eyes, as if that helped him think. He let out a deep sigh.

"Either he was gambling that Mrs. Gustano was still so naive and desperate that she would fall for his ploy or . . . they're all just rubbing it in our faces, how easy it is for them to slip back and forth between the worlds," he murmured.

Chess darted his gaze toward Mom. Even now she had the bat case with the lever inside hanging from her shoulder. She still had on the yoga pants and T-shirt she'd slept in. Her feet were bare. And she hadn't taken the time to pull her hair back into her usual ponytail, so the dark strands hung down into her face.

But she had the lever. So, really, any of them could go back to the other world any time they wanted, too.

Except, the way the other world works, unless we were really, really careful, we'd probably be caught right away and taken to prison. Maybe we'd also be experimented on like the Gustanos were, exposed to horrible smells that made us feel even more hopeless than ever. . . .

Chess's stomach churned.

From overhead, he heard a thin cry revving up, growing more and more angry.

"Kafi's awake, Dad," Kona said. "You got food for her when you bought the diapers, right?"

"Yeah, sure, but . . . where's the kitchen in this house?" Joe mumbled. "Natalie put Kafi's food in the fridge for me last night and . . . well, I think she did that. I was busy with the surveillance equipment, and . . ."

"Dad, you really aren't very good at multitasking, are you?" Kona teased.

"Never claimed to be!" Joe muttered. He took off sprinting for the stairs as Kafi's cries turned into wails.

And then it was just Kona, Chess, Emma, and Finn clustered around the useless laptops and iPad. Chess glanced toward Natalie, but she was with Mom and Ms. Morales, all of them comforting the Gustanos.

Later, Chess thought. *We've got time. I'll tell her everything Kona told me, and she'll fill me in on everything she heard before Kona gave me the earbud last night.*

Beside him, Kona plopped down onto the couch.

"Are things always this exciting around here?" she asked.

"They weren't until about a month ago," Finn said. "That's when we found out about the other world."

"Guess I'm about a month behind you," Kona said with a shrug. "I didn't find out until we were an hour away from—what was that restaurant called? The Cuckoo Clock? Until then, I thought the only thing different about this weekend was that Dad was going to take me to my gymnastics meet alone, because Mom had to work."

"But you were so calm about everything," Chess marveled. "You didn't even seem upset."

"I've moved seven times in the past eleven years," Kona said. "I've lived everywhere from Hawaii to Maine to . . . well, we got to Atlanta just before Kafi was born. Adaptable is my middle name."

"Really?" Finn breathed.

"She's joking," Emma told him. "Nobody's middle name would be 'Adaptable.'"

"You moved because of your dad, right?" Chess said. "Because he was the one handling all the secret records for people from the other world like my mom, and so he was the most visible person and . . . he had to keep moving to hide."

Kona gaped at him, her gaze locked on his. Chess would have said that it would have been the most awkward and uncomfortable thing ever, to gaze into anyone's eyes like that besides Mom or Emma or Finn. Or, lately, Natalie's. But it felt okay for Kona to stare at him like that, and for Chess to stare back.

"Dad didn't tell me that, but . . . you're right," Kona whispered. "I'm sure you're right. So . . . if we fixed everything in the other world, then my family could just stay in one place for once? That'd be great! I'd do anything for that!"

"Kona, it's not that easy," Chess moaned.

"Wait, what?" Emma said, looking back and forth between Kona and Chess. "Did I miss something?"

"Kona and I kind of eavesdropped on the grown-ups last night," Chess said.

"I thought the grown-ups trusted us now," Finn said forlornly. "I thought they were telling us everything."

"Well, we're keeping secrets, too," Emma said. She pulled a coin from her shorts pocket—the coin that had rolled out into Chess's hand when he'd touched the carved angel at the Cuckoo Clock the day before. "We should show this to Mom and Joe, and then I bet they'll want us to all work together to figure out the code. I'm sure it's connected to the other world somehow. I don't want this to be like last time, where I'm trying to solve some code while we're running toward danger. And when we don't know who's trustworthy and who isn't."

This stung a little, because the last time they'd had an unsolved code and had to make a decision anyway, Chess had guessed the answer completely wrong.

"You've got a coin with code on it?" Kona asked. Her voice came out a little oddly. "Can I see?"

Emma handed her the coin. But Kona didn't dip her head

down to study it. Instead, she dug her other hand into her own shorts pocket. Then she lifted both hands toward the light that was coming in around the edges of the blinds.

"If your coin has code, then . . . is this code, too?" Kona asked.

She was holding up a second coin beside the first.

And it, too, was covered with mysterious symbols.

SIXTEEN

FINN

"Did you press the angel wing at the Cuckoo Clock, too?" Finn asked Kona. "How did you know to do that? And how did you get another coin out of it? I pushed it six or seven times after Chess did, and nothing happened. Did someone have to like, reload it? If we went back and pushed it again this morning, would we get more coins?"

"Angel wing at the Cuckoo Clock—what?" Kona said, looking from Finn to Emma to Chess as if Finn were *talking* in code, and she wanted the other kids to translate.

"That's where we found our coin," Emma said, waving

her hands impatiently. "At the Cuckoo Clock. Where'd you get yours?"

"At a rest area somewhere in Tennessee—or maybe Kentucky, I wasn't really sure—when we were driving here," Kona said. She lowered her voice. "Don't tell Dad, but I put Kafi down on the floor in the bathroom and it wasn't very clean and she started crawling away and she picked that up and I just barely managed to stop her from putting it in her mouth . . . I put it in my pocket just to get it away from her. And then, with everything else, I forgot about it until now."

"A rest area in Kentucky or Tennessee, and the Cuckoo Clock here in our own town," Emma murmured, slumping back against the couch. "That's, like, too coincidental. Maybe neither of these coins are connected to the other world. Maybe we're just clutching at straws. Looking for patterns where there aren't any."

Chess rubbed his hands across his face and back through his hair. Any other day, Finn would have laughed at how crazily this made his hair stand on end. And it had already looked pretty crazy.

"So we don't have any clues except . . . we know the bad people from the other world are taunting us," Chess said. "They're coming back and forth any time they want and scaring us and, and . . . we're helpless."

Before a month ago, Chess never would have said something like that around Finn.

And Finn wasn't going to let him get away with saying it now.

"No, no, no," Finn said, as if he were the big brother and Chess was the little kid who didn't understand anything. "We're not helpless. We rescued Mom and Joe and Ms. Morales from the other world, remember? And that was when it was just us Greystone kids and Natalie working together. And, okay, Other-Natalie and Other-Natalie's grandma and the Judge. But we've got all the grown-ups and the Gustano kids *and* Kona on our side now. And even Kafi, if you count her helping by picking up random things nobody else sees."

"She is good at that," Kona agreed. "As long as you catch her before she puts those things in her mouth."

"And you *did* catch her, at that rest stop," Finn said. "And we've still got Emma's big brain and Chess's bravery, and Natalie's still good at lying and . . . Emma, why don't you at least *look* at the coin Kafi found?"

"Okay, okay," Emma grumbled.

She half-heartedly took both coins from Kona and turned them side to side in the light. And then suddenly she bolted upright. She clutched both coins in her hand and scrambled up and took off racing for the stairs.

"These *are* connected to the other world!" Emma exclaimed. "And I know how!"

SEVENTEEN

EMMA

Emma could hear the other kids calling after her—"Wait, where are you going?" "What did you just figure out?" "Emma?"

But she didn't look back. She took the stairs three at a time, sped down the upstairs hallway, and turned the corner into the bedroom so quickly that she clipped the wall. She knew she'd end up with a bruise, but right now she didn't care.

Her hands shook as she reached inside her pillowcase to pull out a piece of paper.

And there it was: the sheet of gibberish math calculations she'd brought from her own house the day before. The only thing she had left from her father.

The paper she thought had only sentimental meaning.

But she laid the paper down on the floor and put Kona's coin right beside it, and she was right. Unlike the coin Emma and her brothers had found at the Cuckoo Clock, Kona's coin had numerals mixed in among the incomprehensible symbols.

And the numerals imprinted on the metal coin might as well have been written by Emma's father. Emma hadn't seen the connection when she just had one coin. But now that there were two . . . If you could say that the way someone formed their numbers (and other mathematical symbols) was handwriting, then everything engraved on Kona's coin—or Emma's—was Dad's handwriting.

"Emma? Is something wrong?" Mom stepped into the room. Even stressed and distracted and troubled, she was still the first to reach Emma.

Evidently Emma screaming and suddenly running up the stairs at full speed, out of nowhere, was enough to trip Mom's "something's going on with my kid" instincts.

Emma dropped the paper and held out the coins to Mom, one in the palm of each hand.

"This is Dad's writing, isn't it?" Emma asked. Her voice shook. So did her hands. She felt cruel even talking about Dad, when Mom was already so worried. But she had to know. "Dad died eight years ago, in the other world. Why does it look like he wrote this code on these coins Chess and Kona found yesterday?"

Mom gasped and put her hand over her mouth. Her eyebrows shot sky-high.

"Where?" she whispered. "How—?"

Before Emma could answer, everyone else crowded into the room behind Mom, even the Gustano kids. They looked like they'd just stumbled out of bed.

Emma knew she should probably apologize for waking them up. But she could barely look away from Mom. It wasn't surprising that Mom looked stunned. But why did she also look happy?

Or is that . . . hopeful? Emma wondered.

The Gustano kids shoved closer to Emma—past Mom, even. Then Emma Gustano's voice rang out: "Don't you know Rocky has a coin like that, too? Show them, Rocky!"

That made Emma pivot toward the Gustanos. Rocky dug into his pocket. Emma's head flooded with questions even before he had the coin out and lying flat on his palm.

"Where did *you* find a coin yesterday?" she asked, staring at the coin, which was the same size and color as the ones in Emma's hands. "And—"

"Yesterday?" Rocky repeated. His face twisted mockingly. "I didn't find this yesterday. I've had it for years—ever since I was four!"

EIGHTEEN

CHESS

"Four?" Chess said. "When I was four, my dad died."

He didn't realize he'd spoken those words aloud until Natalie gave his shoulder a squeeze. Finn reached out and clutched his hand comfortingly.

Mom stepped closer and put her arm around Chess, too. But she kept peering toward Rocky, her gaze laser-focused.

"Explain," she said. "Did you find this coin or . . . did your mom?"

"Kind of both, I guess," Rocky said. "How did you know?"

"Tell us," Emma said, sounding just as intense as Mom. "Tell us *everything*."

Everyone seemed to be holding their breath. Even baby Kafi had fallen silent.

Chess felt like he was going to faint.

This is about Dad, he thought. *Emma says that's Dad's writing on those coins. . . . I'm going to find out something new about Dad.*

"It was weird how it happened," Mrs. Gustano said. Her eyes locked on Mom's, as if she couldn't look in any other direction either. "It was Rocky's fourth birthday."

Distantly, Chess heard Finn tell Kona, "Chess and Rocky have the same birthday. They're *exactly* the same age. So that was Chess's fourth birthday, too."

Chess couldn't remember his fourth birthday. Too much else had happened right afterward.

"Mom was trying to make me take a nap," Rocky said, rolling his eyes. "Before my birthday party. But I didn't want to, and Mom put her head down on the pillow to show me how soft it was. I put my hands over her ears—and there it was. This coin was in her right ear."

"I kept saying, 'Rocky! You're a magician!'" Mrs. Gustano said. "But it didn't make sense. You know how four-year-olds are with magic tricks—they can't hide anything. And none of us had ever seen that coin before. It really did seem to materialize out of nowhere."

"You've been carrying around that coin since you were four?" Kona asked skeptically.

"*No,*" Rocky said, rolling his eyes.

"He would have lost it," Finn Gustano teased. "Rocky always loses things."

"I never lost this," Rocky countered, holding the coin up high. It was about the size of a quarter. Chess was having a hard time imagining it coming out of Mrs. Gustano's ear. "We always called it my lucky coin. And after . . . after being kidnapped, I thought I could use all the luck I could get. I put it in my pocket before we flew back here."

"That doesn't have code on it, like the others," Emma objected. She'd moved in close enough that if she'd blinked, her eyelashes would have brushed the coin. "It has actual words. It says—"

"I know, I know—it says PLEASE LISTEN," Mrs. Gustano said. "But I swear to you, it did have some bizarre code on it when Rocky first held it out to me."

"And then you touched it," Mom said. She almost sounded like she was in a trance. "You touched it, and the code transformed into something you could actually read. . . ."

"Okay, this is too weird," Mrs. Gustano said. She pulled all three of her kids closer, as if she wanted to protect them against everything odd. "What you're saying . . . it's like you were there. But how could you possibly know what happened to Rocky and me eight years ago? When I was in Arizona and you were in Ohio and . . . no, wait, if I'm supposed to believe everything else you told me, back then I was in this world's version of Arizona and you were in the other world's version of Ohio, and . . . How can you expect me to believe anything you've told me?"

"Because it's all true," Mom said. "And because . . . I'm the one who sent you that coin."

Mrs. Gustano's expression crumpled and it looked like she was about to cry. She put her hand over her mouth, mirroring Mom.

"We were always connected, weren't we?" Mrs. Gustano asked, her hand sliding down helplessly. "Even before my kids were kidnapped. Even before I got that coin. Even before I was born, probably. From the moment my parents met—"

"It was probably the exact same moment Mrs. Greystone's parents met in the other world," Natalie said from behind Chess. "Don't blame Mrs. Greystone for any of this. It's not anyone's fault. Doubles just are connected. They're like, the same person in different circumstances. Or the same person, except they've made different choices because they're in different worlds. But they're still linked, no matter what."

"I don't understand these coins yet, but I can promise

you—Mom didn't mean you any harm," Chess said. Mom still had her arm around his shoulders, but it felt like he should be the one protecting her. "Mom would never want to hurt anyone."

"Chess is right," Mom said. "That coin was supposed to be a good thing. . . ." She snorted, and then the snort turned into a giggle. "Can you understand what it's like for me to find out that that coin actually reached you? For the past eight years, I thought that Andrew and I had failed completely. But you got the coin. You got the coin!"

"Um, Mom, could you back up and explain what that coin was supposed to do?" Emma asked. "And how and why you sent it to Mrs. Gustano eight years ago?"

Practically at the same time, Kona was turning to Joe: "Dad, did you know about any of these coins? When you lived in the other world, were you sending coins to anyone in this one?"

Joe shook his head and gave a perplexed shrug.

"It was a secret," Mom said. "Everything always had to be secret, even from people we trusted. Because we never knew who would be caught, and what they might be forced to reveal. . . ." A shadow crossed her face. "My husband, Andrew, and I had always worked as journalists. But it became too dangerous to do that publicly, because the people in control of the government only wanted the country to believe lies. We felt like we had to keep doing our jobs—we felt like it was our calling to keep gathering information, and telling people what was really going on. But we had to do that underground, anonymously. And if you can only spread the truth in secret, like gossip, do you know how much it starts sounding like just another lie?"

"Nobody knew what to believe," Joe said grimly. "So no one believed anything."

"Andrew and I, we knew we had to do something drastic," Mom said. A little of her grin came back, and she hugged Chess, Emma, and Finn close. "Would you believe we got our idea for the coins from reading *Horton Hears a Who* to you kids when you were little?"

"The Dr. Seuss book?" Finn asked. "Was it from the 'A person's a person no matter how small' part or the 'Yopp!' part?"

"I bet it was the part about seeking help from a different world," Emma said. She was practically jumping up and down with excitement now. Chess could tell that she, at least, loved this story.

"Right," Mom said. "Our world had become so grim. It wasn't just one thing or just one leader making the changes—it was a thousand tiny decisions over the years, everyone acting out of fear and distrust and hate, until no one had any freedom. No one could speak the truth openly. No one was even allowed to ask questions of our leaders."

"And if the leaders said, 'The sky is green and the grass is blue,' everyone had to agree, 'Yes, yes, you're absolutely right,'" Joe added. "Nobody was allowed to say, 'Are you kidding? I have eyes of my own, and that's not what I see!'"

Mom reached out and gripped Joe's shoulder, linking the two of them.

"Can you understand now why Andrew and I had to keep everything secret?" she asked beseechingly. "But the two of us, we were friends with a physicist who had told us about the possibility of other worlds outside our own. We worked with her to figure out how to send a message between worlds. I couldn't explain the science of it then, and I can't now, either. But our friend knew what metal to use, how to design the tiny electronics inside the coin, why we should use the thumbprint authentication to make sure a voice-coin from one person only went to his or her double in the other world. . . . Andrew and I decided to put codes on the coins in his handwriting—just to keep track—and I would record the first message. We decided to send the first one out on Chess's fourth birthday." She flashed Mrs. Gustano and Rocky a significant look. "Then, if it was safe, we planned to send out a second a week later, a third the week after that. . . ."

"I never got any other coins," Mrs. Gustano said.

"Neither did Rocky or my Emma or Finn. Or my husband."

Mom let go of Chess, Emma, and Finn. It fell to Chess to mutter, "Everything changed. Our dad was killed five days after my birthday."

"So was our physicist friend," Mom whispered. "And then the kids and I moved to this world, and I shifted to trying to make sure no one in my family crossed paths with anyone in yours. Before Andrew died, I thought you could be a help to me in my world. But once I was here, I believed I could only be a danger to you in yours."

And that's what happened, Chess thought with a pang. *It's because of us Greystones that the Gustano kids were kidnapped. And even though we rescued them, we messed up their lives. They don't have their dad with them right now, either. This whole world is in danger from the other world.*

Was that the Greystones' fault, too?

"But what did you think when you heard my message—when you got the coin originally?" Mom asked Mrs. Gustano. "Could you tell my voice was the same as yours? Did you have even a moment of thinking, 'I need to go rescue her'?"

Bewilderment spread over Mrs. Gustano's face.

"Kate, I'm sorry," she said. "I never heard your voice or any sound at all coming from your coin. Rocky, did you—?"

But Rocky was shaking his head, too.

"So the coin did the hardest thing—traveling between the worlds—but it failed to even work like a simple recorder?" Mom asked.

She sagged down onto the bed, as if having hope—and then losing it again—had taken too much out of her.

"But, Mom, now we have these coins, too," Emma said, holding her hand up again. "Maybe we just need the right person to press them. Maybe the technology improved in the last eight years."

She began passing the coins around, letting everyone in the room finger them. When the coins circled around to Chess, they just felt cold and fake in his hand, not even as valuable as a penny. The numbers and symbols on the surface stayed indecipherable.

Chess handed the coins on to Kona and Emma, and they each slid one into a pocket. Rocky did the same with the coin that proclaimed, PLEASE LISTEN.

"Maybe . . . maybe we'll figure out more about the coins later," Chess said, because everyone had fallen back into grimness.

"Right," Mom said. "Maybe if we take a break and eat breakfast, we'll think of a solution."

Chess thought probably even baby Kafi could hear the fakeness in Mom's voice. They all seemed stuck again. Chess felt Natalie's hand slip off his shoulder, and he turned.

Natalie wasn't even looking toward him. She had her head tilted back, watching something fall from the ceiling.

At first, Chess saw only a streak of golden light. Natalie stuck out her hand and caught it. She flattened her palm, and Chess saw what lay in the center: a coin that looked like the ones Kona and Emma had pocketed, covered with indecipherable code.

"This one was meant for me," Natalie said, her voice ringing with confidence. "I can feel it."

Emma asked, "What do you mean by that?" and Emma Gustano asked, "Can you describe that feeling more precisely?" But everyone else began shouting, "Your thumb!" and "See if your thumbprint matches!"

Natalie lowered her thumb toward the coin as if she were taking part in a sacred ceremony. She raised her thumb again and breathed, "It's words now! It says FIND US!"

"Press it again," Mom said breathlessly. "It's the second touch that activates—"

And then she stopped, because Natalie was already doing that. And Natalie's voice flowed from the coin.

No, Chess thought. *That's not Natalie's voice, even though it sounds the same. We're hearing her double in the other world. Other-Natalie, who's just like our Natalie.*

He saw the excitement burst over Emma's face, the excitement and pride and hope springing back to life on

113

Mom's. Chess could tell what Mom was thinking: that the idea she and Dad had come up with eight years ago actually worked.

Finn bounced joyfully up and down. Chess wanted to throw his arms around Natalie.

Then it registered what Other-Natalie's voice was saying:

"This is a warning. We're all in danger now. I need your help. You need mine."

NINETEEN

FINN

"That's it?" Finn asked. "Isn't she going to tell you *how* to help?"

He heard a clatter out in the hallway—the exact sound that a handful of coins would make hitting a wooden floor.

"Oooh," Finn cried. "She's sending you more coins!"

He heard Ms. Morales say behind him, "Some of those might be for me. I . . . I feel like they're calling to me. . . ."

But Finn was already sprinting out into the hallway and scooping up coins to hand to Natalie and Ms. Morales.

Ahead of him, he could see even more coins gliding down from the ceiling. In the sunlight streaming through the upper window, the coins twirled and twinkled, as bright as stars.

It was the most beautiful thing Finn had ever seen.

Except for his own mother's face, of course.

"Everyone!" he shouted over his shoulder. "Come and look!"

The others spilled out of the room and down the stairs behind him. The whole group spun into the living room, their heads tilted back to stare in awe at the coins floating down. Finn chased the coins as if they were fireflies flitting across a backyard on a perfect summer night. He scooped them up and poured them into the other kids' cupped hands, too. He felt dizzy with joy. The coins were answers; they had to be. He didn't know how everything was going to work out, but he was certain it would.

Emma, Kona, and the Gustano kids laughed and traded coins back and forth with Finn, each coin seeming shinier than the last. All the parents smiled indulgently. Natalie gathered up coins and dropped them one by one into Chess's hands as if she were sorting them by touch: "This one's mine. This one's Mom's. This one's Mom's, too. . . ."

Then the front door rattled.

It was an odd sound to notice in the midst of their glee. Maybe Finn wouldn't have paid any attention at all if it hadn't been for how the coins reacted: Except for the ones held tight in someone's hands, all the coins suddenly skittered out of sight, like frightened animals. They slipped down into the cracks between the floor's wood panels; they jammed themselves under couch cushions.

The front door began to open.

Did someone have a key?

Finn remembered the fake police officer. He remembered Other-Natalie's message from the other world: *We're all in danger now.*

And then he saw who'd opened the door.

It was only Natalie's dad, Mr. Mayhew.

Natalie's dad happened to be a great friend of Finn's. Mr. Mayhew and Natalie's mom were divorced, but everyone got along really well. Now, anyway.

In this world, Finn's brain reminded him.

Finn clutched the coins in his hand a little tighter, so they wouldn't escape. But he stepped out from behind the couch.

"Mr. Mayhew, you won't believe what you just missed!" he cried.

Mr. Mayhew barely glanced at Finn. His eyes darted around like he was trying to keep track of everyone all at once.

Then he flashed a cheesy grin and seemed more like himself.

"Oh, sorry—didn't mean to barge in," he said. "I thought

everyone would still be sleeping." He held up a stack of boxes labeled in garish shades of pink and orange and brown. "I just wanted to leave these in the kitchen so you'd believe the doughnut-and-bagel fairy had been here overnight. . . . I heard you had quite the houseful, and I figured you might all be hungry."

"Doughnuts!" Finn squealed at the same time that someone behind him—Other-Finn?—cried out delightedly, "Bagels!"

Finn saw Natalie's shoulders slump in relief. She dropped her last coin into Chess's hand, and tripped forward to give her father a hug.

"Dad, that was really nice of you," she said.

Mr. Mayhew awkwardly shuffled the boxes of doughnuts and bagels to the side so he could draw his daughter close.

"Here. I can take those," Finn said, reaching out. He grinned. "If you trust me not to eat them all myself."

But something was wrong. Mr. Mayhew didn't laugh at Finn's joke. He also didn't let go of the doughnut and bagel boxes.

And Natalie was already pulling back from her father.

Finn stopped reaching for the doughnuts and glanced back and forth between Natalie and her dad. Mr. Mayhew was wearing a neon yellow golf shirt that almost seemed to glow against his tanned skin—this was a perfectly normal look for him. But Natalie shook her head and alternated between blinking and widening her eyes at Finn, as if she were trying to send a secret message in Morse code.

Finn wanted to say, *You know Emma's better at code than I am! I don't understand!*

In one smooth move, Mr. Mayhew threw the boxes of doughnuts and bagels past Finn's outstretched hands. They landed on a bare patch of floor that only moments before had been covered by glistening coins.

"Hey, why'd you do that?" Finn demanded. "You wouldn't want to ruin good doughnuts, would you?"

"Five-second rule!" Other-Finn crowed behind him. Finn heard a clinking, as if Other-Finn had dropped his coins to scurry over and grab whatever doughnuts and bagels might roll out.

But it wasn't doughnuts or bagels that spilled from the sagging, splitting boxes. Instead, a thin line of smoke or ash or some other kind of pollution wafted up. Finn couldn't help himself: He sniffed. And he didn't smell chocolate or maple or the glorious aroma of fried dough. He smelled an odor that sent him back into his worst nightmares. It smelled of dead animals and burning garbage and despair.

It smelled like the other world.

And suddenly Finn understood what Natalie had been

trying to tell him: This wasn't actually Natalie's dad. This was his double from the other world. The Mayor. The worst double any of the kids had met.

And what he'd brought instead of doughnuts and bagels?

He'd brought weapons. He'd brought fear and lies.

He'd brought evil.

TWENTY

EMMA, AT THE SAME TIME

Emma just wanted to keep thinking about the coins.

But she could hear Joe muttering beside her as he put Kafi down and snatched up a laptop: "All the security cameras I set up around this house—they're being jammed! Somehow they're looping all our old footage again and again . . . that's how I didn't see Roger Mayhew coming. We're flying blind here!"

She could see Kona dashing back up the stairs to peer out the only uncovered window.

"*I* can see!" Kona cried. "This neighborhood is crawling with police cars! Or—fake ones!"

Emma whirled around, and now she could also see Chess and Natalie and Finn trying to shove Mr. Mayhew out the front door.

No, that's Other—Mr. Mayhew, Emma realized. *The Mayor. He must have used that fake cop we saw before as his scout. Or as a decoy, to throw us off from the real danger. So what we should do now is . . .*

The first tendrils of odor from the Mayor's boxes reached Emma's nose. The tendrils whispered, *Don't think. Don't listen. Don't look. Just smell . . . Smell, and think what I want you to think. Hear what I want you to hear. See what I want you to see. . . .*

Emma clamped her mouth shut and shifted all the coins she was holding into one hand so she could pinch her nose shut.

"That's poison!" Emma screamed through gritted teeth. "They're poisoning our air! Hold your breath, everyone! Open the windows!"

She started to bolt toward the nearest window, but Mom grabbed her by the shoulders and spun her in the other direction.

"Run!" Mom yelled. "All you kids—escape! And, Emma, you guard this. . . . Keep it safe. . . ."

Mom thrust something into Emma's arms. It was the bat bag containing the lever.

And then Mom slumped down toward the floor.

Emma shouldered the bat bag but tugged on Mom's arm, too.

"Mom! Run away with us!"

"Can't," Mom murmured. "Need to stay . . . and fight. Should have stayed . . . and fought . . . back home. . . ."

She means back in the other world, Emma thought.

Mom didn't even think of home the same way Emma did. What if Emma couldn't even trust her own mother?

Emma realized she'd accidentally taken a tiny breath of air. *That* was why she'd had a moment of distrusting her mother.

"Mom!" Emma dropped her coins and tried to shake her mother out of her stupor. Dimly, she realized that the other moms, Natalie, Joe, and Finn Gustano were also sinking toward the floor. Emma's brothers, Other-Emma, Kona, and Rocky were all still standing, but only barely.

If Mom gets back up, the others will, too, Emma thought. *I'm sure of it.*

"Save . . . ," Mom murmured. "Rescue . . ."

Emma was starting to feel a little dizzy herself. Her mind screamed, *Air! Air! You need to breathe!* But she resolutely locked her jaw and clenched her teeth and avoided the instinct to inhale deeply. Swaying slightly, she sprinted toward the front door. Natalie, Chess, and Finn had almost succeeded in closing it behind the Mayor. But Emma yanked it back open and gulped in the sweet, precious, untainted air from outside.

Only then did she realize that the Mayor was still on the porch. Except, he looked like a monster now.

Oh. He'd slipped a gas mask over his face.

"And I thought you were supposed to be the smart one, Emma," he chuckled, his voice distorted because of the mask. "Thanks for bringing me exactly what I wanted."

He began yanking the bag containing the lever directly from Emma's shoulder.

"Get away from me!" Emma screamed, pulling back on the bag.

But the Mayor was a strong man who played sports a lot, and she was a ten-year-old who'd been on the verge of oxygen deprivation a moment ago. If it was just a battle of the muscles, Emma was never going to win.

So use your brain, she told herself.

The last time the kids had encountered the Mayor, they'd used his own allergies against him. Now the gas mask protected him against that, too. But . . .

She reached up and tugged off the Mayor's gas mask.

"Stop that, you little brat!" the Mayor gasped, quickly yanking it back into place.

But he reeled and his grasp on the lever bag weakened,

as if he'd breathed some of the contaminated air flowing out of the house, too.

"Chess, Finn, Natalie—help me!" Emma screamed.

She filled her lungs with as much of the outdoor air as she could, jerked away from the Mayor, and struggled to slam the door again. Belatedly, Finn and Chess sprang up to shove against the door, too. Natalie spun the lock at the top of the door—the deadbolt.

"Let's hope . . . he doesn't . . . have a key . . . to that . . . ," she murmured.

But with each word—and without any more fresh air—she began sliding toward the floor again.

"The bagel and doughnut boxes actually held . . . stink bombs?" Other-Emma whispered. She was valiantly trying to pull her younger brother away from the boxes on the floor. She dropped the last coin from her hands to get a better grip on Other-Finn's shirt. Emma didn't dare take another whiff, but she could tell by the way Other-Emma and Other-Finn grimaced that the boxes were still leaking their foul odor.

We've got to have fresh air to be able to think, Emma told herself.

She stepped toward the nearest window. Because she felt herself starting to black out, she allowed herself one small sip of air.

The window latch looked incredibly complicated—too complicated for Emma to figure out. This was hopeless.

"Break the window!" Finn shouted behind her. "Use the lever and break it!"

Oh yeah. That would work.

Emma swung the lever bag toward the window. But having so little air made her weak. The lever bag crashed into the blinds and warped them, but did no damage to the window.

Emma had just yanked the lever bag back for another swing at the window when she heard the crash of breaking glass above her.

"Oh, thanks!" she cried, jumping back from the little shards of glass raining down on her. She also had to avoid the now-broken blinds swinging back and threatening to stab her. She took a deep breath of the sudden fresh air. "Who figured out you could just *throw* something through the window? Chess? Kona? Emma? Nat—"

The fresh air she was suddenly swimming in woke up her brain. It made her realize that if someone had thrown a vase or paperweight or something equally heavy from inside the house, the little bits of shattered glass from the broken window wouldn't have fallen *toward* Emma. They wouldn't have landed in her hair and on her shoulders. They would have been carried out of the house along with the vase or paperweight or whatever had been thrown.

And the broken blinds would be out on the porch, not sagging toward Emma.

So someone threw something into *the house?* Emma wondered, shaking bits of glass out of her hair. *But what? And why?*

The fresh air she was breathing stopped seeming so fresh. The smell of death and despair and fire and fear rose around her even as another window shattered and more falling glass crashed to the floor.

And then another window broke.

And another.

And another.

And another.

"They're attacking everywhere!" Emma screamed, because the others had to know. She had to make them understand. "Everything's poison now!"

TWENTY-ONE

CHESS

"Kids, really! Save yourselves! I . . . can't!" Mom wailed. "And . . . the lever! You have to keep the lever away from . . . Oh, Chess, please! Save Emma and Finn!"

It felt like an eternity since the last time Chess had taken a breath. Along with the sounds of crashing glass, he could hear footsteps out on the front porch. Too many footsteps to just be Mayor Mayhew. It had to be more people from the other world.

How much time did they have before those people came climbing in through the broken windows?

Was it just his imagination, or were there sounds at the

back of the house, too? Were people from the other world already coming in through the back door?

"There's nowhere to go!" he screamed back at Mom. But Mom was just lying on the floor now. Finn was crouched over her yelling, "Don't breathe! Don't take in any more of this bad air—what if it kills you?"

"Won't . . . kill . . . me," Mom murmured. "I'm . . . no threat . . . like this. But you kids . . . more power . . . more danger . . . the coins . . . . the lever . . ."

She was weeping now. Weeping more hopelessly than Chess had ever seen before.

Chess still hadn't taken another breath, but Mom's murmured "more danger" hit his brain like a jolt of electricity.

He tore his gaze away from Mom and Finn and frantically glanced around.

The air in the house seemed murky now, as if the stench was so intense it'd become visible. Or maybe Chess was just seeing the effects of the stench: All the other grown-ups and Natalie had collapsed to the floor like Mom, all in the foyer near the door and the doughnut boxes. They'd given up. Oddly, little Kafi seemed the least affected—she was crawling toward Kona, still back on the stairs.

Oh no—babies near stairs—that's dangerous, too, Chess thought. *They can fall. . . .*

He took a step toward Kafi, then saw that Rocky had

done the same thing. Rocky pulled away from his siblings, who were clumped and wailing over Mrs. Gustano and the doughnut boxes.

Behind him, the front door rattled in its frame. Mom sobbed harder.

"Save . . . Finn . . . Please . . . Chess . . . and Emma . . . and the lever . . ."

With one arm, Chess scooped up his little brother and held him sideways. Then he looked around for Emma.

She was crouched by one of the couches in the living room near the stairs. She was trying to shove the lever bag under the couch—trying to hide it.

But the stench—or the lack of air—had made her slug-gish and clumsy, and the end of the lever bag kept snagging on one of the couch legs.

"Diagonal," Chess tried to shout at her. "Sideways. Slide it in at an angle. . . ."

Normally Emma would have known that. She must have breathed in more of the stench than Chess had.

Emma also should know it was totally stupid to try to hide the lever under the couch. The gap between the bottom of the couch and the floor was huge—the lever would still be in plain sight.

Chess switched to struggling to yell, "Get up! Take it . . . someplace else!"

But where?

Still clutching Finn—and with one quick glance to make sure Rocky was still headed for Kafi—Chess stepped from the foyer into the living room with Emma. He reached past her to grab the lever bag.

Chess wasn't Emma (Emma on a good day, that is—Normal-Emma); he couldn't figure out angles and actions and opposite reactions in a split second in his head. So he didn't see that pulling up on the lever bag while Emma was pushing forward would make it bounce against the couch.

He also hadn't spared a thought for calculating how the lever was aimed.

But even from inside the bat bag, the lever was still powerful.

Chess saw a flash of light, and for an instant it seemed like the lever was going to latch onto the couch just as he'd seen it latch onto walls and into closets. In that instant, it felt like the lever might open a secret tunnel to the other world straight through the couch.

But then Emma got a better grip on the lever bag and pulled it back just before the lever totally engaged.

"Sheesh, what's in that bag?" Rocky asked behind them. He'd scooped up Kafi and held her safely in his arms. "You hiding the Incredible Hulk in there?"

Chess saw that the end of the lever bag was shredded

now. The part of the lever that he'd hit against walls before was sticking out, completely revealed.

Completely ready.

The front door rattled again, and burst open. Chess caught a quick glimpse of multiple men in gas masks streaming into the foyer. Somebody screamed. Maybe everybody screamed.

Chess was so terrified he gulped in air. But some of it must have been fresh and untainted, coming from outdoors. Because suddenly he knew exactly what to do.

"Hide!" he screamed. "Follow me!"

He yanked the lever out of the bag, out from Emma's grasp. And then he swung the lever as hard as he could—directly at the floor.

TWENTY-TWO

FINN

"Oh, cool!" Finn screamed, even as he tumbled forward. "You opened a slide this time, not a tunnel!"

The hole that had suddenly opened right in the floor beside—and then *around*—Finn and Chess and Emma was like something out of an amusement park. Finn could see shadowy twists and turns, and he imagined that there might even be loop-de-loops ahead. Of course he couldn't see all the way to the end of the slide, but he had a pretty good idea where he would land.

"Come on, everyone!" Finn shouted over his shoulder as he spun around, speeding toward curves and corkscrews.

"Get away from the bad guys!"

He decided he didn't want to look completely back toward the front door; he was leaving anyway, so why scare himself by seeing how close the men in gas masks had gotten?

"But won't this take us to the other world?" someone screamed behind him. "Exactly where we *don't* want to go?"

That was Rocky, tumbling alongside Finn and the other Greystones. Rocky was clutching little Kafi and looked a hundred times more terrified than the little girl. She looked completely unruffled. The yellow bows tied in her hair weren't even crooked.

"Right, but we'll be in Judge Morales's house in the other world, and *she's* on our side," Finn countered. "It's okay!"

He somersaulted out of Chess's arms, grabbing for Emma and Rocky as he turned head over heels beyond them.

"But maybe we should think through this . . . first," Emma was saying even as she tumbled around and around with Finn.

It was too late. They were both—no, wait; all three, all four, all *five*—slipping and sliding and twisting and banking off the turns of the slide that had suddenly appeared beneath their feet. The slide was spinning, too, so it felt like a combination slide and amusement park ride. Kafi seemed to be shrieking with glee, and all five of them were so jumbled together that Finn couldn't figure out whether it was Rocky's elbow or Chess's that had lodged itself in his ear. He couldn't tell whether it was Emma's knee or Kafi's that kept bumping against his leg.

"Kafi!" he heard someone yell behind him, and he realized it was Kona's voice. "Don't worry! I'm coming after you!"

And then there was a foot—Kona's?—that kept tapping on his head whenever Finn slowed down in the twisty curves of the slide.

Then, as if it came from a million miles away, he heard a man's gruff voice calling out, "Here's where they escaped! Do we follow them, or just take their lever?"

Finn shrieked. Twisting a lever could shut a tunnel; surely it would shut a tunnel-slide, too. And if the people from the other world took the lever away completely, then . . . then . . .

It didn't seem like it would be safe to still be in a tunnel-slide when that happened.

And it would mean the Greystones and Rocky and Kona and Kafi had lost the lever.

They couldn't lose the lever. They'd be trapped.

Still shrieking, Finn hit the floor, landing in a heap with the other kids. He didn't want to think about how he could fall straight down through the floor and land on the exact same floor in the other world—thinking too much about how the worlds connected always made his head hurt. Emma moaned on one side of him, Chess on the other, as if both of their heads hurt, too. Rocky, Kona, and Kafi were a little farther away, but only Kafi sat up immediately.

Kafi was just a baby. Rocky and Kona didn't know as much as the Greystones did about levers. And Emma and Chess always had a harder time recovering from traveling between the worlds than Finn did.

So maybe everything depended on Finn?

He groped around on the floor, and—yes! There was the lever. Or, at least, *this* world's version of the lever, the mirror image of the one they'd left behind on the floor at Natalie's house. Finn wrapped his hands around the lever the same way a really little kid would clutch a blankie. But in his mind, Finn replayed another moment with this lever—a time when Chess had tried to hold on to the lever while someone in the opposite world ripped the corresponding lever away . . . and the lever had vanished from between Chess's fingers.

Finn couldn't let that happen again. He couldn't let his family be left without this lever.

Straining every muscle, Finn yanked the lever straight up from the floor and hugged it close to his chest.

Instantly, the tunnel-slide at his feet vanished completely.

"Mom? Chess? Finn? Natalie?" Emma moaned beside him.

Only then did Finn realize: They'd left Mom and Natalie behind. And Ms. Morales, Joe, and all of the Gustanos except Rocky. The others had been in the foyer, not the living room, when the floor opened up. So they'd been trapped with all the men in gas masks smashing into the house and throwing stink bombs.

And Finn himself had just taken away the lever that would have allowed Mom and the others to escape.

TWENTY-THREE

EMMA

Emma felt so groggy. She couldn't quite remember why she needed to get back to her senses immediately, but it seemed like a good idea. Maybe because someone was shaking her shoulders and calling her name: "Emma? *Emma?* EMMA!"

She opened her eyes and blinked away the darkness. And there was Finn staring down at her, practically nose to nose.

"How far from a closed tunnel-slide do you have to go to open a new one?" he asked. "Where's the best place to swing the lever? Should I hit the floor again or aim for the wall?"

"Finn . . . slow . . . down," Emma moaned, because he seemed to be talking twice as fast as usual.

Or maybe Emma's brain was just working twice as slowly as usual.

"Hurry up and start thinking again!" Finn begged. Did he have tears in his eyes? "We've got to go back for Mom!"

Go . . . back? Emma had to puzzle out the meaning of both those words.

Then she remembered. Doughnuts. Mayor Mayhew in a gas mask. Broken windows. The adults and Natalie slumped to the floor. The spinning tunnel-slide.

So she and Chess and Finn were in the other world now?

Oh yeah, Emma thought. *Since the lever opens a spinning room if you hit it against a wall, then it must open a spinning slide if you hit a floor. Because it's spinning plus gravity.*

"Shh." She shot her hand up and slipped it over Finn's mouth. Then she hissed, "It's dangerous to make so much noise."

"But we're in Judge Morales's house," Finn whispered, despite the hand over his mouth. "She's on our side."

"Don't say that out loud! Someone might hear!" Emma whispered back. "It's a secret, remember? And she has enemies even in her own home. . . . We have to make sure it's really safe here before we go back for anyone else."

Dizzily, Emma sat up.

Chess was straining to prop himself up against the side of the couch, too.

"We . . . should get out of sight . . . ," he moaned. "As soon as . . . we can . . ."

"Where . . . are we?" Kona asked dazedly. She was still lying flat on the floor, with Kafi sitting beside her, patting her cheek.

"Same house, different world," Emma muttered.

On the other side of Kona, Rocky sat up unsteadily and began peering around.

"Same couch, same staircase, different windows, no exploding doughnut boxes or stink grenades . . . ," he murmured. He took a deep breath and started coughing. He seemed to be at least *trying* to do it quietly. He grimaced, and seemed on the verge of gagging. "Ugh. I take that back. The stink grenades have been here, too."

He bent down and peeked under the couch, as if he expected to see the same small round rubbery bundles of poison stench that had come flying in the windows at Ms. Morales's house back in the better world.

"Stink grenades" was a pretty good name for them.

"Don't worry," Emma assured him. "*This* house wouldn't have poison smells. The Judge and the Mayor are leaders here. The leaders use the bad smells to make ordinary people feel hopeless. The Mayor did, anyway. The leaders and their families—they don't have to deal with anything like that themselves."

"Oh yeah?" Rocky asked. "Then what am I smelling?"

"The leftover stink on your own clothes? Your own hair?" Emma asked. "All of us kids?"

"Maybe it's the air inside our noses from the other world," Kona said helpfully, sniffing deliberately. She exhaled, and tried again. "But . . . I smell it, too. It's like they held a rat convention here, and all the rats died."

"It's worse over by this wall," Rocky reported, edging away from the couch. He made a face like he was about to throw up. "Kona, you should keep your baby sister away from here."

"Hey, is that wall *broken*?" Finn asked, squinting as if his eyes hadn't fully adjusted either.

Now all the kids stared at the wall. A shadowy line ran through its cream-colored paint, then turned at a right angle about eight feet up.

"Oh, I see," Chess muttered. "That's a *door*. I bet it leads to one of the secret passageways here. Someone just left it open a crack."

"Why would they do that?" Emma asked. "Then the passageway isn't secret."

Recklessly, she lurched to her feet. It felt like her legs had fallen asleep, and they were just starting to awaken. So she was lucky not to trip as she stumbled toward the crack in the wall. But her brain was fully alert now. And Rocky was right. This house reeked, too. The stench intensified the closer Emma got to the wall.

But I have to know what's in there. . . .

Emma cupped one hand over her mouth and nose and tried to keep from gagging as she tugged on the edge of the door. A dim passageway appeared ahead, just as Emma had expected.

Emma and her brothers had spent a lot of time roaming through the secret passageways of this house on their last trip to this world, so they knew the routes well. She was not at all surprised to see the unfinished beams and drywall of the narrow passageway before her. Only the floor of the passageway seemed to have changed. Someone—the Mayor? The Judge? Some servant?—had laid down a black rubberized surface that seemed oddly bumpy.

Emma blinked, and her eyesight swung into clearer focus.

No. She'd been wrong. The actual floor of the secret passageway hadn't changed.

It was now just covered with stink grenades.

TWENTY-FOUR

CHESS

"Get down! Someone will see you!" Chess hissed at Emma. He lunged toward her to pull her down to the floor and safety. But his muscles were still a little shaky from changing worlds, and he started to fall past her.

Emma caught him, and pulled him up beside her.

"No, Chess—look," she breathed, spinning him around to face out into the living room. "I don't think anyone else is here."

Chess blinked. The house did have an eerie, abandoned feel to it. The front door of the house was hanging wide open, creaking back and forth with the breeze. Chess tilted his head back to look at the upper level of the entryway windows—the extra level, which Ms. Morales's house didn't have back in the better world. Those windows were all broken, and tattered drapes and valances fluttered in and out.

"This house was attacked, too," Rocky said grimly, pulling himself up alongside them. "Maybe it was attacked first. And then . . . and then . . . the way these attacks work . . . was everyone just taken away? *Kidnapped?*"

Chess remembered the words from the first coin Natalie had received: *We're all in danger now. I need your help. You need mine.* He remembered how, the last time the Greystone kids had been in this house, there'd been a behind-the-scenes battle raging between the good Judge and the evil Mayor. The Judge had seemed to win that battle. But now . . .

The Mayor's out running around, attacking the better world, Chess thought. *The Judge is nowhere in sight. That's not a good sign.*

"This must be what the coin from Other-Natalie was warning us about," he said, wincing. "Both of the attacks. Here and there. Except . . . we didn't help Other-Natalie and her mom. We got distracted playing with the coins."

Chess felt his face flush. Just thinking about the coins back at Ms. Morales's house made him dizzy. When the coins were drifting down, when Natalie placed them so carefully in his hands . . . how could he have felt anything but wonder and awe? How could he have done anything but peer into her face and smile?

Chess looked down at the coins he still held clutched in his left hand. He'd managed to hold on to most of the Natalie coins, even though he'd dropped the Ms. Morales ones.

"The coins made us all giddy," Kona said. "That does *not* seem like a good system for sending messages."

"Hmm," Emma said. She began digging in her pocket. She pulled out the coin she'd brought from the other world and handed it to Chess.

"Wait a minute—no, just thirty seconds—then give that back to me," she told him, letting go.

Then she dived into the pile of stink grenades in the secret passageway.

Instantly she began weeping and wailing.

It was a horrible sound, as if Emma's heart was completely broken, and she believed everyone she loved was dead, and she knew her life would never contain so much as a glimmer of happiness ever again. She flailed her legs and clutched her face in her hands.

Chess couldn't take it.

"No, Emma, please! Stop that!" Chess pleaded. "Get away from there! Everything will be okay, I promise. I—" Desperately, he shoved the coin back into Emma's hand, even though he hadn't timed anything.

Emma popped back up. Her eyes still glistened with unshed tears, but the overwhelming distress was gone. The corner of her lips trembled, as if she was trying to smile again.

Finn gave both Chess and Emma a big hug, as if they'd both just escaped an attack all over again.

"What are you guys doing?" Rocky complained. "We don't have time for playing with the stink grenades any more than we did with the coins. Not when my mom and brother and sister are still in danger."

He looked around, as if he expected Kona to say, "Or my dad." But Kona had a gleam in her eye that almost matched Emma's.

"She's figuring out the coins," Kona said. "The coins and the stink grenades and the different worlds and . . . and *us*. Right, Emma?"

Emma rewarded Kona with a full-on grin. It wasn't exactly like watching Natalie and her double, Other-Natalie, have a moment of mind-meld. It wasn't even like watching Mom and Mrs. Gustano together. But Emma and Kona were definitely on the same wavelength.

"I don't know what else they can do, but around the stink grenades, the coins are, like, *immunity*," Emma said. "Protection. A 'Get Out of Jail Free' card."

Rocky dug in his pocket and brought out the PLEASE

LISTEN coin he'd been carrying. He looked like he was considering dropping it to test Emma's theory, but didn't quite dare.

"I'm holding this coin in my hand, and that stink still makes me feel awful," he said. "It's still like I've got this voice in my head saying, 'You may never see your family again. They might be suffering right now, and you're not doing anything about it.'"

"Right," Emma said. "'You *may* never see them. . . . They *might* be suffering. . . .' If you put that coin down, the smell would make you think, 'I know for sure I'll never see my family again. I know for sure they're suffering, and there's nothing I can do. I hate myself. I hate everything. There's no hope.'"

Rocky closed his fingers around the coin in his hand and shoved his hand back in his pocket. He kept his hand there, holding on to the coin.

Chess clutched the coins in his own hand even tighter, too.

"Did you notice that every single one of us who escaped from the Mayor's attack had coins?" Emma asked.

Chess looked around. Kona patted the coin she'd placed in her own pocket. Finn clenched his hand around his coins so hard his knuckles turned white.

"Not Kafi," Kona reported, checking the little girl's

hands and clothing. "Oh, wait . . . Kafi, how did you manage to get one stuck in the toe of your sleeper?" She unzipped the girl's sleeper and pulled out a coin. Instantly, Kafi screwed up her face and began to wail. Kona put the coin back. "Okay, okay, Kafi—I'll leave it there!"

Kona rezipped the sleeper. Kafi stopped crying, snuggled against her big sister, and stuck her thumb in her mouth.

"I think we need to get as far away as we can from the smell, so we can think straight," Chess said, pulling Finn and Emma along with him, away from the secret passageway.

As soon as they were out of the way, Rocky shoved the door completely shut. Then he gave the door an extra kick.

"*That* felt good," he announced.

Finn grabbed the lever again as all the kids moved into the open area of the living room.

"We go back, we use the coins like shields, we hand out coins to Mom and Natalie and everyone else. . . . It's a plan!" Finn said, practically dancing now. He was definitely cheering up, almost back to his usual self.

Chess looked down again at the coins in his hand. Away from the secret passageway full of stink grenades, it felt safe now to unclench his fist, to hold the coins loosely. He noticed that Natalie's touch had transformed whatever code had been there originally, so he could read the words on all the coins now: HEAR US, SEE US, HELP US. . . .

The last message repeated twice.

Why didn't we hear Other-Natalie's voice through these coins, when they transformed? Chess wondered. He remembered Mom saying to press the coins twice—maybe Natalie just hadn't done that.

Or maybe Other-Natalie's voice had spoken, and Natalie and Chess had missed hearing it in all the chaos.

Then Chess realized something else. He held only four coins; Finn, he'd seen, had three. Everyone else had only one. So if they all kept one for themselves, that left only five to give to Mom, Natalie, Joe, and the three left-behind Gustanos.

Five coins, six people, Chess thought.

He was away from the awful smell, and he still didn't feel very cheerful. But maybe this was his natural self: wondering, worried, stymied. . . .

"Somebody else take all my coins," Chess said, holding out his hand. "I'll hold on to Emma or Finn, and maybe their coin will work for me, too. So we can hand out my four coins and the two extra ones Finn has, then—"

"Chess, that doesn't seem fair," Emma said. "We don't want to risk losing you. Let's work on this—we've got a lot more to figure out."

"Oh, come on," Rocky groaned. "We're going to keep talking and talking about this, and the rest of my family is still in danger, and . . ."

He looked around frantically, as if being farther from the stink grenades had freed him to move decisively again.

Then he grabbed the lever from Finn's grasp and swung it at the nearest wall.

TWENTY-FIVE

FINN

"Go, Rocky!" Finn cheered. "I agree!"

Rocky was worried about his mom and brother and sister; Finn was worried about Mom and Natalie and Ms. Morales and Joe. They could still be a united team. Finn raced over to Rocky's side, ready to turn the lever as soon as it latched on.

But something was wrong. The lever didn't burrow into the wall. It skittered to the side, leaving a gouge in the cream-colored paint.

"It's okay," Finn said. He put his coins into his pocket so

he could pat Rocky's back. "I know what happened. Someone must have used that spot before. Levers have rules—they can't latch on in the same place twice. We'll try somewhere else."

He eased the lever out of Rocky's hands.

"Finn, Rocky—wait!" Emma said. Maybe Chess and Kona were screaming the same thing. Their voices blended together. Finn heard, "—logical plan—"; he heard, "—work out strategy—" and "—before we do anything else." And then he looked into Rocky's eyes and tuned out the others.

"We can't wait!" Finn shouted, even as he swung the lever at a lower spot on the wall than Rocky had hit. "You plan. Rocky and me, we'll get the lever ready."

But the lever bounced off that part of the wall, too.

"What?" Finn wailed.

"Finn, it's really not a good idea to—" Chess began.

Finn didn't listen. He slammed the end of the lever down into the floor, as if he were hammering a nail.

Nothing happened this time either.

The others fell silent.

And then Finn went a little wild. He began swinging the lever again and again and again—at every wall, at every panel of the wood floor, at the stairs, even at the coffee tables. Nobody stopped him, even though he was like a maniac. He knocked over lamps and vases; he toppled framed pictures from the wall.

But he might as well have been wielding a Wiffle ball bat for all the good it did.

Nothing *changed*. None of the spots he hit opened tunnels or slides or spinning spaces. The lever just wouldn't connect. It was like it had turned into an ordinary hunk of metal, instead of a key to traveling between the worlds.

Finn threw the lever across the room. It crashed into one of the few lamps Finn hadn't already knocked over. That lamp fell to the floor, shattering on impact.

But the lever didn't connect there, either. It slid across the scarred wood floor, completely unmoored.

"Why won't it work?" Finn wailed. He sank into a heap on the floor as if his bones had turned to rubber. Or as if, like Emma facedown in the stink grenades, he'd dissolved into hopelessness.

Only, his hopelessness was real. Not caused by any fake smell.

"How are we going to rescue anyone now?" Finn moaned. "How are we going to save ourselves?"

Chess and Emma crouched beside him to pat his shoulders and arms and back. To comfort him. And then Rocky and Kona and Kafi were there, too. Kona stroked his hair.

Kafi left a little string of saliva on his face.

But nobody answered his questions.

Nobody wants to say it out loud, Finn thought. *Nobody wants to admit . . .*

They couldn't rescue anyone now. Not Mom. Not Natalie. Not Kona's dad or Rocky's mom or brother or sister.

Mom and the others were stuck in Ms. Morales's house, under attack from scary people from the scary world.

And Finn, Chess, Emma, Rocky, Kona, and Kafi were stuck in the scary world.

TWENTY-SIX

EMMA

"Psst," Kona said.

Emma looked up from blindly patting Finn's shoulder again and again and again. Her mind kept spinning out the same thoughts, over and over: *How could every single spot that Finn or Rocky hit be one that was used before? Or just too close to a previous crossing point to work?*

"I have an idea," Kona whispered beside her. "But I want to test it on you before I tell everyone else because . . ." She grimaced in a way that Emma totally understood.

Because why risk disappointing everyone all over again if it doesn't work?

"Okay," Emma said.

Kona pointed to a spot halfway across the room and gestured for Emma to follow her.

"We'll be right back," Emma told the others.

They didn't even seem to notice. Rocky, Finn, and Chess were all just piles of misery.

But it felt good to move. It felt good to think that Kona *might* have figured out something everyone else had missed.

Kona hoisted Kafi up into her arms and led Emma to the exact center of the room.

"If the lever won't work in the same place twice, we've got to find the most out-of-the-way place ever to try it," Kona said.

In spite of everything, Emma felt a smile creeping over her face.

"You're thinking like me!" she exclaimed. Then her smile faded. "Or, at least, thinking about the same problem."

"I think I have a solution," Kona said. She pointed up.

The ceiling above the living room was high overhead—Emma thought it might be what Natalie and her Realtor mom would call a "cathedral" ceiling. Emma gasped, catching on.

"You think we should try using the lever on the ceiling," Emma said. "Because there's no way anyone would have done that before."

"Yep," Kona said.

Emma fished the lever out from under a coffee table, where it had come to rest.

"That's awfully high up," Emma said, cocking her head back again. "If this works, how are we going to get up and over there to turn the lever and open a tunnel? Or would it be more like creating a chimney?"

"Maybe we could zipline over from the second floor," Kona said. "Or get a ladder. And carry ropes with us, in case we have to climb down in the other world. We'd have the element of surprise that way, right? We can work out those details once we see if the lever will attach. Once we . . . have hope again."

It sounded crazy—all except the hope part.

"I like the way your brain works," Emma said.

"Just wait until you see my pitching arm," Kona said, flexing her muscles. "Here. Trade you." She took the lever from Emma and put Kafi into Emma's arms.

"P'ch," Kafi repeated solemnly. She put her chubby hands on Emma's cheeks and tilted her forehead toward Emma's so they were eye to eye. "Ko' p'ch."

"Right—cheer for me, Kafi," Kona said. "Just like you do at my softball games."

Kona grasped the lever tightly, raised and lowered it a few times, and then hurled it toward the ceiling high overhead.

Emma could see why Kona bragged about her pitching. Her aim was perfect. The lever flipped end over end, but rose straight up. It struck the ceiling with a resounding thud.

And then it dropped straight back toward the floor. Emma and Kona had to dart out of the way to keep from being hit. Emma held her hand over Kafi's head as if that would protect her, too.

"Oh," Kona said, gazing disappointedly down at the fallen lever. "I was so sure. . . . Well, I'll try again. Maybe my angle was a little off."

"No, that hit exactly right," Emma said. She hugged Kafi a little tighter, and buried her face in the little girl's curls.

Kona gulped.

"You think we just proved for sure that the lever's broken?" she asked. "I thought we would prove the opposite! I thought that would work! I wouldn't have tried it otherwise!"

"I know," Emma said. She felt like kicking the lever the same way Rocky had kicked the door of the secret passageway.

And I used to love that lever so much, she thought.

She remembered how amazed she'd felt each time the lever worked. And how jubilant she'd felt the night she and her brothers and Natalie had discovered a hidden code on the lever—a code that had then helped them decipher a secret message from her mother, just in the nick of time. The words USE IN A PLACE THAT EXISTS IN BOTH (WORLDS) were still faintly legible on the side of the lever.

Emma gasped.

"Oh no," she moaned. "What if it's not the lever that's broken, but . . . the house?"

"The house?" Kona asked, peering around in bafflement. "You mean because of all those smashed windows? Or . . . ?"

"This lever only works in places that match in both worlds," Emma said.

"Yeah, Dad told me that," Kona said, as if Emma had insulted her. "Oooohh. You think . . ."

"Something could have happened to the house in the better world after we left," Emma said grimly. "Something that made it too different from this one."

Like, what if the Mayor set it on fire? Emma wondered. *What if it exploded? What if . . .*

It hurt just thinking about the possibilities. Especially when Emma's own mother had been lying on the floor of that house, all but unable to move, the last time Emma had seen her.

Her own mother . . . and Natalie . . . and Joe . . . and the rest of the Gustanos . . .

"Stop thinking like that," Kona said, as if she could read Emma's mind. Probably because they thought so much alike. Kona reached down to pick up the fallen lever. "This just means we'll have to find some other place to make this work."

"Good idea," Emma said. "I'm sure we . . ."

Still have time? Won't be too late? Will figure out exactly where it can work?

Emma was *not* going to tell Kona how terrifying it was to think of wandering around anywhere else in this horrifying world.

But Kona wasn't acting normal now, either. She didn't straighten back up. She stayed frozen, hunched over the lever.

"Kona?" Emma said.

"The lever," Kona whispered. "It *is* broken. *I* broke it."

"You mean that rough edge on the one side?" Emma asked. "It looks like that anytime anyone pulls it away from a wall. Or in this case, I guess the last time it attached anywhere, it was the floor. . . ."

"No, *look*," Kona said, sliding the lever into Emma's hands.

The entire rim that encircled the lever was rough now. Maybe the outside of the lever wasn't metal, after all. Maybe it was stone or clay or something else that could crack or chip away. Pieces of the lever were breaking off in Emma's hand.

I shouldn't have agreed with Kona about throwing it. We should have been more cautious. . . .

Then Emma realized what was breaking off.

"It's just paint," she said, her voice awash in relief. "Just really, really thick paint or varnish—something like that."

She began brushing the paint chips away.

Little etchings emerged on the surface below. Etchings that looked like the engravings on the coin in Emma's pocket.

"More code?" Emma asked. She looked a little closer. "No—it's more coins!"

TWENTY-SEVEN

CHESS

"Chess! Finn! Rocky!" Emma called. "The lever is completely made of coins! So I bet we can turn our coins into a lever, if the lever we have is really broken! We're not trapped, after all!"

Chess blinked groggily as Emma and Kona came racing toward him and the other two boys. Emma was talking a mile a minute—which probably meant that her brain was spinning even faster than that. Maybe even at the speed of light.

Finn sprang up and threw his arms around Emma and Kafi.

"I knew you'd figure something out!" he shouted at Emma, as if he hadn't just been lying flat on the floor, in misery.

"We should have had confidence in you, Emma," Chess said, his own spirits rising, too.

"And Kona," Emma said, with unusual modesty. "She's the one who led to this discovery. Look!"

She held out the lever, which now had part of its outer covering torn away. Beneath that, coins were pressed together—glued, maybe? Fused somehow?

Chess could think of lots of problems with Emma's theory. They had only ten coins between them—no, eleven, counting the one in the toe of Kafi's sleeper—instead of the dozens that must be inside the lever, if it was entirely made of coins. Would eleven coins be enough? If not, how could they find more? And how were they supposed to connect them?

But Emma's ideas and theories had gotten them past lots of problems on their last trips to this world. Maybe Chess should stop worrying and have faith that they could all figure out something together this time around, too.

"We didn't want to peel away any more of the covering, because, who knows, we might still need to make this lever work," Kona was saying. "But, look, all the coins inside have already had their codes translated—would you call it translated? The ones I can see say FIND US, HEAR US, SEE US, HELP US. . . ."

"Like the ones Natalie touched," Chess said, holding out his handful of coins again.

Finn put his coins down on the floor and started pressing his fingers against them, one after the other.

"When I touch them, nothing happens," he complained.

"Because those coins were meant for Natalie and Ms. Morales, not you," Emma explained. "It's like you got someone else's text messages, and they were encrypted, so you can't read them."

"But I can still figure them out," Finn said. He held up one of his coins. "This coin has three little symbol thingies, and then a space, then two more. So I bet it's a SEE US coin."

"Whoa, Finn—you figured out a code before I did!" Emma congratulated him.

"But if those messages are for other people, and it's just random words like that, does it even matter what they say?" Rocky asked.

Chess waited for Emma to explode, *Of course it matters! It's CODE! We always need to solve the codes we find!*

But just then Kafi darted forward and snatched two of the coins Finn had lined up on the floor. She immediately stuffed them into her mouth.

"Kafi, no!" Kona cried, yanking them away.

Kafi began to wail, even louder than before.

"She still has her own coin, right?" Emma asked. "So it's not the stink grenades making her sad again, is it?"

"She's a baby," Kona said. "Babies cry a lot. And . . . she's probably hungry."

"*I'm* hungry, so I can understand," Finn said, patting the little girl's back just as heartily as Kona was.

Chess stood up.

"That's a problem I know how to fix," he said. "The kitchen's right over there. I'll go see what I can find."

He tried not to think about how frightened he'd been on his last trip to this house, any time he'd stepped out of some hiding place. He and the others had probably been in the living room for the past half hour, and they'd totally stopped trying to be quiet. Kafi was pretty much screaming at the top of her lungs. If anybody else was in the house, they already would have found them.

And I know the Mayor's in the other world, making trouble there, not here, he thought with an ache.

Of course, it was possible for the Mayor to come back.

That thought made Chess hesitate once he stepped out of the open area of the living room. He inched around corners, noticing that the door to the Judge's office hung open and half off its hinges; the hallway chandelier dangled askew.

What exactly had happened here? Why had this house, of all places, come under attack?

But nobody stepped out of the shadows; nobody hissed or shouted, "Who's there? What are you doing here?"

Chess pressed his back against the last wall before the entryway to the kitchen and listened hard. He could still hear the murmur of the other kids' voices out in the living room, along with Kafi's snuffling, her sobs almost exhausted. But no sound came from the kitchen.

He peeked out, then whirled around the corner before he lost his nerve.

A bright light flashed ahead of him.

No, no—turn back! screamed in his head.

"—see the devastation," a loud voice said.

Chess's knees went weak as he realized what had happened: The large flat-screen TV sitting on the counter opposite him had just sprung to life.

Its volume must have been set incredibly high. When a loud *Boom!* sounded from the TV's speakers, Chess felt it deep in his bones.

"What's going on in there?" Finn called anxiously from the living room.

"Just a TV," Chess called back. "I guess they had it on a timer—or, I know, maybe a motion sensor."

Why would anyone have a TV programmed to come on

anytime anyone walked into the room? Especially showing something as disturbing as a war movie?

People on the screen were running and screaming and falling down. People were bleeding and maybe even dying.

Chess reached out to turn it off. What if Kafi followed him into the kitchen and saw it? Or even Finn?

Somehow, Chess couldn't find the power switch. He realized he wasn't actually standing close enough to the TV. And his hand hadn't actually reached for the TV. He'd just stretched his hand out and turned his hand over.

Then he unclenched his fist.

The coins he'd been carrying dropped straight to the floor.

"It's a superhero movie," he called to the others. Superhero movies always had crowd scenes of everyone running and screaming and being afraid. Then the superhero showed up and saved them all.

Chess could use a superhero showing up right about now.

"Don't you love superhero movies?" he called again. "I do."

Somehow it seemed important to let the others know that.

The running-and-screaming-crowd scene seemed to go on and on and on. It felt familiar somehow. Had he seen this movie before? In the brief gaps between the swirling smoke and the surging crowd on the screen, he caught glimpses of dense hedges and a tall, ramshackle wood fence covered in faded, multicolor paint. So familiar. So very, very familiar.

He knew that street. He knew those hedges and that fence. He knew the house that was beside the fence— barely more than a shape in the midst of all the smoke and screaming.

It was the house where he'd lived the first four years of his life. It was this world's version of the house where he'd lived the past eight, misguided years of his life.

It was the house where he belonged, even now.

Because he belonged in this world.

Dimly, Chess heard shuffling behind him. Dimly, he heard coins clinking to the floor.

"That's not a movie," Finn said, his voice dreamy and distant. "That's real. It's happening right now."

"We have to watch—"

"We have to see—"

"We have to know—"

Chess couldn't pick out whose voice said what. But it didn't matter. He agreed with all of them.

"Yes," he said, his voice gone just as blank as Finn's. "We have to."

TWENTY-EIGHT

FINN

Finn was so glad to be safe.

He knew he was safe, because the TV kept telling him how the leaders of his city and state and country were keeping him safe.

He couldn't stop watching the TV, because it kept telling him how much danger he would have been in, if it weren't for the leaders protecting him.

"Your leaders discovered the existence of a dangerous other world just in time," the deep, authoritative newscaster voice kept saying over the scenes of all sorts of places blowing up. "Terrible, terrible people from the other world invaded our peaceful existence this morning. Of course your leaders are winning against the enemy, because they are strong and powerful and wise. But a round-the-clock curfew is being enforced, to preserve the safety of all. Stay where you are, keep watching our reports, and you and your families will be protected from the evildoers. All those who dare to disturb the peace of our world are being arrested. Our leaders will have everything under control in no time."

It's a battle zone out there, Finn thought. *The other world— the world I just left—is an awful place. They're trying to make this one an awful place, too. I'm so lucky to be here at Mayor Mayhew's house, not anywhere else.*

On the TV screen, there was a flash of light that hurt Finn's eyes. Five or six people fell to the ground.

They deserved that, Finn thought. *They should have listened to their leaders, and stayed in their houses.*

He edged closer to the TV alongside Chess and Emma, Kona and Rocky. Without really thinking about it, Finn linked arms with Chess on his right, and Emma on his left.

He had everything he needed in any world, right here.

Something in his brain tried to protest, ever so softly, *But what about . . .*

He shut the thought down. He stared even harder at the TV.

Distantly, in the moments between booms and crashes

coming from the TV, Finn heard a childish gurgle. Maybe a giggle, too. But he didn't dare look away from the TV to find out what it was.

And then, suddenly the TV went dark. The announcer broke off in the middle of saying, "The other world must be—"

"Kafi!" Kona screamed.

TWENTY-NINE

EMMA

The minute the TV died, Emma's brain woke up.

She blinked, recognizing the Morales-Mayhew kitchen again, recognizing her own thoughts again, remembering her own goals: *Rescue Mom and the others. Figure out the coins. Make it so Mayor Mayhew and the other evil people of this world never hurt anyone again.*

Then she saw why the TV had gone dark: Kafi had pulled the plug.

The little girl sat on the floor by the electrical outlet. In one hand, she held the TV cord. In the other, she held some of the coins the other kids had dropped.

And she was about to put both the cord and the coins into her mouth.

"Kafi, no!" Kona shrieked, dashing toward her little sister.

Emma was a little closer. She ran alongside Kona. So did Chess, Finn, and Rocky. It was like all five kids were racing to save the little girl. But Kona reached her sister first.

"Spit it out!" Kona screamed, pulling a coin from Kafi's mouth and two others from her hand. "You'll choke!"

Emma swiped the electrical cord out of the little girl's other hand. It whipped toward the floor.

Kafi began to scream.

"Here, chew on this instead," Finn suggested, pulling a box of granola bars from a cabinet and unwrapping one quickly. He shoved it into Kafi's clutch.

Chess and Rocky picked up the other dropped coins, so Kafi couldn't reach any of them.

Kona hugged Kafi close and bounced her up and down. Kafi's sobs subsided as she began gumming the granola bar.

"I can't take my eye off you for a minute, can I?" Kona moaned, her face buried against Kafi's curls. "I didn't even want to watch that TV. I just . . . couldn't stop."

Now that Kafi's safe, we should plug the TV back in, Emma thought, reaching for the cord again.

Where had that thought come from?

"Here. This is the one you were carrying," Chess said, slipping a coin into Emma's hand. "Take an extra one, too."

Emma stared at the two coins Chess had given her. Her mind felt totally back to normal now—totally hers.

"I—I—how could I have dropped that?" Emma asked. "How could I have dug it out of my pocket and thrown it to the ground and . . ."

"The TV made you do it," Rocky said. He looked like he wanted to punch someone. Or maybe something—like the TV. "It controlled us just like the stink grenades did."

"Only worse," Finn said. He leaned against Rocky the same way he often leaned against Chess.

He's still scared, Emma thought.

So was she.

She looked down at the TV cord again. She could resist the urge now to plug it back in, but why did it still call to her? The silver prongs of the plug gleamed temptingly in the sunlight streaming in through the kitchen window.

Wait a minute, Emma thought. *Sunlight?*

She raced to the window, leaning across the counter to peer up at the sky.

"Everything was a lie!" she announced. "There's no battle going on in this world! At least, not where the TV was showing it. The TV made it look like it was right in our neighborhood—the bad-world version of our neighborhood,

I mean. And if there was that much smoke and fighting going on there, we would definitely be able to see it from this window!"

The others crowded around her. Outside the window, the yard sloped gently down to a row of trees. A stone wall with guard towers every ten feet or so lay nestled in the trees.

Above the line of trees, the sky was a crystalline blue, with puffy white clouds. It was, in fact, the clearest sky they'd ever seen in this world.

There was no smoke. No smoke at all.

"The TV tricked us!" Finn protested.

"But we believed it," Rocky said.

"And we couldn't stop watching," Chess added. "Here."

Emma saw that he'd found a roll of masking tape in one of the kitchen drawers, and he'd used it to tape two of the coins tightly around his wrist. He was offering to do the same for her.

"That's really smart, Chess," Emma said admiringly. She held out her arm and he began taping coins to her wrist, too.

"It's like the first step toward having another lever," Kona joked. Kafi clapped her granola-sticky hands, as if she approved, too. Kona bit her lip. "Wait a minute—what if that's *how* people figured out to build the lever? Because they were trying to fight off the power of the stink grenades or the TV?"

"The coins worked a lot better against the stink grenades than they did with the TV," Rocky said, frowning as he unwrapped a granola bar of his own. "And the lever was useless."

"Oh no—our lever!" Emma cried, realizing that all of them had just abandoned it in the living room when they'd heard the TV. She jerked her wrist away from Chess even though he'd barely gotten the first strip of tape in place around her coins. She dashed into the living room, careening against the walls. She scooped up the lever, and began racing back toward the others.

But in her haste, she took a corner too fast and knocked into the door of Judge Morales's office. Even half off its hinges, the door scraped back and smashed into the wall.

And then a TV announcer voice came from the office: "Stay tuned for live updates about all the ways your leaders are keeping you safe during the evil attack from the other world. . . ."

"Hey, guys! There's another TV in the office—I guess it was set to be motion-activated, too," Emma called. "And, really, we should find out what it's saying. . . ."

She began to pick at the tape on her wrist, the tape holding her coins in place. The lever slipped down in her grasp. But she was still in enough control of her own brain to hear the other kids shouting from the kitchen, "Emma, no!" "Stay away from there!" "Don't go into that office!"

That was Chess, Kona, and Rocky.

Then she also heard Finn yell, "Emma! We'll come and rescue you!"

He would, she thought, even as the TV announcer in the office still called out to her, "The danger is not past. We repeat, the danger is not past. You cannot trust anyone. You have to watch out for yourself, just as your leaders are self-lessly watching out for you. . . ."

No, Emma thought, and it felt like she was wrenching her own brain away from the TV's lure. *I can trust Finn. And Chess and Kona and Rocky. And even Kafi. They will try to rescue me, and that will just lead to them being trapped, too. I have to rescue myself.*

Emma noticed her own fingers were still picking at the tape around her wrist.

No, she thought again. *It's not just that I have to rescue myself. I have to get away from that TV in the office to keep the other kids safe.*

Emma's fingers stilled. And then she wrapped them completely around her own wrist.

Holding the coins in place.

Painstakingly, groaning with the effort, she turned away from the office with its loud TV and began inching back toward the kitchen.

Not just for my own sake, she thought with each step. *For Finn. For Chess. For Kona. For Kafi. For Rocky. For Finn . . .*

Finally, sweating profusely, her muscles aching, Emma rounded the corner into the kitchen. Her gaze fell on her brothers and Rocky, Kona, and Kafi. Oddly, it looked like they'd been taping their wrists together, linking as many of their coins as possible.

The part of her brain that could still distantly hear the TV in the office told her, *What? They weren't going to rescue you. They were joining together to* abandon *you.*

But Emma knew the truth: They would *always* help her.

She knew something else, too.

"We've got to get out of this house," she said. "Now."

THIRTY

CHESS

Five minutes, Chess thought.

Emma had been away from the others maybe five minutes, tops. But she looked like she'd been through an entire war: her hair sweaty, a bruise growing on her cheek, the lever wielded ahead of her like a sword.

We are in a war, Chess thought. *We've been in a war our entire lives, and we didn't even know it.*

Finn ripped away from the others and threw his arms around Emma.

"We were just coming to rescue you, but now we don't

have to," he rejoiced. "You rescued yourself! You figured out how to fight the TVs!"

"Barely," Emma said. "I don't know if it will work the next time. That's why we have to get away from this house. I bet the Judge and the Mayor and Other-Natalie had at least a dozen TVs here. They're probably all booby-trapped."

"But what if there are just more TVs outside?" Rocky asked, his voice shaking. "Or what if there really is a battle going on out there, one we just can't see? Or there might be security guards and bad police officers like the ones my brother and sister and I saw after we were kidnapped. Before you Greystones rescued us . . ."

He might as well be one of those TV announcers, telling us all to be too afraid to move, Chess thought.

"We have to get out of this house if we have any hope of getting that lever to work," Kona said.

And what she said, that felt like the coins working, Chess thought. *Giving us hope. And courage.*

"Come on," he said, gently patting Rocky's back. "We'll all be together. We'll be okay."

"And we'll go slow and be careful," Finn said.

If everything hadn't felt so serious just then, Chess would have laughed. Finn *never* wanted to be careful or go slow. On their previous trips to this frightening world, he'd always been the one scurrying out ahead of everyone else, never even thinking of danger. Or, just expecting someone else to rescue him.

Well, Chess thought, *I guess Finn can grow up, too.*

"Want to take a box of granola bars with us for the road?" Kona asked.

Quickly, the kids all grabbed something they thought might be useful. Emma found a sack with handles to carry the lever more easily. Finn threw in a handful of candy bars. (Maybe he wasn't too grown-up yet.) Chess dropped the roll of tape into the sack, Rocky added the granola bars, and Kona topped it off with a pile of dish towels as she muttered, "I guess these could serve as spare diapers for Kafi, if we get desperate."

"We're really doing this?" Rocky asked, hesitating beside a long window at the end of the kitchen that was already broken. "We're going to risk everything and—"

"Staying inside would be risking everything, too," Chess said gently.

Risking that we're going to be trapped by another TV springing to life, he thought. *Risking that we never get back to rescue our moms, Natalie, and the others. Risking that the Mayor completely takes over the better world, as well as this one. Risking that we never actually* do *anything, but just wait and worry . . .*

"Here," Chess said. "I'll go first."

He stepped out through the window frame, being careful

to avoid the last shards of broken glass still hanging around the edges.

Nothing happened. No sirens blared; no security system beeped. Chess peered down toward the guard towers at the bottom of the hill, and they all stayed silent and still. As far as Chess could tell, they were all deserted.

"See?" Chess said. "No problem. This is easy."

It wasn't—Chess's heart still pounded too fast. He hadn't recovered from worrying about Emma just a moment earlier. Or about everything else ever since finding out about the alternate world. But he could still move forward. He could still hold his hand out to help the other kids step out the window, too.

Then they were all outside, all of their backs pressed tightly against the wall. The air seemed much clearer now, without any smell of stink grenades.

"I say we run down to the trees at the bottom of the yard," Emma whispered, as if she'd only needed a little fresh air to come up with a plan. "Then we climb the wall and hide as much as we can on our way to the first house that we recognize as being like one in the other world."

"And you think that's where we can use the lever," Kona finished for her. "Or use some lever that we make from our coins."

So many gaps in that plan, Chess thought. *So many things we* don't know about the lever or the coins, that mean we don't know if that plan will work or not.

Also, the expanse of open lawn between them and the trees looked as enormous as a football field. Maybe two. Maybe three.

The longer the kids stood there staring at the wide-open span of grass, the bigger it seemed.

"Umm . . . ," Rocky began.

He's going to chicken out, Chess thought. *He's going to talk everyone else into being too afraid, too.*

Chess could feel how everything was in balance, teetering between fear and action. He could feel how much he was like Rocky—how much he had always been the one saying, *No, wait! Let's think about this before we do anything!*

But he could also feel how much they needed not to be afraid.

How much Chess himself needed not to be afraid.

"Let's go!" Chess called, taking off. He glanced back over his shoulder to call to the others, "Just run, and you'll be safe in the trees before you know it!"

And it was at that exact moment—when he wasn't looking—that someone crashed into him.

THIRTY-ONE

FINN

Finn sped blindly behind Chess. He wanted to shriek, "Take that, Mayor Mayhew!" or "Nobody can catch us now!" or something else just as fun. But maybe it would be smarter to run silently.

He turned back to tell Rocky, "Look how cautious I'm being!"

So it was too late when he saw the girl whip around the corner of the house and smash into Chess. They hit so hard they fell to the ground, and Finn had no time to dodge them. He fell, too. All three of them landed in a heap.

"Sorry!" Finn cried, trying to scramble back up. "Didn't see you!"

The girl was already shoving and kicking Finn and Chess, and struggling to get away. But they were all too tangled together.

"We didn't mean to—" Chess began.

Emma, Rocky, and Kona and Kafi circled them instantly. Emma and Rocky began pulling Finn and Chess away from the girl.

"Stop hitting my brothers!" Emma cried.

Rocky yelled at the girl, "We'll call the police! You're trespassing! Get out of here!"

Kona hollered, "We've got guards with us!"

Finn wanted to laugh. He wanted to yell, "Go, team!" Because that's how it felt: as if Rocky and Kona had joined the Greystone kids' team, and they would always be on the same side.

Then he saw how the girl sat huddled in the middle of their circle, her face hidden in her hands, her shoulders trembling.

She might have even been crying.

"Uh, guys?" Finn said. "I think she's scared of us."

"She should be," Rocky growled.

"It could be an act," Kona said. "She could be a spy."

"Don't start feeling sorry for her yet, Finn," Emma said. "We don't know anything about her." She crouched beside the girl. "Who are you? Why are you here? What are you doing skulking around like that?"

The girl seemed to be trying to peek out, still without showing her face. Her tangled light brown hair was like a curtain over her eyes and nose and mouth. She had her hands over her face, too. Finn caught barely a glimpse of her pale eyelashes, caught in her hair.

"Shh," she hissed. "Please. Don't call anyone. Just . . . be quiet. Let me go without telling anyone, and I won't tell anyone you're here, either."

"There are five of us and one of you," Rocky said. "You're outnumbered. You can't bargain like that. We're in charge."

The girl huddled even tighter against the ground. She darted glances all around, as if looking for a way to break through their circle and escape.

"Rocky, you sound like a bully when you talk like that," Finn complained. "Maybe she just wants us to be nice to her."

"We're, like, in a war zone," Rocky said. "Nobody can be nice."

"We're nice to each other," Finn reminded him.

"If she tells us who she is, then we can decide if we want to be nice," Emma said.

The girl peeked out a little more. Now Finn could see one terrified gray eye showing between her fingers.

"Be nice by forgetting you ever saw me," the girl said. "I'm not doing anything wrong. I'm just here to check on . . . my friend. I'm a friend of the family. I promise!"

"Which part of the family?" Emma demanded, fiercer than ever. "Who do you support—the Mayor or the Judge?"

Emma was so good at asking questions. That was what it came down to, wasn't it? If the girl supported Mayor Mayhew, she was on the bad side. If she supported this world's Natalie and the Mayor's wife, the Judge, then . . .

Then it's only a maybe that this girl is on the good side, Finn thought sadly. Because everything was so awful in this world, Other-Natalie and the Judge had never been able to stand up and say to everyone, "I'm on the good side! Let's get rid of all the bad leaders!" They had had to pretend they were mean and awful, too. They could be good only in secret.

Finn didn't like maybes. He didn't like not knowing what people were like, right away. He looked to Chess, because Chess hadn't said anything yet.

Chess was mouthing the word "friend" again and again, like he wasn't entirely sure what it meant. He looked puzzled.

"Chess?" Finn asked.

"What if . . . ," Chess began. "What if we know who she's

187

friends with? What if this girl is someone we've seen before? Or heard, anyway. Her voice . . . I recognize her voice."

Now everybody else looked confused, too.

"*I* don't recognize her voice," Finn said.

Emma, Rocky, and Kona all shook their heads, agreeing with Finn. Even Kafi got into the act, imitating the older kids and turning her head side to side.

"It was from when we didn't have enough earbuds for everybody," Chess said. "Only for me, Natalie, and . . . Other-Natalie."

"Oooh," Finn whispered, just as Emma exploded, "You think she was there that night at the party?"

Chess crouched down beside the girl, too.

"We're talking about the night of the political fundraiser at this very house a week ago," he told the girl. His voice sounded as gentle as if he were talking to Finn. "The night that . . . people got shot. You probably thought you were there with your friend Natalie. But really . . ."

"It was the Natalie from the other world," the girl whispered. She let her hands slip down, almost uncovering her face. She gazed side to side, paying special attention to Chess, Emma, and Finn. "Some of you were there with that Natalie, too."

Finn began tugging on Chess's arm.

"I know who she is now!" he cried. "She helped Natalie escape!"

"Lana," Chess said. "You're Lana."

The night of the horrible party, this girl had been in a navy blue dress—but then, everybody there had worn navy blue or orange, and all the decorations were the same colors. Those were the colors of the political party that ran this world. The one that all the evil leaders belonged to.

Just thinking about those colors together made Finn feel sick to his stomach.

But now Lana was wearing dark jeans and a dark green, long-sleeved T-shirt that could almost have served as camo. Maybe she'd picked that outfit to blend in around the trees and bushes down by the guard wall. But out here in the open, the clothes made Lana stand out.

Finn waited for Lana to sit up and reveal her whole face and cry, "You're right! You figured out everything! We're all on the same side!"

But she kept her shoulders hunched and jerked her head back and forth, as if still looking for an escape route.

"We won't hurt you," Finn crooned, the same way he would have spoken to an injured baby bird found fallen from its nest. "We know you were a good friend to Natalie. She told us. Now that we know who you are and you know who we are, we can trust each other."

Lana laughed. It wasn't a nice sound.

"Trust?" she repeated mockingly. "*Trust?* I'm not even

sure I can trust Natalie anymore, and she's my best friend!"

Ouch.

"She's nice," Finn said. "We know."

Then he remembered that none of them knew where this world's Natalie was.

He remembered how the house behind them was destroyed, and how it held TVs that had made even the Greystone kids, Kona, and Rocky think that terrible things were true.

What if that had happened to Other-Natalie, too?

What if the TVs had made her *do* terrible things?

There was so much Finn didn't know.

He didn't even know for sure that Other-Natalie had survived the night of the party. Maybe Lana was mad at Chess, Emma, and Finn, because they hadn't rescued Other-Natalie, too.

Maybe she should be.

Or maybe she should be mad because they hadn't rescued *her*.

"Is your friend Natalie okay?" Finn asked, as a start toward making peace. "I mean . . . not hurt? Healthy?"

"Is anyone healthy in this world?" Lana muttered.

"Hey," Rocky said, peering around as nervously as Lana. "It's really stupid to stand here talking out in the open, where anyone can see us."

"Right," Lana said. She shoved Emma and Chess away and started to stand up. "Finally someone's talking sense. You let me go on my way, I'll let you go on yours—none of us talk to anybody, and nobody will be any wiser."

"And now *you're* right," Emma said, gently putting her hand on Lana's shoulder. She sounded almost as sad as if she'd been around stink grenades again. "If we do that, it's true: nobody will be wiser. And we all need to be wiser. We need to trust each other. We need to share information."

"That'll never happen," Lana snarled.

Finn started patting her on the back, because she *really* seemed like she needed someone to be nice to her. Lana jerked away from both Finn and Emma. It was like she thought they were going to hit her.

But the movement threw her off-kilter—she completely fell over.

And . . . something fell out of the back of her shirt.

Coins.

Finn, Emma, Chess, Rocky, and Kona all reached for the coins, and Lana shrieked, "Stop! No! You can't have those! Don't even look at them!"

She scrambled to pick them up, even grabbing them out of the other kids' hands. She didn't seem like a defenseless baby bird anymore—she was more like a tiger, hissing and snarling.

But Finn saw how she cradled her coins, how she hugged them close.

Maybe . . . , he thought.

He peeled back the masking tape circling his right wrist and thrust his wrist directly under Lana's nose.

"We're not trying to steal your coins!" he cried. "We just want to see. Because we have coins, too. We match! We fit together! We're on the same team!"

Lana froze, staring at the coins.

"Oh," she said. "Oh." She sagged back down to the ground, all the fight gone out of her. "Are you right, too? About us fitting together?" She looked up, straight at Finn's face. Her hair slid back, and he could see all of her face, too: her terrified gray eyes, her wrinkled-up nose, her worried mouth. And then, something like hope spread over her face.

"I want you to be right," she whispered. "I want us to be on the same team."

THIRTY-TWO

EMMA

Only Finn, Emma thought.

He was so innocent, he was the only one who could have calmed Lana down. The only one who could have made her feel like part of the team.

Emma could still think of reasons someone could have coins and not be on the same team.

For all we know, there are different kinds of coins, Emma thought. *Good coins and bad ones. Or Lana could have stolen these from good people, and . . .*

But Natalie had trusted Lana.

And Emma trusted Natalie.

"Where?" Lana was asking, peering frantically around at all of the kids. "Where did you get your coins?"

It would make sense to give a vague answer, to protect the coins. To try to pry information out of Lana before giving away any of their own.

But maybe sometimes Emma needed to act more like Finn.

"In the other world," Emma said. She pointed to her wrist, so Lana could see she had coins, too. "We're all carrying coins."

Lana's face lit up. It was like seeing fireworks burst to life in a dark sky. She was every bit as jubilant as Mom had been when she saw Mrs. Gustano's coin back in the other world.

"So you found them," Lana murmured. "In the other world. You're *from* the other world! Our plans worked! All our hard work, all the risks we took—it all paid off! You found the coins and you came here! And here I thought it was all too late. . . ."

"Uh, yeah," Finn said. "That's right. I mean, not all of that. It's a little confusing to say which world we're from exactly—well, for everyone but Rocky. He's *definitely* from the other world. The rest of us are kind of . . . connected to both. Anyhow, it's not too late. I don't think. What do you mean, talking about *your* plans? What have you been doing with the coins? Are you one of the people who's been sending them to the other world?"

Emma was glad Finn was smart enough to ask those questions. Lana would probably take them better from him than Emma.

But a shadow crossed Lana's face.

"Don't you know?" she asked. "You say you found the coins, but you don't know the plan? Didn't you come here to save us?"

Emma tried to signal the others with a glance. She wanted to say, *Be careful! I think we're going to have to bargain for information! Don't give anything away until Lana tells us more!*

But Chess, of all people, was already answering.

"We'd *like* to help you," he said. "But we don't know how."

"How can that be, if you found the coins?" Lana moaned. "Didn't the coins tell you what to do?"

"The coins we have weren't meant for us," Kona said. "I mean, two of them are kind of mysteries—we don't know *who* they were meant for, or why they showed up. They just appeared. But the one Rocky has actually belongs to his mother. And the ones Chess and Finn brought, those were sent from this world's version of Natalie to the other world's version. Or from this world's version of her mom—the Judge—to the Ms. Morales in the other world."

"But that Natalie and that Ms. Morales—*they* didn't

195

bother coming here?" Lana sounded even more heartbroken now. "They didn't care about helping their doubles, even after they heard what the coins had to say?"

Emma had so many questions she wanted to ask right now. But Lana seemed to be in such anguish.

Emma answered Lana instead of asking more.

"Natalie and her mom both *wanted* to help their doubles," she assured the other girl. "I'm pretty sure they wanted to listen to all the coins and find out what they said. But . . . there wasn't time. Because the Mayor attacked the other world. I guess you thought you were going to get help from the other world but . . . now people there need help, too."

The color drained from Lana's face, making her already-pale skin deathly white.

"That's what we feared the most," she said. "If Mayor Mayhew is already in the other world, then, then . . . He's winning. Maybe he's already won."

She peered all around. The air was still crystal clear around them. Birds chirped in the distance, and a soft breeze whispered through the trees down the hill. Emma loved how peaceful everything seemed.

But Lana acted like she was gazing at a battle—maybe even at one of the scenes the TV had shown.

What did she see that Emma was missing?

"Come on," Lana said, grabbing up the last of her coins

and scrambling to her feet. "We've got to tell Natalie! My Natalie, that is!" She whirled toward the broken, silent house behind them.

"Natalie's not there," Chess said. "I mean, we didn't search every room, because we kept running into these horrible TVs we could barely get away from, but . . ."

Emma wondered how they could possibly explain the pull the TVs had had over them. But apparently they didn't have to: Lana gasped and pressed a hand to her face.

"The mind-control TVs are even in Natalie's house now?" she groaned. "Even there?" She aimed a fearful glance back at the giant house, her gaze lingering on the broken windows and torn drapes. It didn't seem possible, but her face turned even paler. She spun away from the house. "That's it! We're in so much danger here. We've got to get to safety."

She began racing down the hill. When nobody else moved, she called back over her shoulder, "Come with me!"

Emma exchanged glances with Chess, Finn, Kona, and Rocky. All of them seemed to decide as one: They started running, too.

Maybe Lana will take us someplace the lever will work, Emma thought as she tried to catch up. *And if she's with us, she can give good answers if any guard tries to stop us. . . .*

The dash down the hill went quickly. But the swath of trees at the bottom of the hill was wider and denser than it had looked from above. Emma was glad the trees hid them better than the open lawn had, but it hurt to fight her way through brambles and lashing branches.

And . . . is that poison ivy? Emma wondered, dodging a suspicious-looking vine.

"The Judge and the Mayor were in charge of everything," Finn muttered behind Emma. "Couldn't they have made a *path*?"

"This is like an extra security system," Lana explained as the woods made her slow down, too. "If the guards and security cameras and the wall didn't stop people, the thorns and thistles would. But Natalie showed me a good route."

She did seem better than anyone else at avoiding the branches catching at their sleeves and shorts and skin. Emma wished she'd had time to change out of the T-shirt and gym shorts she'd slept in the night before into something a little sturdier, a little more protective.

Like, maybe, armor, she thought ruefully.

But she followed Lana, and the route became a little easier.

"When you visited Natalie normally, didn't you just use her sidewalk?" Chess asked, pulling away briars caught in his hair. "You were on the approved guest list for the party. People saw you together. You were allowed to be friends, right?"

"We didn't always want others to know we were

meeting," Lana said. "Especially not this past week, when . . . oh, never mind. I'll explain when we get to safety."

They reached the wall, and Emma began to wonder how they were going to scale it, especially carrying Kafi. The wall was smooth and gray and about twice as tall as Chess. It didn't seem to have any divots for holding on.

But Lana put her hand against the wall and a small section slid to the side.

"Keep this secret," Lana said, glancing around once again. "I . . . I'm trusting you."

After the wall, they had another swath of trees and bushes to scramble through. And then they faced a row of large houses.

"Do any of those look like the ones by Ms. Morales's house back in our world?" Kona asked softly, as though trying not to let Lana hear. "Would *they* be places the lever might work?"

"I . . . don't know," Emma said. She hadn't memorized all the houses in Ms. Morales's neighborhood. These houses were grand enough to fit in there. But here they were all sectioned off with chain-link fences topped by razor wire. It made them look scary and strange. Did everyone in this world need walls and fences? Was every neighborhood dangerous?

"These are officials' houses," Lana explained. "Just not

officials as high up and important as the Mayor and the Judge."

She reached down for a handful of pebbles, and threw them up in the air. Emma caught a glimpse of movement in the nearest trees.

"Are there motion-activated cameras up there?" she asked Lana. "And you're confusing them with gravel?"

"You got it—run!" Lana cried.

All of the kids dashed across the street, following Lana to one of the larger houses. They ducked in past a tall metal gate that had been left open. Then they wound down a long driveway to the house. Lana pressed a finger into a scanner beside the front door, and the door swung open. Everyone rushed inside and Lana shoved the door shut behind them.

And that was when Emma saw the people sitting in rows of chairs in the grand entryway.

No—the people *tied* to their chairs in the grand entryway.

Emma scrambled back toward the door.

"You tricked us!" she gasped. "This is a trap!"

THIRTY-THREE

CHESS

"No, no—wait—it's no trap—I should have explained—" Lana began as all the kids shrieked and clutched for the door handle.

The door handle which . . . wouldn't budge.

"We *asked* to be tied to these chairs," one of the people in the chairs said.

It was a woman with the same gray eyes and long chin and wispy hair as Lana.

"Yes, Mom—you explain," Lana said. "Or Dad."

Lana's mother was surrounded by nine or ten other people also imprisoned in the chairs. One of them was a large man in a dark business suit—Lana's dad? The others wore uniforms that probably meant they were guards or maids or maybe even butlers.

Chess didn't care about making sense of the uniforms right now, or figuring out anyone's identity. He looked around for something to throw at one of the windows so they could escape. A paperweight, maybe? A lamp?

"All the windows are shatterproof," Lana's dad said, as if he could read Chess's mind.

Chess decided mind-reading *that* wouldn't be much of an accomplishment. Rocky, Kona, and Emma were also frantically glancing about. Rocky had even gone over and put his hands around the bowling-ball-sized globe on the newel post at the bottom of a grand staircase.

"So just listen," Lana begged Chess and the others.

Lana's dad frowned, deepening the lines on his face. His suit looked expensive, the kind that should have made him seem powerful and decisive. But it sagged on his slumped shoulders. His face and his suit both looked crumpled.

"Do you know the stories about sailors who had to be tied to the masts of their ships?" he asked. "Because that was the only way they could avoid being so mesmerized by mermaid songs that they sailed their ships onto the rocks and died? We are those sailors."

"You're afraid of *mermaids*?" Finn asked. Now he was the

one peering all around. "You think this house is a sailing ship? And you're on the ocean?"

"Figuratively," the man said.

"Dad," Lana complained, "they don't need to hear about myths and legends and analogies. Just what's true now."

"In there. *That* is what we're afraid of," Lana's mother said, straining against the ropes on her wrists to point into a formal living room off to the side. The furniture in that room was just as ornate and imposing as at the Judge and the Mayor's house. But on the largest wall, over a huge fireplace, a blanket covered with childish purple daisies was draped over . . . was that another TV?

Lana's mother was pointing straight at the daisy blanket.

Or, more likely, a TV behind it.

"Ooohh," Finn said. "We didn't like what was on the TV back at that house, either." He pointed toward the Judge and the Mayor's house. "Why didn't you just unplug it? That's what we did."

"We couldn't," Lana's dad said. "And every time Lana managed to cover it, we couldn't stop ourselves from uncovering it. She had to blindfold herself and put cotton in her ears and tie us to our chairs, and *then* cover the TV. She had to do all that just to be able to leave the house."

"Why can Lana resist uncovering it, when you couldn't?" Emma asked.

"We don't know," Lana's mom said.

Chess saw Lana's eyes dart about.

She knows, but she doesn't want to tell her parents? he wondered.

"Perhaps you should move away from that room." This came from one of the tied-up men, who seemed to be wearing a guard's uniform.

Chess realized that all of the kids had started drifting toward the TV covered with the purple-daisy blanket. Even he'd turned toward the TV; he caught himself sliding his feet forward.

But I didn't decide *to walk in that direction,* he thought. *I didn't plan to move at all.*

If he thought, *I am just going to stand right here. I'm not going anywhere,* his feet stayed in place. But if he stopped thinking that, the TV drew him like a magnet.

"Do you have any rooms without TVs?" Chess asked.

"Uh, no," Lana said, almost as if she were embarrassed.

"I am—or was—in charge of the local TV station," Lana's dad said. "I *needed* TVs in every room in my house."

"Turns out, you didn't," one of the women in a maid's uniform said. "Turns out, it was bad for you, too."

Emma tilted her head, watching the woman. Chess decided Emma was probably trying to figure out how the woman had the nerve to say that to someone who was clearly her boss. He sniffed. This house smelled a little like the bad odor that had infected the Judge and the Mayor's house. But the smell seemed to be growing fainter and fainter.

"Whatever the TV does to people—that must have replaced the odor as a way to control everyone," Emma said. She turned to Lana's father. "Did you know that was going to happen? Do you know how it works?"

The man shifted uncomfortably in his seat.

"We were just trying to sell our advertisers' products," he said. "I mean, sure, we knew some of our techniques were a little . . . oh, addictive . . . but . . . we didn't expect the government to start using the same techniques."

"You mean, you didn't expect the government to start using them on *you*." It was the same maid again.

Chess tried to catch Emma's eye. He wanted to ask, *Could this woman help us, too?*

Maybe not, if she would just go straight to the TV if she escaped from the chair.

Emma was busy appealing to Lana.

"We have to go somewhere safe and have you explain everything to us," Emma begged.

Lana shot a glance at all the adults in the chairs.

"Come on," she said. "Let's try my room."

All the kids trooped up the stairs together. Even though the house was nearly as grand downstairs as the Judge and the

Mayor's place, the upstairs looked shabbier.

"We don't actually have as much money as my parents want people to believe," Lana said, as if someone had asked.

They turned the corner into a room that seemed like a smaller version of Other-Natalie's. One wall was dominated by the same poster they'd once seen in Other-Natalie's room: It showed a group of teenagers wearing menacing expressions and orange-and-navy-blue clothes. Other-Natalie stood front and center in the group; Lana was in the back row. Solemn lettering hovered at the top of the picture like a threat, announcing, "When we stand together, no one can oppose us."

"Other-Natalie had a poster like that, and she tore it down," Finn said. "Why didn't you do that?"

"I . . . was afraid," Lana said. "It just didn't seem like . . . I could."

Her gaze darted toward the opposite side of the room, where a tattered quilt hung from a large rectangular object on the wall. Chess didn't need to walk over and pull down the quilt to be certain that it was covering another TV screen. But his feet turned him in that direction anyway.

He wasn't the only one. Emma was three steps ahead of him—three steps closer to the TV.

"Emma, no!" he cried. "Don't do it!"

The others started shouting along with him, and rushing after Emma. Finn screamed, "Here, take my coins! That'll help you!" Kona yelled, "Kafi wouldn't even be able to reach the plug on that TV!" Rocky hollered, "Fight back!"

Emma moaned, "I can't, I can't, I can't . . ."

All five of them grabbed for Emma.

And we're all wearing or carrying coins, Chess thought. *Maybe that will help? Maybe . . .*

Emma kept moving toward the TV anyhow. Chess barely managed to get one unsteady hand on her shoulder.

Emma reached for the TV.

And then, suddenly, she grabbed the lever out of her bag and swung it at the quilt over the TV screen.

The sound of breaking glass filled the room.

THIRTY-FOUR

FINN

"Emma, you're amazing!" Finn cried. "I didn't even think of doing that! I'm so glad you're a genius!"

He watched the broken shards of glass trickle down from under the tattered quilt. He grinned wider and wider with every bit of glass he heard hitting the floor.

"You even had great batting stance," Kona congratulated her.

"I wish you'd told us you were planning to do that," Rocky said. "I thought I was going to have a heart attack, watching you walk over there. If you'd turned on that TV, I—I . . ."

"We all would have watched it," Chess finished for him. "We all would have been trapped."

Emma stared down at the lever in her hands. She didn't look as triumphant as Finn thought she should. She was sweating and gasping for air, as if she'd narrowly escaped falling off a cliff.

Well, she kind of did, Finn thought. *We all did.*

"I . . . really wasn't sure what I was planning to do," Emma said, grimacing. "It could have gone either way, until that last minute when I felt Chess's hand on my shoulder. But then I hoped . . . Why didn't the lever open a tunnel to the other world? Why didn't it work, even here?"

"Was *that* what you were trying to do?" Finn asked. "You really are a genius, if you could think about swinging the lever and making a tunnel and all that, even when the TV was calling to you."

Emma slammed the lever against the wall directly below the TV.

Nothing happened.

She dropped the lever.

"Just when I had hope again!" she moaned.

Lana slid her hands under the lever and scooped it up as gingerly as if she were handling priceless jewels.

Or, maybe . . . eggs.

Seeds.

Something that could turn into something else.

"You thought this was going to open a route to the other world?" she asked. "Is this actually one of the coin-levers?" She turned it over and over in her hands. "Oooh . . . So this is what the coins look like when they've succeeded together. And united."

"'Succeeded'?" Finn repeated, pouncing on the word as if it were another coin to be discovered. "What does that mean? The lever *didn't* succeed, or else we'd be on our way back to the other world right now."

"I mean, the coins in here all must have reached the right person in the other world," Lana said. "See how they all have messages like SEE US and FIND US and HEAR US instead of just a bunch of code? That must mean the messages have been delivered. And listened to. I've only heard whisperings about this, but people say if someone has enough coins delivered to them, they can bind them together to open doorways that anyone could travel through, between the worlds. Not just one double reaching another."

"We've seen that work before with this lever!" Finn assured her, picking up the one Emma had dropped. "It brought us here! It can take us back, as soon as we find the right place to use it! And then you could come with us to the better world, and you'll really be safe there. And . . ."

He remembered suddenly that the other world wasn't so

safe now either. Not with Mayor Mayhew attacking.

Not with Mom and Natalie and the others frozen in place by all the stink grenades.

"No," Lana said, shaking her head sadly. "Not if that lever stopped working for you. Not if you say Mayor Mayhew went to the other world. He's probably setting up mind-control TVs in the other world, too. That would stop the coins from being able to travel between the worlds. Or from letting any*body* travel. No matter how many coins or levers they have."

"But that's just your theory, right?" Emma asked. "You don't know for sure that any of that's true, do you?"

It was like she was begging for there still to be a way out.

And a way to defeat Mayor Mayhew and every other horrible person who wanted the TVs and the stink grenades to win.

"I know the coins can't travel between the worlds anymore," Lana said. She sounded like she was announcing that somebody had died. Somebody she loved. "They stopped working at nine thirty-eight this morning. And if the coins stopped working, so would levers."

Finn hadn't looked at a clock or a watch even once since he'd gotten up that morning. But it couldn't have been 9:38 a.m. yet when all the coins had rained down inside Natalie's house. And it was probably still earlier than 9:38 when Chess opened the tunnel-slide in the floor.

But it could have been *after* 9:38 a.m. when Rocky swung the lever at the wall in Other-Natalie's house, and it didn't work.

"There's stuff you aren't telling us," Emma said. "Where were you at nine thirty-eight this morning? What were you doing? How did you find out any of this? What are your sources? What research have you done?"

Emma was *such* a scientist. She always wanted all the facts.

Lana sat down heavily on her bed.

"It's not that I don't want to answer you," she assured them. "I'm just . . . not used to trusting anyone except Natalie. There's no one else I've ever been totally honest with."

Emma shot a glance at Finn, as if she were just begging him to help.

But what was Finn supposed to say?

"Pretty," Kafi said, straining out of her sister's arms as if she wanted to pick up one of the shards of glass on the floor and—knowing her—probably put it in her mouth.

"Here," Finn volunteered. "Let's move the bed over and let Kafi crawl around between the bed and—" He'd started scooting the bed away from the wall. He was kind of proud that he could do that even with Lana sitting on the bed. But he stopped when the bottom of the bed ripped off the tops of a row of cardboard boxes hidden beneath it. "Whoa. Is this where you have your whole world's supply of those coins?"

The coins were spilling out of the boxes by the hundreds. Possibly even by the thousands.

"Nooo," Lana moaned. "I just have . . . a few. And you shouldn't have seen that. You can't tell anyone they're here. Especially not my parents. They'd turn me in. You can't . . ."

Finn sat down on the bed beside Lana. He touched the coins taped to his wrist against the coins that he now saw she had in pouches in the back of her shirt.

"You're friends with this world's Natalie, and we're friends with the other world's Natalie," he said. "Really, we Greystones are even friends with *both* Natalies. And you have coins; we have coins. You want to fight the TVs; we want to fight the TVs. I bet you want to fight the stink grenades just like we do, too. We *are* on the same team."

Lana leaned against Finn's shoulder, as if she'd been longing for someone to lean on for ages. After a moment—almost as if they'd all silently agreed—Chess, Emma, Kona, and Rocky sat down on the floor in a half circle by the bed. Kona plopped Kafi down in the center of the half circle, where she could crawl or totter back and forth between the kids.

They all sat waiting on Lana.

Finally, Lana whispered, "There are ways to control people. The *government* controls people."

"We knew that already," Rocky said with a skeptical snort.

"Look, it's not like they teach us this in school," Lana said. "Some of this is just what I've found out from eaves-dropping. And from spying on officials at rallies and fund-raisers I went to. From spying on my own parents and their friends. Most people think I'm just the not-too-smart, not-too-pretty daughter of—"

"You're pretty!" Finn said quickly. "And I bet you're smart, too. It's just that I can't tell that by looking at you, and knowing it right away."

Lana gave him a smile that made him think she was both very pretty and very smart. And very nice, too.

"It's okay," she said. "I didn't *want* people to notice me. I was just kind of there. Around."

"I'm the kind of kid who's just 'around,' too," Chess said quietly. "At school, the other kids don't really see me."

"We see you!" Finn and Emma shouted practically at the same time. Then Finn added, "And *Natalie* sees you now, too."

Chess seemed to be trying not to smile too widely, just at the thought of Natalie.

"Anyhow," Emma said, turning back to Lana.

"Right," Lana said. "Some of this happened before I was even born. First, a group of scientists invented a foul-smelling chemical that affected people's brains, and they offered it to the military as a weapon."

"That's illegal," Kona said confidently. "We studied that in school. Chemical warfare was outlawed after World War One."

"In *your* world, maybe," Lana said. Then she winced. "Or maybe it was outlawed in mine, too, years ago, but people ignored that law. It's not something I ever learned about."

"How does the smell work?" Emma asked. "I guess it must trick people's brains into thinking they should be terrified and sad. And that they should give up. Is it pheromones? Does it affect the hippocampus or the thalamus or—"

"You think you're going to figure it out scientifically?" Rocky asked incredulously. "And then, what, come up with an antidote?"

"Don't be mean!" Finn told him.

Emma put her hand on Finn's knee, like she needed to calm him down.

"*Somebody* might be able to come up with the antidote," Emma said. "I'm not saying I know enough about chemistry, but if we could get a really smart, really brave chemist to come from the good world, then—"

"The smell doesn't matter that much now," Lana said. "Because the leaders moved on. The smells were just the first step. Like, I don't know, bicycles with training wheels. And now the leaders are using the equivalent of rocket ships."

"You mean the TVs people can't stop watching," Kona said.

"Yes," Lana said.

Finn reached over the opposite edge of the bed and grabbed a handful of coins.

"But your side—*our* side—we have these to fight back with," he said, letting the coins sift down through his fingers. "Right? You have all these coins under your bed, and your parents don't know, and that's how you can resist the TVs and they can't. How *do* you have all these coins? Where did they all come from?"

Was this what it felt like to be Emma—to always have more questions to wonder about?

Lana kept her lips pressed tightly together.

Finn patted her knee the same way Emma had patted his.

"Our mother—Emma's and Finn's and mine—she told us about the beginnings of the coins," Chess said. "Or the first coin, anyway. When our family lived in this world, eight years ago, our mom sent a coin to her double in the other world. And her double was Rocky's mom."

Lana raised an eyebrow, looking back and forth between Rocky and the three Greystone kids.

"And we know Natalie and her mom got coins from their doubles in this world," Kona went on, taking up the story from Chess. "Lana, did you help the Natalie here send those?"

Lana shook her head.

"No, but I was the one who told Natalie about the coins," she said. "A week ago. After the party where Natalie could have been killed. Natalie wanted to *do* something. Something big. She said she was sick of everybody lying all the time, everyone having to pretend that everything's great. When, actually, everybody is scared all the time in this world. Nobody is allowed to think for themselves or make any decisions on their own—did you know that there's only one political party for anyone to belong to? We hold elections, but they're just for show. Fake. There's only ever one candidate for anyone to vote for, for any office. The government can arrest anyone they want, and just make up a reason. And the 'criminals' can't even defend themselves. If they even get a trial, it's just, like, make-believe. Propaganda, to make people hate the criminal. Who might not have done anything wrong at all."

"We saw that happen!" Finn exclaimed. "They put our mom on trial, and they made it look like she was lying, and admitting she was guilty!"

"Multiply that by a hundred," Lana said bitterly. "By a thousand. By ten thousand, or a hundred thousand. I don't even know how many people have been punished like that, just because some official doesn't like them. There's so much I *don't* know, because no one's allowed to tell the truth."

"Our parents told the truth," Chess said quietly. "Even when they knew it could lead to their deaths, they still kept trying. They still kept gathering and sharing the truth."

Finn felt a surge of pride. He wanted to brag, *That's my mom and dad, too! You should hear how brave they were! How brave my mom still is, and how hard she's* kept *trying!*

But then Emma said, just as quietly, "And then our dad was killed. Eight years ago."

"I'm sorry," Lana whispered.

"Others died, too," Kona said. She hugged Kafi close for an instant, before gulping and going on. "Like the physicist who figured out how to make the first coins. And Natalie's grandmother in the other world."

"Did you and Natalie know you were risking death?" Rocky asked. "For . . . coins?"

He didn't sound like he was making fun of Lana, or trying to bully her. It was more like he just couldn't understand.

"The coins seemed like the only way to change anything," Lana said. She began to pick at the threads of her comforter. It was lumpy—maybe it had coins sewn into its stuffing. "I was just at the lowest level of the people working with the coins."

"You joined the rebels," Kona said, sounding awestruck.

"The resistance. The freedom fighters!"

Lana looked terrified again.

"We never called ourselves any of that," she said. "We didn't dare to. We just said . . . we were helpers. Or, we thought of ourselves that way. We mostly didn't dare to talk to anyone else working with us. It wasn't safe. I would just get notes, hidden under a rock by my family's fence: Pick up coins stored here. Move them over to there. Store them until it's safe to send them out again. And sometimes I used coins to record my own messages, and sent them out when I felt really brave. After I talked Natalie into helping, too, she was also recording messages and transporting coins. And I know she was planning to send hers into the other world. She must have done that today. With the ones that were my own, I could just drop them and they would disappear, and I would know they'd gone to my double."

"But why?" Emma asked. "What good did any of that do?"

"FIND US, SEE US, HEAR US—that all sounds pointless!" Rocky agreed. "I guess there's HELP US, too, but . . . how does that help? What's it all for?"

"I don't know," Lana whispered, her voice so soft now that Finn had to hold his breath, because even drawing air into his lungs might be too loud for him to still hear Lana. "Not entirely. But we all thought our doubles could rescue us. We thought they would come here and take care of us. Make all our decisions for us, maybe."

"That's what you want?" Finn asked. "I like making my own decisions. Like if Mom says, 'Do you want spaghetti or tacos for dinner?' sometimes I want Italian, and sometimes I want Mexican. It can depend. And she knows I like being able to choose."

"But my people have made such bad choices. . . ." Lana was still whispering. A tear rolled down her cheek, and she wiped it away. "Never mind. None of this matters now. The coins stopped working. Your lever doesn't work, either. The TVs are telling everybody in my world how to think and what decisions to make. We no longer have *any* choices. And now Mayor Mayhew's in the other world making sure no one has choices there, either."

Everybody else was squinting at Lana. They all looked like they were about to cry. Even Kafi, and there was no way she understood what the big kids were talking about.

Finn hoped his face didn't look like crying. Because he wasn't going to do that.

"But the coins do still protect us from the TVs," he said. "They still work a little."

"So what?" Lana asked, with a helpless shrug. "At some point, one of us is going to give in. And then we will be trapped, and the coins will be like Rocky said. Pointless."

It's not fair that the bad guys have two weapons, and we only have one, Finn thought.

Finn glanced at the TV across the room. Even broken, it seemed too scary to think about.

So he thought about the game rock-paper-scissors instead.

This is like if Rock and Scissors ganged up on Paper! he thought, getting mad all over again at Mayor Mayhew and all the other leaders of this awful world. *Only, for us, it's like the game is smells-coins-TVs, and Smells and TVs are on the same side! Coins don't have a chance!*

But maybe Finn wasn't thinking about things right. In rock-paper-scissors, you chose what you were, you won or you lost, and then you could be something different in the next round.

You got to choose a different "weapon" every time.

What if . . . What if . . .

Because he didn't want to look at the TV, Finn looked down at Kafi, cuddling against her sister's knees. Maybe his thoughts were as crazy as her saying "Pretty" when she saw the pile of broken glass under the TV.

But she was right: Some of the broken glass did kind of gleam in the sunlight coming in through the window. If you didn't know the TV was evil—and broken—it did look pretty.

Most of the time Finn didn't care if things were pretty or ugly. He was a lot more concerned if things were fun or not. Oh, and if food tasted good.

But if something ugly and broken could look pretty, then . . . then could something bad be used for good? he wondered.

Could the TVs be used by the people on the good-coins side, not the bad-smells side?

"What if *we* go on TV?" he asked. "What if we go on TV and tell the leaders they have to let levers and coins work again, and they have to be nice to people in both worlds, and, and they should only give people *good* choices? The coins and the TVs both deliver messages. So if we can use the coins for good things, why can't we use the TV for good messages, too?"

THIRTY-FIVE

EMMA

"Finn, you're a genius," Emma cried. She stood up and threw her arms around her brother's shoulders.

"No, no, no," Finn said, playfully shoving her away. "You're the smart one."

"Well, we can both be smart," Emma said. Finn seemed willing to compromise: He let Emma keep one arm draped around his shoulders. And he let Emma keep talking about how smart he was. "You being smart doesn't make me any less smart. And this time you were the one to remember this fact: Scientific discoveries usually aren't good or evil just by themselves. Science is neutral. It's what people do with their knowledge that matters."

Finn's eyes grew big.

"Emma," he said. "I didn't know any of that!"

"But you knew that if the bad guys can use the TV, we can use it, too," Kona said. "Only, we'll use it for good reasons, not bad."

"That's a nice theory," Lana said grudgingly. "It's just impossible."

"It *is* possible," Emma insisted. "Lana, if your dad worked at the TV station, then he has a key, right?"

"If nothing else, we could sneak in and turn off the power at his TV station," Chess said thoughtfully. "The . . . what would it be called? The transmitter?"

"But wouldn't there be lots of TV stations?" Rocky asked. "So if we turn off one station, the others would just keep controlling people? I keep thinking about all the TV interviews my mom and dad did when my sister and brother and I were kidnapped—there were so many stations who sent reporters to their news conferences. And people from online news services and radio stations and newspapers and magazines . . ."

"Really?" Lana said. It was like she was hearing of a situation too strange to even be a myth. "That's another difference between the worlds. We do only have one TV network. Only one channel. All the others were outlawed. Just like political parties were outlawed, except for the one the leaders are in."

"Unh! Unh!" Kafi pushed against Emma's leg.

"That's it," Kona said, snatching up her sister and spinning her around. Kafi still struggled in her sister's arms. "We have about a minute before Kafi starts screaming to get out of here."

"Then we escape to the TV station and let Kafi escape that way, too," Emma said.

Rocky and Chess both frowned, but they started to stand up. Kona put Kafi into a "You're an airplane now" pose over her head and "flew" her toward the door. Emma and Finn followed.

"You think it's that easy?" Lana asked. "You'll just . . . go?"

"We're hoping you'll come, too, to help us," Finn said, with a particularly charming smile that showed his dimples.

"I don't . . . I'm not . . . ," Lana began. But then she stood up, too. "You think we should walk?"

"I think maybe that one woman downstairs could drive us," Emma said. "The one who kind of scolded your dad."

"You mean Irmine?" Lana asked. "With the gray hair and the lavender streak?"

"We could ask her," Emma said.

Everyone traipsed toward the stairs. At the top, Emma was thinking, *Maybe I should swing the lever at all the TVs in this house.* But by the time she got to the bottom, she could barely keep herself from going over and ripping down the purple-flowered blanket that hid the TV from view. She felt herself longing to turn it on and watch.

That would just be acting like a scientist, she told herself. *Go look at the TV so you can study what it makes you think and do. . . .*

She caught herself turning toward the TV room. Just being this close to the TV, even without looking at it, was enough to make her think differently. And it was trying to trick her into believing those were her normal thoughts.

"Here," Lana said behind Emma. She pressed a little cloth bag into Emma's hands. Emma could feel the outline of coins inside the bag. "Wear this as a necklace, or tie it around your waist, under your clothes. Just in case."

"To protect me even more against the TVs and smells?" Emma asked. "Or do you mean, in case it becomes possible to send them into the other world again?"

"Both?" Lana said with a weak smile.

"Why not?" Emma agreed. She slid the looped drawstrings of the bag around her neck. Now the little collection of coins hung at the same level as her heart.

Lana moved on to offering bags of coins to the other kids as well. Kona didn't let Kafi have one, because she would have tried to eat it. But everyone else took one.

It was strange how much better Emma felt to have the little bag of coins, along with the ones taped around her wrist. But maybe it just helped to know that Lana cared. Either way, the pull of the TV seemed to recede. Emma trusted herself to walk over to the maid—Irmine?—and ask, "If we untied you, would you drive us somewhere?"

"Honey, if you untied me, I would go straight to that TV," Irmine replied, struggling against the ropes to point longingly into the side room. "That's all I can think about."

"What if one of us broke the TV?" Finn asked. "What if we broke every TV in this house?"

Emma was glad Finn had thought of that, too. And that he could still think about it, even so close to a TV.

"I can't lie to you," Irmine said. "I'd be running to the TV in the next-door neighbor's house as fast as I could. I'd be a track star, getting over there."

"We could break all those TVs, too," Finn said.

"We can't break every TV in town," Lana said.

"Or in the whole country," Rocky added. "Or is it in this whole world?"

"You don't have to break any TVs!" Lana's dad gasped. He was clutching his heart as if just talking about breaking TVs made him feel like he'd been stabbed in the chest. "Untie me, and I'll drive you anywhere you want!"

But his eyes kept darting toward the TV room.

"Dad, I don't know if you mean to or not, but you're lying to us," Lana said.

"Then I'll drive you!" Lana's mom volunteered. "Untie me instead!"

The other adults took up the cry: "No, me!" "I'll help! Pick me!" "Lana! I'm your family's chauffeur! I should drive you!"

"Oh, brother," Finn muttered, backing away. Emma saw that he'd pulled his coin bag from under his shirt and was clutching it so tightly that his knuckles turned white.

"What if we gave the adults some coins?" Emma asked Lana. Emma tiptoed closer to Irmine and waved her own bag of coins before Irmine's eyes. It probably looked like she was a magician trying to hypnotize Irmine.

Isn't that kind of what the coins and the TV do? Emma wondered. *Isn't it a lot like hypnosis?*

"Child, I do like money," Irmine said, watching the bag of coins sway before her. Then she snapped her gaze back to Emma's face. "But you could toss me into a whole swimming pool of coins and dollar bills—even one-hundred-dollar bills!—and I'd trade it all in a heartbeat for getting back to that TV."

"We can't trust any of these adults," Lana said. She looked like she was about to cry. "We'll have to walk. It'll

228

take forever. And I'm not sure how safe we'll be. . . ."

"Lana, baby, you are giving up too soon," Irmine said. "I can't trust myself to drive you. You're right not to trust any of us adults. But there is something you know how to drive. . . ."

"Irmine, I'm *thirteen*!" Lana protested. "I've never driven a car! I'd wreck it! I'd hurt people!"

Irmine put a hand on Lana's arm.

"What if I told you I know where the keys are to your daddy's golf cart?"

THIRTY-SIX

CHESS

This is crazy, Chess thought.

All of the kids were piled onto the golf cart. Lana was driving, with Kona and Kafi beside her—Kona had declared herself ready to grab the wheel if Lana weakened and started veering toward any house where a TV might draw her in. Rocky and the three Greystone kids huddled together on the second, backward-facing bench behind Lana and Kona. And propped between them, they had a giant duffel bag full of the coins from underneath Lana's bed.

"Who knows how many we'll need?" Lana had said, tying it in place.

Finn kept hugging the duffel bag and announcing, "Okay. I feel better now."

Were the coins affecting Chess, too? Maybe it was a major achievement that he wasn't jumping off the cart and running over to hide in any of the bushes they passed. Maybe he should feel proud that he'd managed not to start screaming, "This is hopeless! We're all doomed! We should give up now!"

It was insane that they were driving around in a completely open vehicle where anyone could see them. This was the bad world, the nightmare world, and they knew they were in danger. It made no sense to show their faces in public. If one of the evil leaders—or the police or the military or the security forces the leaders commanded—saw them, the kids didn't even have a fast vehicle to speed away in.

Chess was pretty sure that the top speed for a golf cart was something like twenty miles per hour.

But as Chess leaned his head back against the duffel bag of coins, the breeze ruffling his hair, he felt less and less like running or screaming. Driving to the TV station felt *right*.

Were the coins helping him think that? Or was it just what he would naturally think, all on his own?

Anyhow, as they putt-putted along, there *weren't* any evil leaders or police officers or military or security forces springing out to capture the kids. The streets around them were eerily quiet and deserted. Flickering images lit up the windows of many of the houses they passed—*no, no, don't think about the TVs in all those houses*—but that was the only evidence that anyone else still existed in this world. There were still walls and fences and barbed wire and razor wire everywhere, as if every resident was prepared for riots or warfare. Once they passed out of the luxury of Lana's neighborhood, the green lawns were replaced by yards of bare, trampled dirt and, here and there, clumps of weeds. The fences looked rustier; the walls around many of the yards had peeling paint and sagging planks. The streets had more potholes, and Lana had to slow down to dodge them.

But if Chess narrowed his vision to the one brave stretch of ivy curling around the pole of a street sign, or the one valiant dandelion blooming in an empty lot—or the cheerful, puffy clouds sailing by in the sky overhead—he could view everything around him as . . . peaceful. The stillness was pleasant.

As long as he didn't see any evil leaders or police officers or military or security forces springing out to capture them, Chess could feel hope.

It also helped not to think about the scary images he'd seen on the TV screen back at the Judge and the Mayor's house.

He was absolutely certain now that those images were lies.

"Should we make plans as we're driving?" Emma asked.

"Figure out exactly what to do when we get to the TV station?"

"What we say could be . . . overheard," Lana whispered. "This whole street probably has listening devices and security cameras. We'll need to keep . . . the element of surprise."

This seemed ludicrous to Chess, too. Weren't they already doomed regardless, if anyone was watching or listening to them right now through any surveillance system?

Maybe the leaders are just planning to capture us once we get to the TV station, Chess thought. *Maybe they figure we can't do any damage before that.*

He still didn't jump off the golf cart or run screaming for the bushes looking for a place to hide.

Even traveling at such a slow speed, they eventually passed out into the countryside. Now Chess could see a tall TV tower in the distance.

"Is that it?" Kona asked.

"Yep," Lana said, clenching her hands tighter on the steering wheel of the golf cart. She kept her gaze resolutely pointed ahead, as if she'd lose control if she glanced to the left or right.

Finally they reached the base of the TV tower, where a ramp wound around a low, elegant building that seemed to be mostly glass.

"Hope no one's looking out any of those windows," Rocky muttered.

Lana pulled the golf cart into a parking space at the edge of the lot. They were somewhat hidden by the number of huge SUVs around them. But no one sat in any of the cars; no one was rushing between the cars and the building. And no guard stood in the booth at the entrance to the ramp up to the building.

"I'm the general manager's daughter," Lana muttered under her breath. "I'm just following his instructions. He told me to come here. I—"

"Are you practicing?" Finn asked.

Grimly, Lana nodded.

"You're the general manager's daughter," Kona said. "They wouldn't arrest you just for trying to go into the building. What's the worst that could happen—they say, 'Go away'?"

Chess could think of worse things.

All the kids spilled out of the golf cart. Chess thought they probably looked like a clown-car act at the circus. Kafi was chewing on Kona's sleeve. Finn's hair looked like he'd been through a tornado. Emma kept absent-mindedly twirling the string of her coin bag around her finger. Even when it bonked her on the nose, she didn't seem to notice.

"Maybe if we were wearing nicer clothes, they'd pay

more attention to us," Chess said. Everyone but Lana still wore the same clothes they'd slept in the night before—all shorts and T-shirts, except for Kafi's sleeper. "We'd look more official."

"Even if we had tuxedos and ball gowns, we're still kids," Rocky muttered. "We'd still just *look* like kids."

But he turned resolutely toward the ramp up to the building, his jaw set. So did the girls and Finn. Chess swallowed hard and followed along.

After the hum of the golf cart, the silence of the parking lot felt ominous—like it was a lie, too. A trick. Chess strained his ears, listening for the crackle of some security guard's walkie-talkie, or some TV executive calling over his shoulder as he walked out of the building, "Okay, good show. But we'll do even better tomorrow."

No, the TV people in this world would be like, "Great job making up so many lies! Make up even more tomorrow!" Chess thought.

But he couldn't hear anything.

They reached the bottom of the ramp, and breezed right past an empty security booth. They climbed up toward the first set of doors.

"We'll have to be buzzed in," Lana mumbled. "I'll give them my dad's password, and . . ."

The first door hung open, a full inch away from the latch embedded in the doorframe.

"People must have just rushed inside to watch TV, because it had a magnetic pull on them," Emma theorized. "So they weren't careful about shutting the door behind them."

Or it's a trap, Chess thought.

He didn't say that, though. Instead, he wrapped his fingers around the bag of coins in his pocket and followed as Lana opened the door the rest of the way for all of them.

Now they faced a wide counter that could have been a receptionist's desk or another security guard's stand. It didn't matter, though, because this area was deserted, too.

"We should be able to see the security feed for the whole building here," Lana said, circling to the other side of the counter. "Yes!"

Chess followed her. He saw a bank of screens embedded in the desk. One showed the parking lot they'd just left. One showed the front door from outside. One showed silent images of people screaming and punching and—

Lana dropped the duffel bag full of coins onto that screen.

"Don't watch that TV," she said.

Oh. That one showed the TV broadcast. And it had almost drawn everyone else into watching, too.

Chess took a bunch of deep breaths.

"This is the one we need to pay attention to," Lana said, pointing to a screen off to the side. It must have been from a security camera in the company cafeteria, because Chess could see signs on the walls that said, "Soup of the Day: Split Pea" and "Daily special comes with two sides." But this was the only screen showing any people, unless Chess counted the one Kona had covered (*Don't think about moving the duffel bag. Don't do it. Don't . . .*) Chess rubbed the coins in his pocket and made himself focus on the images from the company cafeteria. Dozens of people were crowded onto chairs around the cafeteria's round tables. But no one seemed to be eating. They were almost eerily still, everyone just staring and staring and staring.

They were all watching TV. Chess stared, too. Through the security camera feed, he could still see the images on the TV screen in the company cafeteria. On that screen-within-a-screen, people were fighting. People were being thrown to the ground by earth-shattering explosions. People were . . .

Kona sat down on the screen showing the scene in the company cafeteria.

"Hey!" Rocky complained. "We need to watch that! We need to know—"

"You were getting hypnotized again," Kona told him. "You all were. We *don't* need that."

"It helps to rub the coins around your eyes," Finn suggested helpfully, demonstrating. "That keeps me from wanting to push Kona and the duffel bag away and see the TV stuff no matter what. Or, I know—we could *tape* the coins around our eyes . . . Aha!"

He'd dug out the masking tape from the sack they'd brought with them, and began ripping off strips. In moments, he had a row of coins across his forehead and on either side of his eyes.

"Anyone else want some?" he offered.

"I think we're okay," Lana said.

And then, in spite of everything, Chess wanted to giggle. Even in their terror, none of the older kids wanted to look as ridiculous as Finn did right now. Even Emma regarded him doubtfully.

"Is this the TV studio?" Rocky asked, pointing to another screen showing a dimly lit room with large cameras on wheeled tripods.

"Yes," Lana said. "And . . . that's where we should go."

"Who knows the most about running a camera?" Chess asked as Lana began leading them down a bland hallway painted—of course—navy blue with an orange border. "We might not have much time."

"I learned some things from my dad," Kona said at the same time that Lana shrugged and muttered, "My dad taught me a little. . . ."

Then both girls laughed.

"I guess there are different ways of being doubles," Emma said.

And how many things would our dad have taught us, if he'd lived? Chess wondered, an old, familiar ache rising in his chest. *How much would he have protected us?*

He turned to Emma and Finn to see if they were thinking the same way. Maybe Chess would need to comfort them. But Emma had an even more intense look on her face than usual; she was swiveling her head side to side as if trying to observe every detail of the TV office building. She was completely in scientist mode, not *I miss my dad* mode. And Finn was bouncing along as goofily as ever, the coins taped to his face jiggling as if the tape might come unstuck at any moment. And then the coins might be transformed into something like bungee jumpers, dangling from his face and bouncing along with Finn's every step. . . .

Chess realized that just looking at Emma and Finn had comforted *him*. It was like they were coins, too.

Lana led them through a maze of hallways, and then stopped in front of a dark, unmarked door. She lifted her hand toward a keypad above the doorknob.

"I know Dad's code," she said. "I *think* it will still work. But if an alarm goes off, we should probably run in opposite directions, and hope some of us manage not to be caught."

She began entering numbers. The door clicked. Lana grabbed the doorknob and twisted it to the side.

"No alarm," Emma breathed.

"We're not in yet," Lana said. She seemed frozen, with every muscle tensed. "Actually shoving the door open might be what triggers the alarm. . . ."

"We've got this," Kona said. "We're ready."

"Here," Chess offered, reaching for Kafi. "I'll take your sister. You take off running for the nearest camera as soon as we're in."

So he was in the midst of pulling baby Kafi into his arms when the door swung open and the bright light clicked on around them. Jolted, he jerked his head toward the light. He could make out two sets of glowing red letters below a huge glass lens:

RECORDING LIVE

and

ON AIR

Frantically, he looked around, and caught a glimpse of yet another TV screen off to the side in the TV studio room. This one showed a familiar scene: Finn with his goofy forehead full of coins. Emma looking intense. Chess taking Kafi from Kona. Rocky and Lana both frozen in the midst of striding forward.

"This door wasn't set up with an alarm to go off if someone tries to break in," Chess gasped. "It's set up to *film* whoever comes in here—and put them on live TV! Everybody's seeing everything we do!"

THIRTY-SEVEN

FINN

Finn unfroze first.

"Hi, everybody!" he said, waving as he stepped forward. Because if you were going to end up on live TV in front of thousands—or millions?—of people, it seemed rude not to say hello.

Behind him, the other kids were arguing in stressed whispers: "It could just be another security camera. . . ." "No, no—that 'ON AIR' means we're on air *now*! And look, there's the control room over there, and you can see the image on all the screens. . . . It's all Finn!" "The leaders must have had it set up this way for *themselves*. . . ." "But what if this is a trick?" "What should we do?"

Finn smiled wider at the camera.

"Okay, so you're probably wondering why some little kid is on your screen right now, when you've been watching nothing but awful, horrible 'The world is a really bad place' scenes for, I don't know, hours," he began. "I can't really explain all that. I don't know everything that's going on in your world, and even if I did, I'm not sure I could understand it. I'm only eight!"

He couldn't help giggling a little at that. How many eight-year-olds ever got to go on live TV?

And then he almost giggled again because he thought of what his best friend back home, Tyrell, would tell him to say on live TV: "Fart jokes! You could make the whole world laugh!"

But he could look back at the big kids and see how worried and scared they were—so worried and scared that none of them stepped forward to tell him what to say or do. Finn had a lot of experience himself now with being worried and scared. He was worried about Mom and Natalie and everyone else they'd left behind in the other world; he was scared that Mayor Mayhew and the other leaders of this awful world would win once and for all.

A fart joke would make *Finn* feel better.

But he didn't want to talk only to other second-graders.

Right now he needed to say something that would help everyone in both worlds.

"So, anyhow, I don't know everything, but I do know that your leaders have been lying to you. A *lot*. And the TV you've been watching for however many hours today has been lying to you, too. That's *how* your leaders have been lying to you. So go look out a window. All that war and bad stuff isn't really going on. Your leaders just want you to be scared and sad so you'll do what they want. They want you to stay inside and keep watching. And I think they want you to hate the other world, so you'll think it's good your leaders are trying to take it over!"

Behind him, Lana muttered, "But there's been bad stuff going on in our world for years. They're going to think you're lying, too, if you say everything's good!"

Finn paused to press one of the coins taped to his forehead tighter against his skin.

"Okay, yeah," he said. "I'm not saying there's no bad stuff anywhere, but it's not all bad. There's good stuff around you, too."

He remembered how much fun he'd always had with Mom and Chess and Emma, before he'd known about the dangerous world they'd come from. Even after he found out, he'd had some of the happiest moments in his life: Rescuing the Gustano kids. Rescuing Mom and Joe and Ms. Morales.

Just being hugged by Mom . . .

He was going to make himself cry, and that wouldn't help.

All of those things were personal just to Finn, and he needed something that could be personal for a whole country. Maybe even a whole planet.

What could make *everyone* feel like they'd been hugged by their own mom or dad?

Maybe Emma was right, and Finn really was a genius. Because suddenly he knew what to say.

"You know what you should do?" he asked, as if a whole planet worth of people watching him on TV could answer him right there. "You should turn off your TV set and go outside. Go outside and look up at the sky. It's really blue today, and there are lots of puffy clouds. Or if it's night where you are, you'll see stars. And that's where you'll see that your world's not all just about people fighting with each other, and lying, and forcing everyone to make bad decisions. You do that, and then, you know what, I bet you're going to want to get different leaders and make your own decisions and make this world a better place. Okay? Go outside now! You're free! You can be good now, and do good things and, and have fun! You can decide for yourself whether you want tacos or spaghetti or hamburgers or anything! Even if you want split-pea soup, that's your decision! Maybe even have succotash! I don't care!"

This last part about succotash was an inside joke with Emma and Chess, because that had been their code word when all of this started, when Mom first went away and got trapped in this world. Finn knew the worlds were totally separated right now, but he still felt a sliver of hope. Maybe Mom had found a way into this world despite what Lana had said about the pathways between the worlds being closed. Maybe Mom was watching him right now, and succotash could make her giggle, too.

Kona stepped up behind Finn and announced, "Okay, we're shutting off your TV now, so you *have* to go outside."

She found some switch on the back of the camera. The lit-up words, ON AIR and RECORDING LIVE, blinked out.

Emma and Chess threw their arms around Finn.

"That was perfect!" Emma announced. "You said what really mattered—well, except for the tacos and spaghetti and hamburgers part. That was kind of extra. But everything else was what people needed to hear. Now we can just wait to see if people do what you told them, before we turn the camera back on and tell them anything else."

"Good job," Chess added.

"N-Nobody's come to arrest us yet," Lana stammered. "But maybe we should get out of here before that happens."

"Let's go check out that security monitor first," Emma

suggested, gesturing toward the control room off to the side.

Finn raced toward the monitors, which showed all the same security camera scenes they'd watched before.

"The people in the cafeteria! They're getting up! They're heading for the doors!" Rocky announced excitedly. He high-fived Finn. "They're *obeying* you, little dude!"

"If they look up when they go outside—that will be proof," Kona said.

On the security monitors, the first surge of people reached the front door and began spilling out into the sunlight. And—yes!—they all tilted their heads back at the same time, almost as though they were all hearing the same music and all doing the same dance.

"Go, Finny. Go, Finny," Emma chanted, dancing around. "You made that happen. You!"

But then something strange occurred. The whole crowd began streaming back into the building. For the first time, Finn noticed that one of the monitors in the bank of TV screens before them showed a scene from near the Public Hall, where his mother's trial had been held downtown. And on that screen, people were also stepping outside, looking up, then darting back into the building.

"What's going on?" Lana asked.

"Everyone's not returning for the split-pea soup or succotash, are they?" Kona said.

Finn no longer felt like laughing at the funny word.

On the security monitors, Finn could see the progress of the clump of people: back through the doors, past the receptionist desk, down the hall—and then back into the cafeteria.

It looked like all forty or fifty of the people who'd originally been in the cafeteria were moving in unison and sliding back into the same seats they'd sat in before. They turned back toward the TV screen at the front of the cafeteria and went back to watching in silence, even though the screen was completely blank now.

"Our plan didn't work at all!" Finn wailed. "Me talking on TV—it was totally useless!"

"That's it," Lana moaned. "Let's get out of here before someone catches us. Come on!"

She started tugging on Finn's arm. Finn reached for Emma and Chess, because there was no way he'd leave them behind.

But Emma pulled away. She put her lever bag down and leaned toward the monitor.

"No, wait," she murmured. "Is there any way to play back that security footage? I think I saw . . . I think I saw . . ."

"What?" Kona asked, even as she fiddled with the controls. "How far back do you want to go?"

"There!" Rocky cried. "I see it, too!"

Kona had zipped back to the moment when everyone

from the cafeteria was out in the parking lot, their heads tilted back to look up at the sky.

"What?" Finn asked, squinting at the entire crowd frozen on the screen.

"That man!" Emma said, pointing to a fuzzy shape off to the side. "Doesn't it look like he's dropping coins onto the ground? I bet he's on our side! We've found someone else to help us!"

THIRTY-EIGHT

EMMA

Emma took off racing toward the cafeteria.

An ally! she thought. *We've found another ally besides Lana!*

Didn't it logically follow that anyone who had coins would be on their side?

She could hear the others running behind her, Chess calling, "Emma, be careful! Maybe we should think about this first. . . ."

Emma did not slow down. Nobody had caught them on their drive to the TV station—or when Finn was on TV—so she wasn't concerned about being caught now. Especially not if there was a chance to get help.

Emma burst into the cafeteria, panting from her long run. Her gasps for air sounded hideously loud in the quiet cafeteria. But nobody even looked at her until she strode out in front of the crowd—between them and the TV. Then everyone began to mumble and complain:

"No, no, sit down. . . ."

"Sit down and join us. . . ."

"Join us and watch. . . . The next instructions will be coming soon. . . ."

"Who said the next instructions will be coming soon?" Emma demanded, even as she scanned the crowd looking for the man she'd seen with the coins. She could ask questions in her sleep; it took no effort to ask about the TV while she was also trying to find help.

People from throughout the crowd answered this time.

"TV . . ."

"TV always has more instructions. . . ."

"We do what the TV says. . . ."

"TV makes everything official. . . ."

"Nothing's real if it's not on TV. . . ."

"TV is what our leaders want us to know. TV's the only thing we can trust. . . ."

It was almost unbearable to listen to these answers.

"Newsflash: That TV's not saying anything!" she shouted, pointing to the TV overhead even as she shifted to the side, still looking for the man. Where was he?

It really would have helped if she'd seen his face, rather than just the back of his head.

And if he'd been wearing something besides a navy blue hoodie and jeans.

Lots of men in the crowd were wearing hoodies and jeans.

Wavy dark hair, she told herself. *Look for the hair that matches—and that guy definitely had a bald spot.*

She started to circle toward the back of the room, so she could look for bald spots. But just then, the crowd let out a sigh of contentment, in unison. Emma turned her head: The TV had flickered back to life. It made Emma think of a zombie in a horror movie—some monster that couldn't be killed. Emma squinted, trying to figure out how it all worked.

On the screen, people huddled under a broken, sagging roof while flashes of light exploded around them.

Ooooh . . . bombs, Emma thought. *Who cares how the TV works? It's just good that it does, to warn us. A war must have started outside after we all came into the TV station. And after the crowd came back in. Probably because of people from the other world. It's so good that the TV is telling us what's really going on, so we know to stay here and be safe. . . . And we have to keep watching. . . .*

"Emma!"

That was Chess, shouting in her ear. He began pulling

on her arm, pulling her toward the door out of the cafeteria.

Emma's feet wanted to stay in place. Her heels tried to dig into the floor.

"We watched the security footage again—it doesn't look like that man came back inside!" Chess yelled.

"Ooooh . . . ," Emma moaned. But her brain was fighting back against the TV's influence again.

To steady herself, she stared at Chess's face: his ordinary, entirely familiar face. One of his nostrils was ever so slightly larger than the other, and he had a tiny, tiny scar in his right eyebrow, where Finn had accidentally hit him once with a hockey stick. Emma knew the whole story; she knew Finn had been so sorry he'd apologized every day for a month.

Emma *knew* Chess. She knew he loved her, and wanted good things for her.

The TV did not love her. It did not want good things for anybody.

I can think that now, she thought. *I can think with my own brain again, even though the TV's still on. And that's just because of looking at Chess.*

Chess began tugging Emma toward the door. Emma's feet kept fighting her—once or twice, Chess's feet seemed to be fighting him. But finally they were on the other side of the cafeteria door, out in the hall.

Chess slammed it behind them, shutting out the noise of the TV.

"You rescued me," Emma murmured. "You saved me. If it hadn't been for you, I'd still be there, even with all the coins I have. Why am I so . . . susceptible?"

"We all are, Emma—don't be so hard on yourself," Chess said. He grinned in a way that almost seemed happy. At least temporarily. "This makes up for the times you were right during our other trips to this world, and we *needed* to be braver, or we *needed* to solve some extra code. We're a good team. We balance each other out. So does Finn."

"Chess, Emma, come on!" It was Finn shouting from down the hall. He, Rocky, and Kona were clustered around the desk in the entryway again. But they were staring out the front window instead of looking at any of the security footage. "That guy's right outside. Let's go meet him!"

"Is it safe?" Chess called back, and Emma almost laughed because her brother was so predictable.

Of course, if it weren't for him, she'd still be stuck in front of the TV in the cafeteria.

"Maybe we should wait a few minutes?" she called, to back up Chess. "Spy for a few minutes, until we can tell what that guy is up to?"

She and Chess caught up with the others. Lana had the

duffel bag of coins strapped over her shoulder again. Finn had picked up Emma's bag with the lever inside—how could she have dropped it and left it behind? Rocky and Kona were handing Kafi back and forth, as if they needed to do that to keep her out of trouble.

Outside in the parking lot, the man was slowly rotating toward the building.

"In just a moment, we'll see his face," Emma breathed. "We'll be able to tell if we know him or—"

"In just a moment, he'll see *us*," Lana muttered back. She ducked down behind a potted plant, and motioned for the others to take cover, too.

Emma slid down beside a waiting room couch. She could see the man's ear. She could see the first part of his eyebrow. She could see the profile of his nose.

And then Rocky bolted straight up, crying, "I know who that is! It's my dad!"

THIRTY-NINE

CHESS

Chess felt more sorry for Rocky than ever before.

The other boy was already sprinting out the door, screaming, "Dad! Dad! Dad! You came! You found me! I knew you'd rescue me!"

"No, no, Rocky—that's just going to be the version of your dad from *this* world," Chess called after him.

Rocky kept running.

Outside, the man turned to face Rocky full-on. Chess had only ever seen Rocky's dad on televised news reports—the ones broadcast after Rocky and his brother and sister were kidnapped. This man certainly *looked* like Rocky's dad had then. He had the same mussed dark hair, the same saggy jowls, the same worried eyes.

So he looks like a terrified man who doesn't know where his kids are—not someone seeing his missing son for the first time in days, Chess thought.

"Rocky!" Chess screamed, chasing after him. "Be careful!"

Emma, Finn, Kona, and Lana ran, too, crashing through the door with Chess. Kafi straddled the duffel bag of coins on Lana's shoulder as if it were a toy horse. She shrieked, "Faz-er!"

Right, Kafi, Chess thought. *Faster! We've got to get to Rocky before . . .*

Chess was three long strides behind Rocky when Rocky leaped, launching himself toward the man and throwing his arms around him in a joyous hug.

The man didn't wrap his arms around Rocky in response. He just stood there, stiff and stunned and silent.

"That's *Other*–Mr. Gustano!" Emma shouted. "Your dad's double! The one the police say was in our basement—the one who might have been involved in your kidnapping!"

"Kidnapping?" the man said in a panicky voice. "I didn't have anything to do with any kidnapping!"

Rocky peered up at the man's face in horror.

"You're not my dad!" he screamed. And then he crumpled

to the ground, hitting the dirt hard and burying his face in his hands. "It's not fair that you look like him! Oh . . . what if I never see my dad again? Or Mom or *my* Emma and Finn . . . what if I'm stuck here forever?"

This was worse than watching the fake battles on TV, worse than the stink grenades plunging everyone into despair. Rocky's despair was real.

And it matched Chess's despair almost exactly.

But . . . didn't that mean that Chess might know how to comfort Rocky?

Chess closed the distance between him and Rocky and immediately knelt beside him.

"Rocky, it's okay," he said, patting the other boy's back, as if Rocky were as young as Finn. Or maybe Kafi. "I know how you feel."

A memory hit Chess, full force. Not long after his dad died, Chess had been at the grocery store with his mom. Chess couldn't be sure which world they'd been in then, but it didn't matter. He was sad, regardless. Then Chess had spotted a tall man in the checkout line ahead of them. At four, Chess was more used to seeing adults' knees than their faces. And somehow that man's blue jeans–covered knees had looked like Chess's dad's. Chess had wrapped his arms as tight as he could around the man's knees and squealed, "Daddy!"

And of course it hadn't been Dad. When the man crouched down, Chess discovered he had red hair and freckles and a full beard—nothing at all like Chess's dad.

Probably that wasn't a good memory to share. Because Chess *hadn't* ever seen his dad again.

But Rocky's dad wasn't dead. There was still hope for him.

And for Rocky.

"Our friend Natalie went through this the last time we were in this world," Chess told Rocky. "It was awful for her to see her parents' doubles here. But she made it home to her real parents again."

"And now she's just endangered in her own world," Rocky moaned.

Finn ran over beside Chess and patted Rocky's shoulder, too. But Finn faced Other–Mr. Gustano.

"If you're some evil kidnapper, don't even think about bothering Rocky again," Finn snarled, sounding as fierce as Chess had ever heard him. "Or any of us!"

"And if you've got coins because you're a bad guy stealing them, not a good guy helping out, hand them over right now," Kona said, grabbing for Other–Mr. Gustano's closed fists.

"There are seven of us and only one of you—you are totally outnumbered," Emma added, joining Chess and Finn by Rocky's side.

Chess wasn't sure it was fair to count Kafi—though she had been good at unplugging the first TV they'd encountered.

Or maybe it was Lana's loyalty he should doubt. She hovered indecisively behind the kids huddled around Rocky. She seemed to be trying to stay out of Other–Mr. Gustano's line of sight. She crouched down to lower Kafi and the duffel bag of coins toward the ground, but said nothing.

"This guy doesn't have any coins, unless he's hiding them really well," Kona reported, even as she patted the pockets of Other–Mr. Gustano's hoodie.

The man's gaze darted toward the ground, then back at all the kids.

"There!" Chess said, following the line of the man's quick glance. Chess pointed, and Kona plucked a few shiny coins from a clump of grass. She held them high in the air.

"Hide those!" Lana and Other–Mr. Gustano screamed, almost as one.

Other–Mr. Gustano reached out, but Kona was too fast for him. She palmed the coins and slid them into her own pocket.

"Unh-uh," she chided him. "I'm not giving those back until you explain what's going on. Why you had them in the first place. How you're still out here when all your coworkers went back inside. Who you really are."

Other—Mr. Gustano looked frantically back and forth between the Greystones, Rocky, and Kona. Chess noticed that Lana still seemed to be hiding behind the duffel bag, just watching.

"You could get me in so much trouble . . . ," Other—Mr. Gustano moaned. "But . . . you said 'this world.' You said 'doubles.' . . ." His gaze lingered on Rocky. "You look like I did when I was a kid, and you really seemed to think I was your dad, even though *I* don't have any children. . . . But most of all, you're not afraid. None of you are. You're standing out in the open in sight of three security cameras and you're shouting all sorts of things. . . . Where are you from? How did you get here?"

Chess stood up and held out his arms as if he could protect all the other kids.

"Nope," he said. His knees trembled, but his voice came out steady and strong. "That's not how this works. *You* explain yourself to us first."

Emma pulled herself up alongside Chess.

"What were you doing with those coins?" she demanded.

"Why were your fingerprints in a basement in the other world?" Kona added.

"That really does make him seem like a bad guy," Finn agreed, popping up to stand with the others.

"He's not," Lana said, finally straightening up and stepping forward.

"How do you know that, Lana?" Rocky growled. "It's like this guy was impersonating my dad in my world—he might as well have *framed* my dad. That sounds bad to me!"

Lana winced, practically withering under Rocky's glare.

"None of you understand . . . ," she whispered. "How afraid we all are, how long we've had to stay silent. . . ."

"You can tell us, Lana," Chess said softly. "You saw for yourself, nobody was watching or listening to the security footage from out here." He started to add, *You're safe,* but he couldn't really promise that. So he settled for something he was more certain of: "It's worth the risk to tell."

Lana gulped. She darted her glance toward a light pole by the parking lot that probably did contain a security camera. Then she trained her gaze again on the other kids.

"I know we can trust this man," Lana began, "because I heard him making recordings for his coins. He's the *reason* I found out about the coins, and started smuggling them into the other world."

That was enough to make Chess feel better, but Lana went on: "And . . . I'm pretty sure he's the one who made your lever."

FORTY

FINN

Everybody started talking at once.

"Why didn't you say so?"

"How do you know that?"

"He made our lever? Then can he fix it?"

"Lana, why didn't you tell us about this guy from the very beginning? He can help us!"

But Other–Mr. Gustano was shaking his head, crying out, "No, no, none of that's true. I'm just an innocent TV sound engineer. I don't even know what you're talking about. Coins? Levers? They've got nothing to do with me. I am a party member in good standing. Blue and orange forever!"

Finn wanted to throw up just hearing the words "blue and orange." But he also felt a little like giggling. Other–Mr. Gustano was such a bad liar. He was like some kid caught with his hand in a cookie jar trying to say with a straight face, "Cookies? I don't know anything about cookies!"

"Dude—*Gus*," Finn said, because it was easier to call someone a liar when you weren't addressing him as "Mister." The other kids nodded, as if they liked the nickname. And they liked Finn calling him out. "We saw you on the security cameras. You dropped a bunch of coins on the ground. And two minutes ago, you and Lana both yelled, 'Hide them!'"

Gus looked around frantically, like a trapped animal. He had beads of sweat on his forehead.

"Just admit the coins I picked up are yours, and tell us about levers, and I bet we can work together really well," Kona said.

"Right," Finn agreed. "We don't want to yell at you about lying. We just want to figure out how to get back to our families. And how to stop the Mayor once and for all."

"Don't say that!" Gus cried. "Don't say anything bad about the Mayor!"

In one quick motion, Gus put his hand over Finn's mouth. With his other arm, he grabbed Finn and rolled with him onto the ground. They landed against a black SUV parked near the edge of the blacktop. The lever in the bag Finn was carrying dug into his back.

The other kids shrieked, "What are you doing?" and "Let Finn go!" But Finn could tell by the way Gus cradled Finn's head that Gus wasn't trying to hurt him. The man peered frantically around the edge of the back bumper of the SUV.

"If they come for you, say . . . say that wasn't your voice," Gus hissed. "Say they must have heard interference in their security feed. That's all. Because you would never say anything like that about the Mayor, you're nothing but grateful for all he's done for the city, you—"

"If nobody came for me when I was on TV, nobody's coming for me now," Finn protested, squirming away. "I'm fine, Gus, but you—you're a nervous wreck."

This time Finn said "Gus" as if the man were a friend he wanted to help, not someone Finn had just accused of lying.

Gus leaned his head back against the side of the SUV. He gasped for air as if he'd run up and down a football field several times, not just tackled a kid half his size.

"Can't trust . . . anybody," Gus murmured. "Can't tell . . . Can't speak the words . . . aloud . . ."

"Give me one of his coins," Lana said to Kona.

Kona tilted her head doubtfully, but she dug into her shorts pocket and handed Lana a coin.

Lana crouched beside Gus.

"Please?" she said, holding out the coin to him.

Was she *paying* him? Asking him to let her keep the money?

Or should Finn not even be thinking of it as money?

Finn decided not to ask. Everyone was silent, watching Lana and Gus.

Gus groaned and closed his eyes, as if he were too weak to keep them open.

Or too scared.

"You're my boss's daughter," he said. "Does *he* know about the coins and levers? Did he know you were spreading truth even as he got paid to spread lies?"

Lana shook her head, then seemed to realize Gus still had his eyes closed.

"You know my father would have turned me in," she said. "You know he was loyal to the party. To the Mayor, to the government, to all the benefits of propping up the people in power. . . . You know he got a lot of money and power from spreading lies."

Now Gus peeked up at her, his one eye half-cracked open.

"And you say you heard me make the recording for one of my coins—was I that careless?"

"No, I was that *sneaky*," Lana corrected. On someone

else's face, her grin would have looked cocky. But she still seemed too frightened for that. "You were in a soundproof recording studio but . . . I was, too. Out of sight. It was how I found out a lot of things my parents and teachers wouldn't tell me. I hid there all the time. Studio 2-B."

"That studio," Gus repeated dreamily. "Such a perfect name. I went there just 'to be.' To exist. To reassure myself I was real, and that what I was thinking and feeling was true, no matter how much I had to tell lies everywhere else. Some days, that was the only thing that got me through, thinking about how I could go there and tell the truth. . . ."

"And the way these coins work—you thought you were sending them to my dad?" Rocky asked. His face twisted as if he were still about to cry. "It didn't happen. My dad never got any of your coins."

"No, no, I was too much of a coward for that," Gus said, shaking his head sadly. "Pathetic, isn't it? I saw others being brave, but . . . I never tried to send any of my own coins. Not until . . . until . . . just now. . . ." He gritted his teeth. "Here," he told Lana. "I'll do it."

He reached out and pressed one shaking, sweaty thumb against the coin in Lana's hand. When he pulled his thumb back, Finn saw that the coded message on its surface had transformed into three words: TELL OUR STORIES.

Gus pressed his thumb against the coin a second time.

Now his voice came out of the coin, rich and strong: "Here's something else I have to tell you . . ."

"Oh, right," Chess whispered. "You have to hit it twice to hear the message."

"And you can activate your own message?" Emma asked. "It's not just your double in the other world who can do that?"

"Shh!" Finn hissed at them both.

"This story's about one of the bravest things I ever did," Gus's voice continued, coming from the coin. "I heard through back channels that the Mayor and his people had stolen the lever Kate Greystone had in her basement in the other world. I knew she was in prison then, and there was nothing I could do for her directly. But I thought it would help her kids if I stole the lever back and returned it to her basement. And then I spread the rumor that the Mayor himself had wanted that to happen. I used the Mayor's own lies against him."

"You really did help us!" Emma gasped. "We did need that lever, and that was how we were able to rescue Mom!"

The last time, Finn thought. *The only time we succeeded. And then we just lost her again. . . .*

But that was something else he didn't say.

Gus stared directly up at Rocky.

"I never dreamed my fingerprints in that basement

would get your father into trouble," Gus apologized. "I thought of your world as perfect—I didn't think anything bad could happen there."

Rocky flinched.

"You sound just like my dad in that coin-recording," he muttered. "His voice, it's good and true like that and . . . he isn't perfect, and our world isn't perfect. But he tries. And he's kind, and . . ."

Rocky turned his head to the side, as if he didn't want anyone to see his face just then.

"Can we hear another coin?" Kona asked. "Or can you just tell us . . ."

Gus motioned for her to dig out another coin.

"There's another story the Greystone kids would probably really like," he said.

Kona held out another coin. When Gus touched this one, the code on its surface transformed into the words HEAR US. Gus touched it again, bringing forth his voice sounding stronger than ever, saying, "I never met Kate or Andrew Greystone. Eight years ago, I could have walked right past them on the street and never known who they were. But they were heroes to me, even way back then. I was friends with a physicist—let's just call her Gina, because she still has family around. There are still people who could be endangered if the government knew her connection to the coins.

Do you understand how awful this is, for all of us who want good things for our evil world? That we have to hide, even from one another? Gina was the only person I was ever honest with. Well, Gina, and now . . . you. Gina told me about this brave, crazy young couple who came to see her. They wanted to tell their story—*our* world's story—to the people they thought were most likely to listen: their own doubles in the better world Gina had discovered. They thought story-telling would help. When Gina told me that the first time . . . I laughed. This crazy couple thought stories were important, when our leaders had guns? And mind control?"

"You thought we'd like this story?" Finn interrupted, his voice shaking. "You thought we'd want to hear you make fun of our parents?"

"Not this part," Gus whispered back. "What's coming."

Gus's voice kept streaming from the coin: "Andrew and Kate had three children. Really little ones. And they told Gina they wouldn't be able to live with themselves if they didn't do everything they could to make the world a better place for their children. Gina invented the coins for them. They made Gina brave, too. She recorded her own story on her own coins. And she told me about it, and I started recording my story, too. And then there was a whisper campaign. People acted in public like they didn't have a brain of their own, like they just did what the leaders told them. Like they *worshipped* their leaders unquestioningly. But behind closed doors, in secret, I'm convinced practically everyone *except* the leaders have been making their own story-coins. I see them sometimes, when I'm out doing my job: a coin dropped here, a coin dropped there. And I'm convinced the coins help fight back against the poisonous odors the leaders developed to control us all. I think we could overthrow the leaders once and for all, if everyone would just stand up and send their coins out into the other world all at the same time."

"You recorded this before you knew about the mind-control TVs, right?" Rocky asked sarcastically. "Why does this even matter now?"

"Shh!"

Finn couldn't even tell how many of the other kids said that—maybe it was everyone except Rocky.

The voice coming from the coin turned sad: "I cannot force you to come and help me. The way things are in my world, that would have been my instinct: If it'd been up to me, I'd have designed a coin to make you think you *had* to travel here and assist me. But Kate and Andrew Greystone had more faith in humanity than I did. Than I do. Or, maybe they just had more faith and hope, period. They believed people from your world would help of their own accord, as soon as they knew our world's story.

"Maybe you have already listened to one of my other

coins, when I tell what happened to the Greystones, and to Gina. Two dead—Gina and Andrew. Four in danger—Kate and her kids. Gina was the first one killed. The first martyr. And I was in despair. But she must have known it was coming, because she had mailed me instructions. She had predicted that upon her death, all her coins—which she hadn't even sent out yet—could be turned into a different type of bridge between the worlds. It's almost like they were designed to . . . mature. Gina told me how to fuse her coins together to make a lever of sorts, that could open a temporary pathway between the worlds. And anyone could travel through that pathway. Not just people with a double in the other world, but anyone, from either world. It was like her bravery, her courageous example—that fused everyone together.

"So I followed Gina's instructions. And then I left the lever on Kate Greystone's doorstep one dark night when all the security cameras in the area were conveniently down for service. . . ."

Finn couldn't help himself: He threw his arms around Gus's shoulders.

"You saved us!" he cried. "Eight years ago, you were the one who gave Mom the lever to begin with! That's why you wanted us to hear that coin!"

Gus looked embarrassed.

"Oh—no!" he said. "I just wanted you to know what heroes your parents were. What they started. And how everything they did, everything they risked—it was always for you and your brother and sister."

Finn reached out and touched the coin they'd been listening to. He thought about how Emma had the math scrawlings that had once belonged to their dad, and Chess had a picture he treasured. But Finn had nothing that had come from their father. He'd never wanted it before, because he didn't even remember Dad.

"Could I . . . ," he began. "Could I keep this coin? Since you weren't able to send it to the other world, anyhow?"

Gus swiped his thumb across the coin, and the words translated back to code.

"I've got another one just like it," Gus said, sounding a little choked up. "Or . . . *she* does." He pointed at Kona. "I made multiple copies, because I heard how much trouble Gina had when she started sending out coins, before perfecting her system. And before everyone else working with Lana . . . and me . . . before we made our own improvements. You know the lettering on the coins, it's always your dad's writing, in tribute to him. But there were so, so many other people who worked on this."

Finn felt dizzy thinking about all those people. If only they'd been able to come out into the open and say, "Hey, do you want better leaders? Leaders who don't lie and try to make us afraid? So do I!" And then everything would have changed.

Or maybe they would have been killed, too. Just like my dad and Gina, Finn thought, with a shiver.

Kona was digging into her pocket.

"Actually, the only other coin of yours I picked up looks like the first one we heard, not the second," Kona said.

"No, I dropped *five* coins," Gus said. "And I'm sure that two of them—"

"I only picked up three," Kona told him.

Gus jolted back, almost clunking his head against the SUV. Then he scrambled to his feet and rushed to the spot where he'd been standing when the kids first saw him.

"You're not hiding any of the coins from me?" Gus asked Kona, even as he knelt down to search in the grass. "You didn't knock any to the side, or—"

"I picked up everything I saw!" Kona assured him.

Now all the kids ran over to Gus and started feeling around in the grass. The grass was cropped short, newly mown, and dense enough that any coin would have shown up clearly.

"Gus!" Lana exclaimed. "Two of your coins fell through all the way to the other world! The pathways must have opened again!"

The others began exclaiming, "Is it true?" "Does that mean . . . ?" "If it works for coins, then . . ."

Finn didn't wait for anyone to answer. He just snatched the lever from the bag he still held looped over his shoulder.

And then he slammed the lever as hard as he could against the ground.

FORTY-ONE

EMMA

"Finn, don't!" Emma screamed. "Not there!"

Because what if slamming the lever in the dirt meant the whole world shifted places? Or the worlds just . . . traded?

It didn't matter. Nothing happened. The lever didn't settle into the ground, ready to be turned. It just knocked a few tufts of grass out of place.

"I thought if the coins got through to the other world again, the lever would, too," Finn said forlornly, dropping to the ground.

"But only two of Gus's coins got through," Emma said gently. "And then three didn't. I bet the routes between the worlds only opened temporarily."

"And I bet it was when Finn was on TV," Kona agreed. She lifted Kafi away from the duffel bag she'd been climbing over and hugged her close. "Those people who went outside to look up at the sky—maybe they were actually thinking their own thoughts. Not just believing everything they saw on TV. Maybe there was a minute when they *wanted* to look at the sky. They weren't doing it just because of Finn."

"But then they turned around and started going back to the TVs," Chess said. "And that's when the routes probably closed. And the last three coins Gus dropped just landed on the ground here, instead of traveling anywhere else."

"They're right about how it worked, aren't they, Gus?" Lana asked.

Gus looked warily up at the light posts ringing the parking lot again.

"Yes," he whispered. "I'm sure that's true."

"But why?" Emma asked. "I can tell that everything's linked—the coins, the levers, the TVs, the smells we were used to before. But how can—"

Gus darted another glance at the light poles and sighed.

"It's a balancing act," Gus said. "Between the worlds. Between good and evil. And between the coins and the TVs. The Mayor and the other leaders—they took a big risk, leaving this world under control of the TVs, and going to the other one to take control there. I heard they started stealing our side's levers, from the very beginning. And they figured out how to make levers of their own. . . . If they can consolidate their control over both worlds, I doubt anyone will ever be able to defeat them. They'll have too much power for any coin, for any lever, for any*one*."

"But . . . ?" Emma said hopefully, because she knew there had to be one.

She knew they still had to have a chance.

"But right now, they're fueling their invasion of the other world by drawing on the power of all the minds under their control in this one," Gus said. "All that brainpower, all that energy—it's all being drained to help the Mayor and the other leaders who have gone to spread their evil in the other world. When people walked out and looked at the sky— suddenly they weren't working for the leaders anymore. They weren't doing what the leaders wanted. It was like . . . a power outage."

"Or a power *surge*," Kona said. "A surge of power for the good guys. For us."

"So we know what to do next!" Finn said excitedly. "I can go back on TV again. I'll tell people to go outside for, I don't know, *five* minutes. That gives us enough time to use the lever, doesn't it? We'll travel to the other world, rescue Mom and everyone else, and fight off the Mayor. Five minutes of telling people what to do—that's all I need!"

Finn was such an optimist.

"No," Gus said, shaking his head even more sadly than before. "You don't need to spend more time controlling people. What matters is how long they spend thinking for themselves. Each of them individually longing for goodness . . . And you had the element of surprise the last time. If you tried the same approach again, people would just shrug and think, *Enh, going out and looking at the sky didn't change anything before. So I'll just keep watching TV.*"

Emma scowled at Gus, because he was such a sad sack, so full of doom and gloom. How could he have worked with the coins for the past eight years when he didn't seem to have any hope at all?

I bet every bit of hope he ever experienced was just because *of those coins,* she thought.

She felt the first prickles of an idea jolting her brain. People always said getting an idea was like a lightbulb turning on, but for Emma, ideas arrived more like lightning. Maybe thunder, too.

"What if . . . ," she began. She could barely get the words together to explain. "What if . . . Gus, Lana, do either of you know where we can get more coins?"

Gus and Lana peered at each other. At first, they looked as secretive as ever, their teeth clenched, their eyes narrowed, their lips pursed. But maybe it helped that there were two of them. Maybe they had started trusting one another. At least a little.

Maybe they had started trusting the Greystones and Rocky and Kona, too.

"Ye-es," Gus said cautiously. The corners of his mouth ticked up, ever so slightly. On anyone else's face, this would still count as a scowl. But from Gus, this was definitely a smile.

"Then let's go!" Emma exclaimed. She grabbed Gus's arm, to tug him to his feet again. "Come on!"

FORTY-TWO

CHESS

Chess didn't feel hopeful.

Emma's plan involved filling an SUV with coins, bringing the coins back to the TV station, and then throwing the coins around in front of the TV cameras for the whole horrible alternate world to see.

"It will work because Gus believes so many people have made coins of their own, whether they've sent them to the other world or not," Emma said. "The coins will remind everyone what they really believe, what they really think and feel—who they really are. What hope they actually have. The coins will change everything!"

If the coins were going to change everything in this world, wouldn't that have already happened? Chess wondered.

But along with all the others, Chess climbed into the SUV they'd been hiding behind—which turned out to belong to Gus. What else was he supposed to do? Tell his own sister her idea was stupid? Cross his arms and sit down on the ground in protest while everyone else drove away?

Give up?

If I were in Horton Hears a Who, *I'd be the kid who doesn't bother chanting "We are here! We are here!" because I didn't think it mattered,* he thought.

It'd been a long time since Chess had read or listened to *Horton Hears a Who.* He couldn't remember if the boy who didn't help thought it didn't matter, or if he just wasn't paying attention.

Chess settled into one of the back seats of the SUV. To his surprise, Rocky claimed the seat beside him.

That was okay—he didn't need to save seats for Finn and Emma. They were up at the front of the SUV, excitedly chattering away with Gus about how many coins he thought there were in the whole alternate world, and how many he thought had made the journey to the other world, and . . .

Finn and Emma are like rubber balls, he thought. *The harder you knock them down, the faster they bounce back up.*

Chess didn't bounce. Knocked down, he had to struggle

to get back up at all. He crawled, he inched . . . he was like some mountain climber who could only move up a sheer rock cliff one fingerhold, one toehold at a time.

"I'm sorry," Rocky said beside him as Gus started the engine and began steering out of the parking lot.

Chess jolted—Rocky couldn't have known what Chess was thinking, could he?

"For what?" Chess asked.

"For back there," Rocky said, tilting his head toward the window and the parking lot beyond. "For falling apart in front of the little kids. It's just . . . at least you have your brother and sister with you. I'm alone. I don't know what's happening with my mom or dad or brother or sister—I'm not even in the same *world* as the rest of my family. And, no offense to your sister, but I don't think we're getting back."

Chess tucked his chin against his T-shirt like a turtle withdrawing into his shell. He knew he should tell Rocky, "No, you're not alone. We're all in this together." Or, "I'm sure your family's fine back in the other world. I'm sure they're just worried about you." But that was just more lies—Chess wasn't sure at all about Rocky's family. Or Mom, Natalie, Ms. Morales, Joe . . .

Maybe there was still a hint of the stink-grenade smell clinging to Chess's shirt; maybe the despair-filled scenes from the TVs had embedded themselves in his brain. Because what came out of his mouth was a bitter "At least you still have a father. At least your dad is still alive."

Chess immediately clapped his hand over his own mouth.

"I'm sorry! I'm sorry! I shouldn't have said that!"

Only then did he notice how red and watery Rocky's eyes were. Only then did he see how tightly Rocky clenched his jaw—a trick Chess himself had learned years ago, when it stopped seeming okay to cry in front of other people about losing his dad.

Now Rocky's eyes widened.

"The whole time I've been jealous of you having your brother and sister with you, you've been jealous of me having a dad?" he asked.

Chess couldn't look at Rocky right now. He fixed his gaze instead on the black leather seat in front of him.

"When you saw that guy—Gus—in the parking lot," Chess began, "when you ran out the door. There was a moment . . . it almost felt like, if that really was your dad, it would be like getting my own dad back. I would have felt that happy for you."

Chess felt his face go hot. Why had he said that to Rocky? He was like all the people of this world, making their useless coins and sending them to people they didn't even know.

Or just making the coins, and then being afraid to send them.

"But you knew that Gus guy wasn't my dad," Rocky said. "You *tried* to stop me. You tried to protect me."

Chess didn't say anything.

"This alternate-world stuff really confuses me," Rocky said. "But if there's a version of my dad in both worlds . . . isn't it possible there's a version of your dad in the other world? A good-world Andrew Greystone? Maybe after all this is over, if it ever is, you and your family could track him down to see, I don't know. See if you like him? See if it helps?"

Chess had never once thought of that before. He wasn't like Emma, who loved puzzling out what was the same in each world, and what was different, and why. Thinking about alternate worlds mostly just made Chess's head hurt.

Rocky's idea made his heart hurt, too. Dad was unique. Dad was special.

Dad was gone.

"Did it help *you* to meet Gus?" Chess asked. "To run up to some guy who looks just like your dad and have him not even know you?"

"*No*," Rocky said. "No, you're right. It makes it worse. Especially when Gus is such a chicken—'Oh no, what if someone sees me? What if someone hears me?' When he's *literally* sending out messages to the universe saying SEE US, HEAR US, FIND US."

Chess snorted out a laugh. Why hadn't he noticed before

that Rocky was as funny as Finn?

Probably because every minute we've spent together, we've been scared or desperate or running away from something. Or all three at once.

Maybe Gus, under different circumstances, would be funny, too. Maybe, if he'd been born in the other world, he'd be a great guy.

Because then he'd be exactly *like Rocky's dad . . .*

"Gus *sounds* scared, but what he's done is brave," Chess said. "Making the lever, giving it to my mom, making the coins, finally sending them to the other world . . ."

Rocky fiddled with the tape holding his coin around his wrist.

"What your dad did was brave, too," Rocky said. "And your mom." He shrugged. "My dad sells insurance. Want to know a secret? My friends voted once, and they decided my dad was the most boring of anyone's."

"I bet he just never had to be as brave as Gus," Chess said. He glanced out the window, at the countryside whipping past. Every house along this route was set far back from the road, but Chess could still see the glow of a TV screen in every window. His heart beat a little faster. "I mean, until you were kidnapped. Until he was falsely accused." Chess turned back to Rocky. "Hey, now that we know Gus, when all this is over, he'll be able to clear your dad's name with the police in the other world."

"Yeah . . . ," Rocky said. "You know what else? After this is all over, you and your family can come visit us in Arizona. Because of our moms being so much alike, it's almost like we're cousins, right? I never had cousins before. And my dad, he'll take you and me fishing. We don't even have to take the little kids with us. They can have a separate trip. I mean, I know it won't be like you having your own dad back, but . . ."

For a second, Chess could almost picture it: him and Rocky and Rocky's dad out in some river lined with red rocks—there'd be red rocks in Arizona, wouldn't there?

"That'd be . . . nice," Chess said. Then he laughed. "But you know the Finns wouldn't let us go without them! Or the Emmas!"

When all this is over . . . After this is all over . . .

Maybe Chess still had hope, after all.

Maybe Rocky did, too.

FORTY-THREE

FINN

"I want to know everything," Emma breathed.

"Me, too," Kona agreed.

Finn almost giggled. He'd snagged the front seat of the SUV, right beside Gus. And when he turned around to look at Kona and Emma behind him, it felt like he was seeing double. Not *exactly* double, of course—Kona's hair was longer, and Emma's skin was lighter, and even though she was his sister, Finn couldn't help noticing that Emma's chin was just a little bit pointy, and Kona's wasn't at all. But their eyes snapped with the same curiosity. And they were both sitting the same way: leaning forward, straining against their seat belts. Kafi had even crawled over onto Lana's lap instead of her own sister's, because Kona hadn't left her enough room.

"Your friend, Gina—how did she even find out the other world exists?" Emma asked.

At the same time, Kona blurted, "Do you know exactly when the two worlds split? And why?"

Normally, Finn zoned out when Emma started spouting off about alternate worlds—or, really, any scientific or mathematical ideas or questions. Emma was the one who loved science and math; Finn loved jokes and pranks. Sometimes she even figured out the science for his pranks, like mixing vinegar and baking soda, or Mentos and Diet Coke. They were a good team that way.

But he was the one who'd figured out the SEE US code on the one coin. He was the one who'd thought of using the TVs for good messages.

And . . . he had questions for Gus, too.

"How come you were the only one who could stay outside when everybody else went back into the cafeteria to watch TV?" he asked. "What made you different?"

"I don't know. I don't know. And . . . I don't know," Gus said as he turned a corner a little too sharply. "I don't know the answers to any of your questions."

"That's not fair!" Finn complained.

Maybe he'd chosen the wrong time to start paying

attention and asking questions like Emma.

"If any of us were your double from the other world, would you tell us?" Lana asked softly. "Have you recorded any of those answers on your coins?"

Gus stared straight out the windshield, as if he were driving through a blinding rainstorm or a terrible blizzard, and he had to concentrate hard.

When, really, the sun was shining, and the road was straight and clear and empty ahead of him.

"Gina said she figured out that the other world exists because the atoms were acting weird in some experiment she conducted," Gus said. "Or maybe it was something with molecules? I'm sorry—her explanation was much too technical for me. And that's the truth. You're kids! You're not going to understand theoretical physics anyway."

"I would like a chance to *try*," Emma muttered, as if he'd insulted her.

Kona high-fived her.

"And how about the way the worlds split?" Kona asked. "Did Gina have a theory about that?"

Gus groaned.

"You'd have to be able to study history—real history—to know that," he said. "Our leaders don't allow that. They only let us know the history *they* tell us. Which . . . is more lies."

"My mom said it was probably a thousand tiny decisions that made the worlds different," Emma spoke up.

"That makes sense," Gus said. "This world, we didn't reach this point overnight." He pointed out the windshield toward a house surrounded by razor wire, the glow of TV battles showing through its windows. "It was people deciding again and again not to trust their neighbors, not to care about their neighbors, not to believe the people who were warning, 'Your leaders are lying. It matters! Look for what's true!'"

"That's what my mom and dad were saying," Finn said proudly. "And, Gus, at least you told the truth when you recorded your coins. And you *did* resist the TVs enough to stay outside."

"It's . . . a fight every minute," Gus said. The veins in his hands stood out where he was clutching the steering wheel so tightly. A muscle jerked back and forth in his jaw. "I'm not sure how long I can do this."

Then he clapped his hand over his mouth, as if he hadn't wanted to admit that.

"I bet you're stronger against the TVs because you knew Gina," Emma said.

"And maybe because you're connected to the Greystones, too," Lana whispered. "Because you gave them their lever. Twice! And because you were in the other world. Even if it was just in the Greystones' basement."

"After all this is over, I'm going to find out all the answers," Kona said. "So I can know things for sure, not just guessing. I'm going to study everything about the two worlds."

This time, Emma fist-bumped Kona.

"But is it ever going to be over?" Lana asked, her voice trembling. "Doesn't it feel like . . . like the TVs around us are getting stronger?"

"Because we're closer to the most populated areas of the city now," Gus said through clenched teeth. "Where there are more TVs."

Finn looked away from all the houses and fences and barbed wire along the street they were on now. Instead, he ducked down to hug Lana's duffel bag with all her coins. For good measure, he hugged the bag containing the lever, too. Both had ended up on the floor at his feet.

Then he decided it was greedy not to share.

"Here," he said, lifting the duffel bag to balance it on the console between him and Gus. "It'll make you feel better to be closer to the coins."

"Maybe it helps to talk about the coins, too," Emma said. "I know you said Gina invented them, but who's making them now? I mean, the earliest version of the coins, before anyone records anything on them. Before you and Lana and people like you smuggle them out."

"I'm sure there's a factory somewhere, but we're not allowed to know its location," Gus said. "It'd be too dangerous, because if the leaders ever caught us, they'd make us take them there. And . . . they'd destroy it."

"I guess we could show you where Gus and I get the coins—right, Gus?" Lana asked.

Gus was staring out the windows too intently to answer.

"I've never seen these streets so empty," he muttered. "Normally, this time of day, there'd be cars and people everywhere! We're almost to the heart of downtown!"

Indeed, they were surrounded by such tall buildings now that Finn couldn't see the tops of any of them.

That's fine. That means I can't see if they all still have those scary blue-and-orange banners, Finn told himself.

But it was eerie to see such empty streets in a place where he'd only ever seen crowds of people packed in so tightly they could barely move.

"It's like a bomb went off, and we're the only ones left alive," Lana muttered. She hugged Kafi even tighter.

Finn tried to think of something to cheer up the others. But just then they passed a soaring building with evil-looking stone creatures carved around all its doors: the Public Hall, where his mother's trial had been.

Finn's stomach began to churn.

The twisted mouths of the stone creatures might as well have been saying, *Give up! You're going to lose! You're just a kid! You can't do anything!*

Maybe the carvings were like the bad smell and the TVs and the coins—maybe they had power, too.

Or maybe they were more like the orange-and-blue banners that wreathed the Public Hall; those just *reminded* Finn of the government's evil powers.

That was bad enough.

"What's with the weird color scheme?" Kona asked, and Finn loved that she could say that so casually.

She hadn't been with the Greystone kids at the Public Hall the last time, when they had to leave Finn's mom and Kona's dad behind. Orange and blue weren't nightmare colors for her like they were for everyone else.

But Lana gripped Kona's arm in distress.

"Don't talk like that!" Lana protested, gazing around as though she feared guards would jump into the car and arrest Kona on the spot.

"Blue and orange are the colors of this world's main political party," Emma explained.

"*Only* political party," Lana corrected. "It's the color for our leaders. For our government. For everyone in power."

"Okay . . ." It sounded like Kona wanted to object, but instead she asked, "Why those colors in particular?"

"The blue stands for the sky and the ocean—meaning it's all around us," Lana said. "It sustains us like air and water. The orange represents fire and energy, the passion we should all have for our political leaders."

She recited the phrases as if she'd memorized them. She probably had.

Finn hadn't known any of that, but it made him feel even worse about all the blue and orange he'd seen in this world.

"The party's like air and water and fire, huh?" Kona muttered. "Or . . . maybe those colors mean that if you don't have any other choice besides 'the party' about what to believe in and what to do, it's like that could suffocate, drown, and burn you."

Now Lana actually put her hand over Kona's mouth, as if she was trying to get Kona to take back what she'd said. Kona jerked away.

"Isn't that true?" Kona asked. "Isn't the party dangerous? Aren't your leaders evil?"

"Shh," Lana said. "It's not that I disagree, but . . . please, just . . . shh. Someone could hear."

"We're in a *car*!" Finn protested. "Who's going to hear?"

"Gus's SUV could be bugged, and we wouldn't even know it," Lana said. Her face had gone almost white with fear again.

"And there are security cameras all around us. Someone

could read our lips," Gus agreed.

"But everyone but us is just watching TV!" Finn reminded them. "We're not in any danger at all right now!"

He looked back at Emma and Kona. Chess and Rocky were peering up from the back seat now, too. Finn grimaced and tilted his head and rolled his eyes, hoping the others could figure out that he was saying, *Are Gus and Lana totally losing it? What can we do?*

The vein in the side of Gus's neck throbbed like it was about to explode. Lana was slumped down in her seat now, her eyes closed.

Then the SUV came to an abrupt stop.

"No, no—keep going!" Finn begged. "Until we get to all the coins you promised us!"

Gus turned his head slowly, as if he were fighting for control of his own body.

"I stopped because . . . we're here," he said.

"We are?" Finn turned eagerly toward the window.

They weren't that far past the Public Hall, but this felt like a different part of the city entirely. An abandoned-looking building sagged alongside the cracked sidewalk. Like the Public Hall, though, this building had elaborate wood carvings all over it. And they were the same kinds of grim wooden shapes: demons, wolves, snakes, and . . .

Wait—isn't that an angel? Finn thought. *Down near the*

ground? With beautiful wings?

He blinked, and suddenly everything made sense. He *knew* this building. He recognized the green tile on the roof, the cut-out shape of the walls, the arches over the boarded-up windows.

Or, at least, he knew it in the other world.

"Guys, I know where we are!" he cried. "That's the Cuckoo Clock! This world's version, anyway!"

"The restaurant?" Kona asked. "Ohhh . . ."

Emma sprang out of her seat.

"And *that's* where the coins are stored?" she asked. "That makes so much sense!"

FORTY-FOUR

EMMA

Emma shoved the SUV door open and scrambled down
to the sidewalk. She could hear the buzz of voices in the
distance—had they parked that close to one of the TVs?
She resolutely tuned out the background noise, and avoided
looking at anything beyond the building immediately in
front of her.

"It's just *wrong* to put all those evil carvings on this
building," she groaned. She patted the wall. "Poor Cuckoo
Clock!"

"Not all the carvings are evil," Finn said, jumping down
beside her. "Look!"

He rubbed his fingers against a carving that was exactly at eye level for him, though not for Emma. She knelt down.

The carving Finn was pointing to was definitely an angel, not a demon. And it was the same kind of angel they'd seen back at their own Cuckoo Clock—and, before that, hidden under Judge Morales's desk.

"What happens if we press this angel's wing?" Emma asked. "Lana, Gus, do you know?"

"Don't . . . We can't. . . ." Gus was still inside the van, still clutching the steering wheel.

But Lana was climbing out of the SUV alongside Kona, Kafi, Chess, and Rocky. She was staring at the angel just as intently as the other kids.

"Go ahead," Lana said, her voice almost mischievous. "Try it."

Finn and Emma tapped the wing at the same time. The angel's mouth opened, just like the angel's mouth back at the other world's Cuckoo Clock. Emma cupped her hands under the angel's jaw.

And then, just as she expected, a coin tumbled out.

"That is so sweet!" Finn roared. "Who does that coin belong to?"

"Nobody," Lana said. "Yet."

Emma ran her fingers over the coin's smooth surface. It

was completely blank. She flipped it over—the other side was blank, too.

"This is a coin *ready* for someone to use," she whispered reverently.

Lana nodded, her face lighting up with joy now, instead of fear.

"My school is five blocks from here," she said. "Most days after school, I come and lean against that wall. To everyone else, it looks like I'm just checking my cell phone. But I have my backpack open on the ground. I put one hand behind my back and press that carving, and the coins spill into my backpack. . . . And then I store them under my bed until I can pass them out in secret places around the city."

Her words bubbled out the same way Emma's did when she was talking about math.

"So you only carried around empty coins?" Kona asked.

"No, full ones, too," Lana said. "Sometimes I hid coins for people who weren't brave enough to send them out yet."

"I always thought there had to be hundreds of us secretly working together, even without knowing each other's names or seeing each other's faces," Gus said behind them. Emma saw that he'd finally stepped out of the SUV. But he was still holding on to one of the doors as if he didn't quite trust himself to walk toward them on his own. "I *liked* believing we were all working together, even if we couldn't acknowledge each other publicly. But . . ."

"But where are all those other people now?" Rocky finished for him. "You and Lana managed to escape the TVs—why didn't the others?"

"Exactly." Gus grabbed the sideview mirror of the SUV, and started breathing hard. "That noise, that noise . . . coming from the stadium . . ."

Emma dared to glance around the corner of the building. There was indeed a large, gleaming stadium just beyond. That was *not* like the setup with the Cuckoo Clock back in the better world.

"We hold a lot of political rallies there," Gus said. Even clutching the mirror, he swayed, as if he was about to fall over. "Maybe the Mayor's back. Maybe that's what we're hearing. Maybe he's already consolidated control in the other world, and it's too late for us to do anything but hide. Maybe we're going to get into trouble for not being at the rally with everyone else. . . ."

"No!" Lana said. "We came for the coins, and we're not leaving without them! Help me!"

She rushed to Gus's side. Emma and the other kids joined her, and the whole group half guided, half carried Gus toward the building. Lana brushed her fingers against another carving on the wall—Emma saw that it was a solitary lamb, looking a little lost in the midst of a lot of fierce-looking wooden lions.

But at Lana's touch, a stairway opened in the sidewalk, leading down to a basement door.

"It's like how *our* Cuckoo Clock has a basement stairway for deliveries," Finn marveled.

Lana began guiding Gus down the stairs, but he pulled away.

"I'm better now," he said. "I'm farther from the noise. Closer to the coins."

Emma and all the other kids were right behind him and Lana.

"Do you know the code to open that?" Lana asked, pointing to a padlock on the heavy steel door at the bottom.

"Three-five-four," Gus said. "Do you know what that stands for? The number of letters in 'air,' 'water,' and 'fire.' Because we're reclaiming them. The natural elements of the world do *not* belong to our leaders!"

Emma noticed that Lana had punched the numbers in even before Gus spoke them.

Ooooh, Emma thought. *She's just trying to distract him, trying to get him to focus on something good. Something besides the noise from the stadium.*

The lock clicked open, and Lana pulled the door back.

She must have hit a light switch, too, because suddenly

everything ahead of Emma glowed.

They were standing in front of mounds of coins—towers of them. It made Emma think of cartoons where people yelled, "I'm rich! I'm rich!" as they rolled around on stacks of dollar bills or gold.

But these coins aren't money, Emma thought. *They don't buy anything.*

Or did they?

Didn't Gus and Lana act like the coins could buy some sort of rescue for their world?

But that's not "buying," Emma thought. *That's caring. Wanting to help. Trying to find other people who can help.*

"Are these blank, too?" Chess asked, leaning down to pick up a handful of the coins.

Emma leaned close to look.

"No, there's code on all of them," she reported.

"Right," Gus said. "These are all coins belonging to people who haven't sent them to the other world yet. Maybe they just weren't ready. Maybe they're too afraid of being caught, and they wanted someone else to take care of it for them."

"But all you had to do to send your coins to the other world was drop them on the ground!" Emma protested. "People are afraid of *that*?"

"The coins didn't always work until recently," Gus answered. A shadow crossed his face. "People remember that. Sometimes it led to people being caught."

"They'll work for what we want," Finn said confidently. "How do we carry them?"

"Buckets," Lana said, pointing to the far side of the room, where stacks of buckets awaited.

The kids and Gus ended up forming a bucket brigade: making a line with each of them standing a few feet apart from the middle of the basement all the way up the stairs and out to the SUV. Emma was at the end, filling the bucket and handing it back to Gus before he handed it on to Finn. Chess and Rocky positioned themselves at the other end of the line, so they were the only ones who had to hear the noise from the stadium.

But this is going really fast, so we'll be out of here and back to the TV station in no time, Emma thought. *They won't be in danger out there for long.*

The buckets were heavy, but it started feeling like they were playing a game. The only way Kona found to keep Kafi from trying to eat the coins was by putting her in a bucket and passing her back and forth in between the buckets of coins. Kafi *loved* that, and squealed and giggled. Finn started pretending he could guess the stories embedded in all the coins, and in his telling, all the stories were hilarious.

"These belong to someone who invented pickle ice cream!" Finn cried, passing a bucket on to Kona. "It's really big here—that's one of the things that's *better* about this world!"

"We don't have pickle ice cream," Lana protested.

But she laughed as hard as anyone at his tales. Even Gus cracked a smile once or twice.

Finally Chess called down the stairs that they'd packed as many coin buckets as possible into the SUV, and if they put even one more in, there wouldn't be room for people.

"When we get back, I can talk on the TV camera before we start throwing the coins around," Finn said as everyone headed back to the SUV. "I can tell a few jokes, make this whole world laugh—that'll help!"

"Of course it will," Emma agreed.

But all of them stopped laughing when they got to the top of the stairs. The booming voices from the stadium were louder now. Emma had to scramble quickly into the SUV to avoid listening.

"Quick, everybody—get in and shut the doors!" she called. She barely missed knocking over a bucket of coins at her feet. "Then we'll be around the coins, we won't have to hear any of that noise from the stadium. . . ."

It felt like everyone was moving in slow motion now. But then the last door slammed. Gus took off before the last person in—Lana—even had time to put on her seat belt.

"That's right!" Kona cried. "Get us out of here!"

Gus squealed the tires. He ran a stoplight.

And then suddenly he turned toward the giant, noisy stadium, not back toward the TV station.

"Gus, what are you doing?" Emma shrieked. "This isn't the plan!"

"I can't help it," Gus wailed back to her. "I don't have a choice!"

And then he slammed on the brakes, flung open his door, and took off running toward the stadium.

FORTY-FIVE

CHESS

"Everybody, stay calm!" Chess called.

His own heart pounded so hard he felt like his chest might explode. His brain felt like a bunch of tangled knots. He jerked his head back and forth, trying to watch out for everybody at once.

Gus—I need to go rescue Gus. . . . But the others need to stay here with the doors closed, and they wouldn't do that, they'd chase after me. . . .

Finn was already too close to the open door. Lana had her fingers wrapped around her own door handle. Emma, Kona, and Rocky had all taken their seat belts off. Even Kafi was crawling over the other kids' laps toward the door.

A loud voice boomed from the stadium, the sound coming in through the open door. The words were distinct now: "Your leaders have everything under control. All you have to do is trust your leaders."

Oh, right, Chess thought. He felt himself starting to fall into the soothing drone of the voice. *That is all we have to do. That's how we stay calm.*

He felt his pulse slow.

I don't have to be in charge. I don't have to be the big brother.

But he could see the strained look on Finn's face as Finn reached past the steering wheel toward the open door. Finn was trying to fight against the power of the voice.

Or was Finn moving toward the door to follow Gus into the stadium?

"Emma!" Chess screamed. "Grab Finn's hand!"

The voice from the stadium tried to take over his thoughts again. But he could hear another voice in his head, one that fit there more naturally: his mother's, saying, "You'll always have each other."

I don't have to be the big brother, Chess thought. *I get to be that. I'm lucky. We're a team.*

"Emma! Hold Kona's hand, too!" he shouted. "Everybody hold hands! We have to stick together!"

Chess grabbed Rocky's hand and reached for Lana's.

Ahead of him, Emma grabbed Finn's wrist.

And then Finn knelt on the driver's seat and yanked Gus's door shut.

The booming voice outside instantly became several decibels softer.

"That was close," Rocky muttered, dropping Chess's hand and drawing back from Lana.

Lana immediately opened the door beside her.

"Lana, no!" everyone screamed at once, even as the roar from the stadium grew again.

Unlike Gus, Lana didn't take off running. She inched one foot out the door, but turned back and clutched Kafi as well. She moaned, "Please . . ."

"Oh no," Kona exclaimed, grabbing Lana's arm even as she protectively swung Kafi out of reach. "You are not going anywhere, and you are definitely *not* taking my sister with you!"

"I can't—I can't—"

Lana had tears rolling down her face. But both her feet were out the door now. She turned so she was on her stomach across the seat, sliding down.

"Lana, you *can*!" Chess yelled. "You're the strongest person we've met here!"

"You're Coin Girl!" Finn encouraged.

"You're smart!"

"You're brave!"

"You're good!"

That was Emma, Kona, and Rocky, chiming in.

"But I'm *alone*," Lana wailed. "I don't have brothers and sisters like the rest of you. I don't have parents who love me. Now I don't even have Natalie anymore—I don't know where she is. . . ."

"You are not alone!" Chess roared. "You've got us!"

He dived over the seat, reaching for Lana. Rocky must have done the same thing, because the two of them landed together on the seats that Emma and Kona had just abandoned. Oh. It was because Emma and Kona had already grabbed Lana, to pull her back into the SUV.

Except, somehow Lana was completely outside of the SUV now.

And a second later, so were Emma, Kona, and Kafi.

And Finn.

"We know what's best for you," the voice boomed from the stadium. "We know everything that you need. You don't have to worry at all."

Maybe . . . , Chess thought. *Maybe . . .*

He longed for that voice to be right. He wanted everything it said to be true.

But it wasn't.

"No!" he screamed. "Rocky, help me! I can't do this without you!"

"We have to get out of the SUV," Rocky said.

Rocky was right—the two of them wouldn't be able to reach the others without stepping down to the ground, too.

But this is how they catch us, Chess thought.

None of them were running toward the stadium, but they were going to end up there, anyhow. All of the kids were together—but that just meant that they were oozing toward the stadium in one big blob, like an amoeba.

But amoebas don't have brains, Chess thought. *We do. We've got seven of them.*

Lana took a step away from the SUV, closer to the stadium.

And then she froze.

"I see everything now," she cried. "I can see who's in the stadium! I see rows and rows of people, all watching TV. . . ."

Without even thinking about it, Chess inched closer to her.

What Lana had seen—and what Chess could see now, too—was the giant screen at one end of the stadium. And the giant screen showed all the people inside the stadium. It was like an infinity loop, people watching themselves watch themselves.

A label stood at the top of the screen:

THESE ARE OUR ENEMIES. THE PEOPLE WHO COLLABORATED WITH THE OTHER WORLD THAT INVADED US.

"It's everyone I ever knew who was brave and good!" Lana wailed. "There's Natalie, there's her mom. . . . What if all the people here . . . what if it's everyone who ever tried to send a coin into the other world? And everyone who ever tried to smuggle an endangered person to safety? Everyone who ever worked against the government? What if they were all captured but me and Gus? Because we were never as important . . . The leaders knew all along what we were doing! They were just waiting for the right moment to punish us! And . . . now they're using us all as scapegoats! And that's what we deserve!"

"Lana! They're tricking you to make you think that!" Emma screamed. "Wait, just . . ."

"But it's true!" Lana screamed back. "We *were* collaborating with the other world! Or trying to! Oh no, oh no . . . what if we were the evil ones all along?"

"Lana, no!" Kona yelled. "What you were trying to do was *good*!"

Lana took another step toward the stadium. At the same time, she turned back to shout to the others, "It's too late for me! But save yourselves! Find a way to go home. . . ."

Chess had so many voices in his head now. One said, *Let her go. You don't even know that girl.*

One said, *Go with her. This is your world, too. You have been a collaborator. The leaders of this world believe your whole family is evil. Maybe they're right. What if your parents had just gone along with what their leaders wanted? Wouldn't you have all been so happy then? Your dad would even still be alive.*

One said, *It doesn't even matter what you do. You don't matter. You're worthless. Useless. Pointless.*

But those were not the voices Chess listened to. The voice he heard loudest kept throbbing through his brain, in time with his pounding heart.

And it said, *Keep trying. Keep trying.*

"Lana," he screamed. "This is not how your story ends!"

She didn't move back toward the SUV.

But she also didn't take another step toward the stadium.

Chess saw exactly what he needed to do.

"Rocky, hold on to the SUV!" he screamed. "Kona, hold on to Rocky! Emma, Finn, hold on to Kona and each other. . . ."

In seconds, they'd assembled themselves into a human chain, the way they would if they were trying to rescue someone lost in a blizzard. Rocky grabbed the sideview mirror of the SUV, the same one Gus had clutched earlier. Kona wrapped an arm around his waist and Emma's, with Kafi clinging to them both. Finn took Emma's hand and reached for Chess's.

They trust me. Why do they trust me? I could be wrong, Chess thought, and he knew that thought wasn't his. It didn't really belong in his head.

If he was wrong, they'd just have to try something else. They'd always keep trying.

Lana stood absolutely still, not moving in either direction.

And then Chess reached out and wrapped her in a big hug, and everyone together pulled Lana back toward the SUV.

FORTY-SIX

FINN

Finn sat with his back pressed against the side of the SUV, right beside the front tire. This was where they'd all landed, everyone jumbled together. Finn dug the heels of his sneakers into the pavement, pushing himself as close as possible to the other kids and the SUV full of coins.

Nobody quite dared to stand up and try to climb back in. Nobody suggested any plans.

Nobody spoke at all, except for the giant, horrible booming voice coming from the stadium, talking about how evil everyone was who'd ever made a coin or sent anything into the other world.

It took every ounce of self-control Finn had not to stand up and run over to the stadium and let the voice take over. Just managing to stay by the SUV seemed like a giant victory—bigger than the Olympics, bigger than the World Series, bigger than the Super Bowl. Bigger than any championship Finn had ever dreamed of winning.

And all he was doing was sitting.

But we have all those coins, he thought sadly. *We were on the right track. I was so sure!*

On his previous trips to this horrible world, Finn had counted on Chess and Emma and their friend Natalie to understand all the scariest details, so he didn't have to.

He understood more than he wanted to now.

The coins aren't enough, he thought. *Not if we just sit here until the Mayor comes back.*

He could just imagine the Mayor coming back in triumph, him and all the other horrible leaders marching into the stadium in some sort of victory parade. Everyone in this whole world would cheer them on, so proud that their leaders had taken control of the other world, too.

That was going to happen. That was what Finn *wanted* to happen.

No, Finn thought. *That's what the voice is making me think I want. Just like it's making me think I want to go watch that big screen with everybody else in the stadium.*

"How . . . how do we fight it?" he asked, his voice coming out scratchy and weak, as if he hadn't used it in a million years.

Nobody answered him. Maybe nobody heard him.

The plan they'd had before wasn't going to work. Gus was gone, and if they went into the stadium to drag him back, they'd all just get trapped, too.

Without him, none of them knew how to drive the SUV. Even if one of the big kids tried, they'd probably just crash.

It'd been a stupid plan, anyhow. It was silly, the kind of thing an eight-year-old boy would dream up when he was imagining being a hero, and the older kids around him were too nice to just say, "Grow up!"

Finn wasn't a hero.

Finn wasn't grown-up.

Finn *was* silly.

But sometimes silly is good, Finn thought. *Sometimes silliness is what everyone needs.*

He remembered how he and Chess and Emma and Natalie had gotten their first clue toward rescuing the Gustano kids because of the Greystones' cat, Rocket, playing with a phone cord.

No—it had begun with Finn *noticing* Rocket playing with a phone cord.

Emma's first good idea for finding a second tunnel into

the alternate world had come after Natalie jokingly threw a pillow at her.

And Chess had found their first coin by pressing a carved wooden angel wing at a restaurant for kids' birthday parties.

Take that, you stupid voice coming from the stadium! Finn thought. *We win by being silly! Because that's what* you *don't understand!*

"Pickle ice cream," Finn said. "Succotash. Cuckoo! Cuckoo!"

It was a perfect imitation of the bird springing out of the clock back at Finn's favorite restaurant—the one in the *good* world.

Emma looked over at him and giggled. Kafi patted his face. It would be stretching things to say that Kona, Chess, Rocky, or Lana cracked a smile, but at least they all stopped frowning so intensely.

Finn dared to straighten his spine and look toward the jumbo screen in the stadium once more. He could see only one small corner of it, but that was enough.

"Our plan isn't ruined!" he cried excitedly. "There are TV cameras in the stadium, too. They're filming here now. We can just go on camera here, and throw the coins around the whole stadium. We're still going to beat the Mayor!"

FORTY-SEVEN

EMMA

Finn's idea wouldn't work.

Emma knew that.

But it wasn't like knowing Fibonacci numbers or the Pythagorean theorem or pi—that was knowledge that made her happy.

This knowledge made her want to cry.

I guess I'm not actually smart enough, she thought.

Emma had *always* been smart enough. She'd been plenty smart enough for school. She'd been smart enough for her own brothers to call her a genius. And she'd been smart enough to figure out Mom's trickiest codes, even when they were layered one on top of the other.

This time around, though, she hadn't even been smart enough to sit down with the coded coins and the uncoded coins to figure them all out. FIND US, SEE US, HEAR US, HELP US, TELL OUR STORIES. . . . She could have found anagrams in the translated words; she could have scrambled and unscrambled the letters and looked for all sorts of extra codes.

But that had never felt necessary. FIND US, SEE US, HEAR US, HELP US, TELL OUR STORIES—that was all the people from this world had asked for. They thought that was enough to change their world.

And things had only gotten worse.

Maybe the real problem is, it's not enough to be smart, Emma thought with a pang.

She *was* smart, and she'd still nearly been trapped by the TVs three times. The first time, they'd all been lucky, and Kafi had unplugged the TV. The second time, Emma had been saved by thinking about Finn, and not wanting him to be trapped, too. The third time, she'd been saved by looking at Chess.

And, oh yeah, I had coins that third time, too, but . . .

But the coins weren't enough, either.

Hmmm, Emma thought.

She tucked herself more tightly into the space between

Chess and Finn. All of the kids had their backs pressed hard against the SUV now. All of them had their feet braced against the pavement like they were playing tug-of-war with an invisible rope.

Their opponent wasn't invisible. Or silent.

Through the entryway to the stadium, Emma could see a swath of the giant screen, the cameras panning across one face after another. Emma was glad she couldn't see Other-Natalie or the Judge; she wouldn't have been able to bear seeing their familiar, beloved faces looking so blank and lifeless and obedient. Not when they looked so much like the Greystones' friend Natalie and her mother—and *their* faces were always so alive and expressive.

And if we went into the stadium—even with a good plan, even with the best of intentions—we'd end up looking lifeless and blank and stupid, too, Emma thought hopelessly. *We'd end up falling under the spell of the screen and that loud voice telling us the leaders know everything, and we should never ask any questions or think for ourselves.*

It wasn't like they could blindfold themselves to avoid peering at the screen. And they didn't have earplugs to block out the voice.

But . . . I am actually managing to block out the voice now, Emma thought. *How?*

Was it because she was thinking so hard about people she loved?

Was it because she hadn't given up?

Emma dared to glance once more toward the giant screen. She fought against the thought, *Finn's idea won't work,* and wondered instead, *How could we change Finn's idea to make it work?* For the first time, she noticed a railing at the top of the screen. She couldn't quite focus her eyes on it. Staring toward the screen was too much like staring into a black hole. Just looking made her feel like she was being sucked in.

That would happen to all the kids if they tried to enter the stadium, if they tried to stand in front of the screen to throw coins at the cameras.

But what if they climbed above it?

FORTY-EIGHT

CHESS, EMMA, FINN, KONA, KAFI, ROCKY, AND LANA

"Everybody, grab a bucket of coins!" Emma yelled. "Grab two! Grab as many as you can carry!"

"That won't work!" Rocky moaned. "We can't go into that stadium! We can't! We'd be trapped forever. . . ."

"You won't have to do that!" Emma exclaimed. "None of us will be trapped!"

And then . . . she stood up. She turned toward the SUV.

The other kids stared at her as if she'd just found a way to levitate. Or fly. It seemed that amazing that she could resist the voice coming from the stadium so easily.

It's because she believes her plan will work, Chess thought. *Because she's still trying. Because she still has hope.*

"Come on," Chess said, hoisting Finn toward the SUV as well. At the same time, Kona lifted Kafi; Lana stood and held out a hand to Rocky.

We can move like an amoeba toward good things, too, Chess thought.

No. They weren't moving like a brainless amoeba—they were moving like a team of individuals capable of thinking for themselves.

A team of individuals who all trusted Emma.

Emma began handing out buckets of coins to the other kids.

"What's the plan?" Kona asked. "Where are we taking these?"

Emma pointed.

To Rocky, who had a fear of heights that he'd never confessed to anyone, it seemed like she was pointing straight into the sun. Lana moaned, "Up there? On the catwalk?"

And then Rocky realized what both girls meant: There was indeed a walkway at the top of the giant screen.

"You want us to go up there and dump all the coins down in front of the screen," Kona said, catching on. "And all the people in the stadium will see them and remember their own stories, not the evil lies the giant screen is putting into their heads."

Chess, Rocky, and Lana exchanged glances. They were the oldest kids; they were also the most naturally inclined to be pessimistic. They weren't doubles of one another—or would it be *triples*? But in that moment, it felt like they were all thinking the same thought: *That is such a long shot. But . . . it's worth a try.*

"And at the exact moment that everyone sees the coins—" Emma began.

"One of us will swing the lever," Finn ended for her. "Because having people think about the coins instead of the giant screen will weaken the bad guys."

"And that could reopen the boundaries between the worlds," Kona added excitedly, bouncing Kafi. "At least temporarily."

"It'll be long enough," Finn said. "We can do this!"

All the kids moved quickly after that. For Lana, it reminded her of the first time she'd picked up a coin, the way just that simple motion had silenced the voices in her head whispering, *You're ugly. You're stupid. You're alone. Nobody cares about you.* Just that one action had made her start thinking, *At least I can do* something. *Maybe this one little change can make a difference. . . .*

Now she stopped hearing the roar of the voices coming from the giant screen. Even as she carried bucket after bucket toward the screen, she could focus instead on the gleam of the coins, the chatter of the other kids around her, the hope that Emma's plan would work.

This is actually better than the first time I picked up a coin, she thought. *Because then I was still alone. Or . . . I thought I was.*

It was eight flights of stairs up to the catwalk above the screen. The kids traveled in a pack: Chess and Rocky carrying four buckets apiece, Kona carrying two plus Kafi. Finn strained to be like Lana and Emma and carry one in each hand.

"If you start feeling scared or hopeless or like the screen is getting power over you, let the rest of us know," Emma directed. "We can cheer each other up. We can make each other brave."

That's what we've been doing all along, isn't it? Chess thought. *From that very first day we heard about the Gustanos being kidnapped . . .*

It made him think about how much Natalie had helped him and Finn and Emma on their previous trips to this awful world, and how much he missed having her along this time. The voice coming from the screen seemed to get louder, and he began to wonder, *Why did Emma, Finn, and I think we could accomplish anything without her?*

He tapped his wrist against the coins he still held in his pocket. He focused his gaze on Finn skipping up the stairs ahead of him. And then he thought, *I am doing this for Natalie, too. I am doing this for her and her mom, and her double in this world, and my mom and Joe. And for this whole world, and for the entire better world, and . . .*

And that was all it took to carry him to the top of the stairs.

The view from the catwalk was dizzying. The kids were so high up now that they could see the entire stadium below them. Hundreds of people—maybe even thousands—stood silently facing the screen, both on the ground and in the stands. From above, it was impossible to pick out individual faces. But all the people in the crowd cocked their heads at the same time; all of them turned toward the action on the left side of the screen at the same time, then back to the right side of the screen at the same time. It was like watching hundreds of people moving as one, because they were all thinking the same thoughts.

Because none of them were thinking their own thoughts.

"Space out the buckets evenly, and then we can topple them all at once," Emma suggested. "That'll get everyone's attention, and that's when we can swing the lever."

"Emma, didn't you say the lever only works in a place that's duplicated in both worlds?" Kona asked. "So it can't be here on this catwalk, right?"

"No," Emma said. Her voice went slightly shaky. "I was thinking I'd . . . run over to the Cuckoo Clock building and use the lever there. We know that building's in both worlds." She pointed, and the other kids gawked. They could see the alternate world's Cuckoo Clock building from this height, but it seemed tiny and impossibly far away.

"You can't go by yourself!" Chess protested.

"I'll go with you," Kona said, looping her arm through Emma's.

"But you have Kafi to worry about," Rocky argued, putting down his buckets.

Kona slid the little girl into his arms.

"I'm trusting you to take care of her," she said.

Rocky squinted at her in confusion for a moment, then he snorted.

"You're doing that to help me, aren't you?" he asked. "Because if I'm busy making sure Kafi isn't eating any coins, I won't get too scared."

"I know what it's like to be the oldest," Kona said. "And—we oldest kids have to watch out for each other!"

This is working, Emma thought. *We're all functioning as a team. It's like we're all doubles of one another in some way—we all have* something *in common with everyone else in the group. And sometimes we think alike. But it's not because anyone's forcing us to. That's a totally different thing.*

She lifted a coin from the top of one of the buckets.

"When Kona and I get over to the Cuckoo Clock building, we'll signal you with this coin," she said. "The sun's at the right angle so that we can flash a message in your direction. I'll do Morse code. Two dashes, one dot, then three dashes—that means 'Go!'"

Of course Emma knows Morse code for "Go!" Finn thought admiringly.

Emma and Kona left their buckets behind and went racing down the stairs. The sound of their footsteps disappeared into the roar of the voices coming from the screen.

And then there was nothing for the other kids to do but wait and try not to listen to the mind-control voices.

"We should stick close together until we see their signal," Chess suggested. His teeth were chattering even though he wasn't cold. He, Finn, and Lana moved in close beside Rocky and baby Kafi. Kafi patted each of their cheeks in turn and giggled.

"Kona left Kafi here to help all of us!" Lana exclaimed. "That was really smart!"

Finn leaned his head back against Kafi's arm. It reminded him of leaning against the coins. And of taping them to his forehead. Maybe that hadn't mattered as much as he'd thought. Maybe it was enough that the coins existed—and that they reminded him that other people wanted to share truth, not lies; good things, not bad.

Being near baby Kafi was good, too.

Finn peered out toward the Cuckoo Clock building. He hoped Kona and Emma were running as fast as they possibly could. They hadn't gotten to the open space yet where he might be able to see them.

Finn touched his forehead—somehow, all the coins he'd taped there had fallen off and he hadn't even noticed. He switched to pulling a coin out of his pocket: the one Gus had given him. The one that contained the story of how Mom and Dad had wanted a better world for their children. The one Finn had intended to keep as a memento of the father he never knew.

Finn held the coin over one of the buckets. And then he let it fall.

Because maybe that one extra coin will make the difference for someone in this stadium, he thought. *Because I'd give that up to fix the worlds and get back to Mom.*

Because he'd never forget what Gus had said about his father, anyhow.

He would always have that, no matter what.

FORTY-NINE

EMMA

Emma couldn't run as fast as Kona. Her breathing grew ragged and her steps faltered as they surged past the abandoned SUV.

"You should . . . go on without me," Emma panted. "I'm really only good at codes and things I can use my brain for, and you're good at that *and* sports, so . . ."

"Emma, are you kidding me? We both need each other to get to that building," Kona said, gesturing toward the alternate world's Cuckoo Clock building, far ahead of them across a vacant parking lot. She slowed down a little. "It's the evil screen making you think you're not as good as me, right?

Because what it's trying to tell me is, 'You can't really be good at both things at once. You're going to have to choose, smarts or sports. And, really, you're not that good at either. . . .'"

Emma tilted back her head as she ran and screamed at the sky, "Kona's good at everything! At heart things, too! Like being a big sister! Look how many times she's saved Kafi from swallowing a coin!"

Kona laughed, and for a moment, it almost felt like they were just two girls running as fast as they could together, just for fun.

Two friends.

"It *is* about the heart, isn't it?" Emma asked. "That's what we have that the other side doesn't have. That's how we're going to win."

Maybe she wasn't as bad of an athlete as she'd thought. She was keeping up with Kona now. But she couldn't get quite enough air in her lungs to both run and explain her idea to Kona.

Emma had relied so much on codes and brainpower on all her other trips to this world. But this trip had involved figuring out *people*, with all their secrets and fears and hopes and dreams and lies and truths.

And that had required both brainpower and . . . was there something called heartpower?

Did I just invent a new word? Emma wondered.

Maybe a simpler name already existed for what she was thinking about.

Love, Emma thought. *It's love. Kona loves Kafi and her dad. I love Chess and Finn and Mom. Rocky loves his parents and brother and sister. . . .*

Somehow, thinking that carried her straight to the alternate world's Cuckoo Clock building.

"We should go inside, right?" Kona asked. "So we don't turn the whole parking lot into a spinning slide or tunnel?"

Emma loved that Kona had caught on to the lever rules so quickly.

"Sure," Emma said.

They used the code Lana had taught them—3-5-4, for "air, water, fire"—on the nearest door. It creaked open, revealing a room that looked even more like the restaurant back home. There were tables and chairs, but they were covered in thick layers of dust, as if they hadn't been used in decades. The far wall even contained the same carved creatures that made up the official restaurant cuckoo clock back home. The clock was just missing its hands.

"Look—there's an angel here, too," Kona said, walking toward the wall. "I'll stand here and swing the lever at the angel wing as soon as you give me the signal."

Emma stepped back into the sunlight. She held up the coin and flashed it twice slowly, once quickly, and then three more times at a slow pace. She knew all the others back on the catwalk above the screen would understand: "GO!"

She let herself stare directly toward the top of the screen, which was barely visible over the seating area of the stadium. She saw a cascade of shiny gold and bronze.

"Now!" she hollered back to Kona. "Swing the lever at the wall!"

She heard the crack of the lever hitting the wall, then a second sound that she could have sworn was the wall growing around the lever, welcoming it in.

"Emma! It worked! The lever latched on this time!" Kona cried. "We just outsmarted the Mayor and all the other bad guys!"

Suddenly Emma remembered that she should have made sure the others knew Morse code for "IT WORKED! COME JOIN US AND LET'S GET OUT OF HERE!"

But then she heard Kona say fearfully behind her, "Emma? Emma? Is it supposed to be moving by itself now?"

Emma turned in time to see the lever seeming to rotate on its own—as if someone in the other world was trying to open the tunnel.

"Emma!" Kona cried again. "Who would be doing that? People on our side? Or our enemies?"

And Emma could only whisper: "I don't know."

FIFTY

CHESS

The last of the coins dropped quickly.

It seemed like the kids had had so many coins when they'd lugged all the buckets up the stairs. And the buckets had seemed so heavy and full as Chess and the others tipped them forward, balanced on the railing. The coins rolled down the screen like a quenching waterfall.

Chess felt so victorious, so powerful.

So happy.

But then the buckets were empty. One by one, Chess, Finn, Rocky, and Lana dropped the empty buckets to the floor of the catwalk.

"Should I throw these, too?" Finn asked, starting to peel off the coins taped to his wrists. "Because these would belong to Other-Natalie or the Judge, and it could help them to see these, too. Right?"

"No—no!" Chess cried, coming to his senses. He realized that Finn had already peeled off the coins he'd taped onto his face. Or maybe they'd just fallen off; Chess hadn't exactly had time to study his brother's face in the midst of fighting off the effects of the big screen.

"You might still need those for protection," Lana said, agreeing with Chess. "Because . . . we didn't plan very well, did we? Shouldn't we have arranged for some sort of conveyor belt to bring those coins back up, so we could *keep* throwing them? So people could keep looking at the coins instead of at the screen?"

"Or we could just shout for everyone to pay attention to us, now that they've seen the coins," Finn said. He began waving his arms and jumping up and down. "Hey, everyone! Up here!"

But Finn was just a little kid on a narrow platform eight stories up in the air. His voice was completely drowned out by the enormous speakers blaring from the giant screen beneath the catwalk.

Don't listen, don't listen, don't listen. . . . Chess thought.

He broke out in a cold sweat with the effort of fighting

against the noise. And against the temptation to climb down and look at the screen.

"*Did* people look at the coins, or was that all for nothing?" Rocky asked.

Chess couldn't quite bring himself to gaze out at the crowd. He looked at Finn. He looked at Kafi. He looked down at the pile of coins they'd poured onto the ground below the screen.

And . . . they were gone.

All of the coins had completely vanished.

FIFTY-ONE

EMMA

We messed up, Emma thought.

Numbly, she watched the lever turning on the wall in front of Kona.

"Should I grab it?" Kona cried. "Break it off the wall before somebody comes through?"

"But we worked so hard to find a place where that would work!" Emma protested. "If you break it off the wall, it won't work in that spot ever again. . . ."

She ran over beside Kona, as if she could protect the other girl. She grabbed Kona by the shoulders and pulled her back. They were still a dozen steps away from the door, but the two of them could cover that distance in a sprint if they had to.

Couldn't they?

The carved angel wing, the angel, and the entire wall around the angel began to shimmy. And then an entire section of the wall seemed to dissolve.

I'm always disoriented and dizzy when I change worlds, Emma thought. *Whoever's coming through here will be, too. So we'll have the advantage. We can wait and see who it is.*

But didn't it seem like, each time she crossed, Emma felt *less* disoriented? What if the person coming through now was an enemy who crossed between the worlds all the time, and had stopped being troubled at all by the crossing?

The wall appeared almost see-through now. Emma had never stood back and watched a doorway opening between the worlds before. She'd always been part of the spinning, the burrowing—the lever working its magic. She'd always been the one arriving, not the one waiting for an arrival. So it stunned her how much she could see into the other world, though it was all as hazy as a dream.

Or a nightmare.

She saw guards. She saw people sitting at tables and screaming, screaming, screaming as they spun.

And she saw a large TV screen high over everyone's heads.

Our Cuckoo Clock restaurant never had TV screens, Emma thought. *Who changed that—the Mayor? Are there stink grenades there, too? All sorts of mind-control weapons?*

She wanted to weep for the other world. The world that had always been the better one.

"Would it be . . . safer . . . outside?" Kona gasped beside her.

Emma was already running toward the door. She and Kona moved like a four-legged creature, both of them propelled by the same fear.

And then, as they burst out the door, Emma couldn't help looking back. She had to know. She had to find out exactly what they were running from.

A man stood just behind them, one step back from the doorway. He didn't look dizzy. He didn't look affected by the spinning he'd stepped through. He flashed a slow, lazy smile.

"Hello, Emma. Hello, Kona," he said. "Thanks for helping me."

His tanned face, his neon yellow shirt, his overconfident smile—everything about him was wrong, wrong, wrong. Because this man had the same features as someone Emma liked: Natalie's dad, Mr. Mayhew.

But this wasn't Natalie's dad.

This was the Mayor.

And he wasn't throwing stink grenades this time. He wasn't wearing a gas mask or screaming commands.

He wasn't doing any of that. . . .

Because he thought he'd already won.

FIFTY-TWO

FINN

"What happened to all the coins?" Finn asked, peering down at the ground alongside Chess. He saw nothing but an empty stage at the bottom of the screen. "Where'd they go?"

"We lost them!" Rocky moaned. He glanced once over the edge of the railing, and seemed to turn slightly green before backing away, clutching Kafi even tighter. "Our plan failed!"

"No, no, maybe . . ." Lana put a gentle hand on Rocky's back. She clutched Finn's arm. "Just let me think. . . . This could be a good sign. It could mean that . . . that . . ."

"You think the coins we dropped all went to the other

world?" Chess asked. "You think the pathways are open again? So maybe the lever worked for Emma and Kona, too?"

"Hurray!" Finn cried, jumping up and down again.

"But why . . . If the coins worked, then wouldn't . . ." Lana seemed to be having trouble getting words out. "I dropped every single coin I had. So . . ."

"Yeah, so did I," Finn said. He picked up one of the abandoned buckets and turned it upside down. "See? Nothing left."

"Right," Lana said. "But those were all other people's coins. I didn't just send out coins that other people made. I sent out all of my own, too. Ones that said FIND US. Ones that said SEE US. And HEAR US, HELP US, and TELL OUR STORIES. The complete set. For the very first time. Don't you see? I sent everything I had to the other world. Every plea! Every hope! Every story about me that mattered!"

"And you expected an answer," Chess said, as if he understood completely.

Lana nodded. The corners of her mouth trembled. She looked like Kafi when she was about to cry.

"Maybe . . . maybe it doesn't work exactly the way you thought," Finn said. He gazed toward the alternate world's Cuckoo Clock building, as if he expected to see another Morse-code message from Emma. "If Emma and Kona got the lever to work, you can just go *visit* your double in the other world. Everything will work out somehow. You'll see."

He was amazed he could say that so cheerfully when the giant TV screen still blared beneath his feet. But it felt like something had changed, just in the last few seconds.

He peered back at Lana. Then he blinked. Maybe the height was getting to him—he was eight stories above the ground. Maybe he'd been pulled back and forth too many times between the hope of the coins and the despair of the bad smells and the TVs. Or maybe his body was telling him that the one little granola bar he'd eaten back at Other-Natalie's house wasn't nearly enough to survive on.

Because suddenly Finn was seeing double.

He saw Lana right in front of him: the tears trembling in her eyes, her wispy hair sticking up, her teeth gritted in pain.

And then, right beside her, reaching out to her, was another version of Lana. One with the same high cheekbones and kind, gray eyes—exactly identical features. But this Lana looked excited and hopeful and a little awestruck.

And *confident*. This second version of Lana looked completely confident, completely at ease, completely comfortable in her own skin.

Even in a totally strange world.

"Lana!" Finn cried, suddenly understanding. "It happened! You got your answer! Your double's *here*!"

FIFTY-THREE

CHESS

Chess was stunned speechless.

The second version of Lana—Other-Lana?—held out her hand. A stack of coins lay across her palm as if they'd been fused together to form something more like a magic wand.

Or . . . a lever? Chess wondered.

"Thank you for trusting me with your story," the new girl said softly to Lana. "I know life has been hard for you, and it took a lot of courage to speak out. I listened to every one of the coins you sent me, starting a few years ago. But I didn't know there was anything I could do until the last coins arrived today."

"I . . . I was always afraid to send out the last ones," Lana mumbled. "I was afraid . . . things could get worse."

"How did you get here?" Finn asked. He reached out and touched Other-Lana's arm as if he couldn't quite believe she was real.

"The last coin came, and I just knew what I had to do," Other-Lana replied, her eyes twinkling a little mischievously. "The coins locked into place together and . . . maybe this wasn't *necessary*, exactly, but this is what I did. I held the linked-together coins over my heart and I said out loud, 'Yes. I'll help you, Lana-in-the-other-world.' And . . . here I am."

"The coins are bridges between the worlds," Lana said. Her eyes glowed, fixed on her double's. "I understand completely now. She and I, we're like anchors on either side of the bridge."

But that's not how our *lever works,* Chess wanted to protest.

And then suddenly he understood, too. He remembered what Gus had explained, about how he'd made the Greystones' lever from all the coins his friend Gina had left behind after she died. Her coin set had been completed in a different way. And so her stories had lived on after she was gone.

And Dad's story lives on, Chess thought, his heart beating faster. *In Mom and Finn and Emma. And me.*

The coin-levers/bridges just needed *something* in common in both worlds. The coins that Lana and Other-Lana shared were anchored in *people* who were doubled in both worlds. The lever that Chess and his siblings had always used needed to be anchored in *places* that were doubled.

Maybe there were dozens of ways the coins could be used that nobody had ever investigated yet, because everything had been kept so secret.

What do you know, Chess thought. *My brain can work like Emma's sometimes. When I stop thinking that it can't.*

"Okay, this is a sweet, touching family reunion," Rocky said. "Or . . . pseudo-family reunion. Whatever. But how are you supposed to help? What can you do that this world's Lana hasn't already tried to do herself?"

"We'll listen to each other's stories," Other-Lana said firmly. "She'll tell me all of hers. I'll tell her mine."

"What good is that supposed to do?" Rocky asked. He sounded like he'd been listening to the TVs again. With the arm that wasn't holding Kafi, he gestured toward the crowd in the stadium. "Don't you see all those hypnotized, brainwashed people out there? Don't you know we're dealing with a crazy dictator who wants to control what everybody thinks?"

"I don't know, Rocky," Chess started to object. "Think

about how scared Gus was when we were around him. Don't you think it would help for him to talk to someone who wasn't scared all the time, but was like him otherwise? *His* double?"

"He means your dad!" Finn crowed. "Don't you think it would help Gus to talk to your dad?"

"My . . . dad," Rocky repeated. His jaw dropped. He leaned far out over the railing. Then he thrust Kafi into Chess's arms and took off running for the stairs. "Dad! Dad! Dad!"

Kafi tilted her head, gazing at Chess. "Wo-ky go?" she asked. "Wo-ky happy?"

Chess held Kafi tight, but leaned out over the railing, too. From this vantage point, he could see the entire stadium—and somehow, since the last time he'd looked out, the crowd seemed to have doubled. People were jammed in tight now, but nobody seemed upset about the close quarters. People were hugging each other, high-fiving each other, putting comforting arms around one another's shoulders.

Everywhere Chess looked, people seemed to be in pairs. Duplicated.

"Lana!" Finn cried behind him. "You're not the only one whose double came! It looks like everyone in this stadium has a double helping them now!"

FIFTY-FOUR

EMMA, BACK AT THE ALTERNATE WORLD'S CUCKOO CLOCK BUILDING

"I'm not afraid of you," Emma told the Mayor.

The Mayor laughed, a harsh, cruel sound.

"Emma, Emma, Emma," he said, shaking his head. "We both know that's a lie. Your parents would be so ashamed of you. I thought your whole family was all in favor of 'truth.'" He made mocking air quotes as he spoke. "'Truth,' 'justice,' 'honor,'—don't you know none of those things really exist? Don't you know those words just mean whatever those of us in power *want* them to mean?"

"You're the one who's lying," Kona spoke up bravely. She kept her arm looped tightly through Emma's. The two girls stood shoulder to shoulder, each drawing strength from the other.

"Math," Emma said. "Two plus two equals four. That's a fact. It's *true*. Science. Water has two hydrogen atoms and one oxygen. That's true, too."

The Mayor laughed again.

"Kindergarten math," he scoffed. "Baby science. Don't you know that even math and science get a little . . . squishy . . . once you get to higher levels? Of course you don't know that. You're only ten. Only a little girl."

Emma *hated* it when people talked to her like that. She wanted to yell, "I know there's such a thing as quantum physics! I know about Schrödinger's cat! Just because something's complicated doesn't mean it's a lie!" But Kona nudged her gently in the side, and Emma reconsidered.

Maybe . . . maybe it's good that he's underestimating us, she thought. *Maybe he's not using the stink grenades or the mind-control TVs on us only because he thinks he doesn't have to. Because he's as lazy as his smile.*

Emma regretted not stocking up on "stink grenades" of their own—maybe filled with all the things the Mayor was allergic to.

But that wouldn't have been enough to beat him now, she

thought. *We're not going to win playing by his rules.*

Emma still wanted to believe they had a chance. She still *had* to believe that.

"And justice? Honor?" the Mayor continued. He rolled his eyes. "Those are squishy concepts to begin with. Whatever helps me, that's justice. Whatever I want to do, that's honor. I guarantee, that's how everyone thinks."

"Not my parents," Emma said at the same time that Kona burst out, "Not my dad."

"Not us," Emma added.

The Mayor snorted contemptuously.

"My dad *died* for truth and justice and honor," Emma said. "My mom and Kona's dad risked their lives and were imprisoned because they tried to rescue kids they didn't even know. Because they didn't think it was fair for another family to suffer the injustice of *your* world."

"It's your world, too, Emma." The Mayor's smile became even more mocking. He flicked his gaze toward Kona. "And you're here now, too, little girl. I guess you made your choice."

"What our parents did, it wasn't just about truth and justice and honor," Kona said.

Emma finished the thought for her: "It was about love. Everything our parents did, they did out of love. And that's why we came here, too."

The Mayor shook his head. His smile was positively evil now.

"If your parents had truly loved you, Emma, they would have just followed the rules," he said. "They would have stayed here and kept their mouths shut and done whatever their leaders told them to do. And *believed* what their leaders told them to believe. Your father would still be alive, if he'd done that."

Emma could think of so many things to yell back at the Mayor: Maybe, "My father wouldn't have been able to live with himself like that!" Or, "You don't know anything about love! Or truth or justice or honor!" Or, "Do you even believe your own lies?"

But just then, Emma was aware of a silence behind her. All along, she'd been subconsciously tuning out the blaring noise from the stadium, the drone of the giant speakers buried in the enormous screen. But that was gone now.

For a moment, everything seemed to hang in the balance, the silence waiting to be filled. And then a buzz began to grow in the stadium—not from any speakers broadcasting one message to everyone in earshot, but from dozens of voices (hundreds? Thousands?) all talking at once.

The Mayor pressed his lips into a narrow line.

"I made that happen," he said. "Now that I'm back, we don't need to use the same techniques here anymore."

"You're lying," Emma said, just as Kona asked, "Isn't he lying?"

The Mayor turned to address a row of people in dark blue uniforms directly behind him, still spilling out from the other world.

"Guards!" he said. "Arrest these girls! Then arrest everyone inside the stadium!"

FIFTY-FIVE

FINN

Finn, Chess, and the two Lanas took off after Rocky. They were halfway down the stairs when the giant screen beside them suddenly went silent.

"How did that happen?" Finn asked.

Lana grinned, and it transformed her face. If she and Other-Lana hadn't been wearing different clothes—Lana in green; Other-Lana in a purple dress—then Finn wouldn't have been able to tell them apart. They looked equally confident, equally certain.

"People stopped paying attention to the screen," Lana said. "Because they're talking to their doubles instead."

"Lana explained this to me through her coins," Other-Lana added. "The TVs got stronger and stronger the more that people watched them. So just now, when people stopped watching . . ."

"The TVs—including this screen—got weaker," Chess finished for her. He gazed out hopefully toward the alternate world's Cuckoo Clock building, where Emma and Kona had used the lever. "Does that mean the Mayor just got weaker, too?"

"I hope so!" Lana said, her grin growing even more.

Hope . . . , Finn thought.

They reached the bottom of the stairs and waded out into the crowd. Finn was pretty sure he could pick out the other-world double in every pair he saw before him: It was the teenager wearing a swimming suit, not the one in drab gray sweats. It was the girl with the fuchsia-colored hair, not the one with hunched-over shoulders and a hoodie hiding her face. It was the old man in the "Wheelchair Athlete" T-shirt, not the one huddled on the ground.

He saw doctors and nurses in scrubs, and men and women in leather jackets who looked like they'd just stepped off of motorcycles. A man in a sweatshirt that said "Proud Stay-at-Home Dad" with smaller print that said "Can't you tell by all the dried Cheerios on this shirt?" A woman wearing bowling shoes and carrying a bowling ball. Someone in a firefighter's coat. People with brown skin and black skin and white skin.

It looked like all types of people had dropped everything to come and help their doubles, as soon as they got their full set of coins.

Finn, Chess, and the two Lanas spun through the edges of so many conversations:

". . . and then I decided to study philosophy because I was curious about . . ."

". . . I think fifth grade was the most fun to teach . . ."

". . . the business I always dreamed of creating . . ."

". . . even though others said I'd never make a go of it, I was able to . . ."

Those were all people from the other world. And the people who looked beaten down and fearful were saying things like:

". . . the saddest day of my life . . ."

". . . if only I'd been brave enough to . . ."

". . . most of all I regret . . ."

Then the deeper Finn and the others got into the crowd, the more he started hearing the same kind of comments from the people of the awful world: "That was possible?"

"How was that possible for you? I never felt that was possible for me. . . ."

"Could I have done that?"

"Is that *still* possible?"

Finn turned around and tugged on Lana's arm.

"It's not fair!" he said. "The doubles are making all the people of your world think that it would be easy to change. To be just like them. But you didn't have all the chances Other-Lana had. You couldn't have made all the same choices. Because she lived in a better world."

He wasn't really thinking about Lana and Other-Lana. He was thinking more about his mom and Mrs. Gustano, his family and Rocky's.

They hadn't had the same lives at all, and it wasn't just because his mom and Mrs. Gustano had married different men. The Greystones had always been in danger; they'd always faced difficult choices, even though Finn, Emma, and Chess hadn't always known it.

Everything would have been fine for the Gustanos if Mrs. Gustano hadn't been Mom's double.

Lana and Other-Lana met each other's eyes and smiled.

"Oh, Finn," Lana said. "I'm not expecting to have the same life as my double. But seeing what's possible for her, knowing she can understand me and I can understand her . . . It helps me see what's possible for me, too. It helps me believe I can change—myself and my world. Even though it won't be easy."

Other-Lana held out the wand she'd made of all the coins Lana had sent her.

"Lana can choose how she wants to tell her own story," she said. "And what she told me so far—her story is really more about her hopes for the future, not just her regrets about the past. Nobody's story is over until they're dead."

"No, it's not over even then," Chess said. He gestured at all the people crowded around them. "All this, all these people here because of the coins—it's because of what my mom and dad and a woman named Gina started eight years ago. My dad and Gina didn't live long enough to know the coins worked. My mom thought for the past eight years that they failed."

"And then Lana and all these other people kept your parents' dreams alive," Other-Lana said. She gazed admiringly at her double. "I've never needed to be as brave as you, but . . . I hope that I would if I had to. I hope that I *will* be."

So it's not just that the bad-world people are learning from the good-world people, Finn thought. *They're learning from each other.*

He was no longer so sure that he could tell the difference between the people of each world. He let himself get a little lost in all the hope and excitement around him. After all the times he'd been drenched in fear in this world, now it felt like he was surfing on joy.

And then he heard shouts from the side of the stadium—a familiar voice amplified by a microphone or a megaphone: "That's right! Those are the orders! Seal off all the exits! Arrest everyone here!"

It was the Mayor.

The Mayor, who . . . hadn't lost all of his power.

FIFTY-SIX

CHESS

Run! Chess thought. *Save Finn and the Lanas! Before the exits are sealed! And, oh, how am I ever going to get over to Rocky and Gus, or Emma and Kona, or Other-Natalie and the Judge? Or . . .*

It was hopeless. Because Chess didn't just want to save his own family, his own friends. He wanted to save everyone in the stadium.

Everyone in the world.

Everyone in *both* worlds.

We can't run this time, he thought. *We need to . . . unite.*

Around him, the happy buzz of voices turned anxious and questioning.

And behind him, the hum of a TV announcer's voice came back to life, though it wasn't quite as booming as before: "The evildoers and warmongers from the other world have now been completely defeated, and our own valiant leaders have returned in triumph. Spontaneous celebrations have begun at rally points throughout the land. . . ."

Chess turned and saw that the giant screen had awakened again, too. Even though the actual Mayor was over to the side, just arriving, the screen showed a scene of Mayor Mayhew standing on a stage at the front of the stadium. On the screen, the Mayor smiled and waved as an adoring crowd cheered endlessly before him.

Around Chess, everyone else began turning toward the screen, too.

Chess couldn't stand it.

"That's a lie!" he screamed. "That's not what's happening here!"

At the same time, Finn stood on tiptoes beside him and hollered, "That's not true! Don't watch!"

"Don't give it power over you!" Lana and Other-Lana screamed, their voices blending perfectly.

Now the people around Chess were looking at him and Finn and the girls, not at the screen.

Chess wasn't like Finn—he hated people watching him. He hated speaking in public.

But right now, he had a voice.

And he was going to use it.

"Lana, you know about TV cameras, right?" he called urgently. "Other-Lana, are you enough like her that you do, too?"

"Absolutely," they both said, in unison.

"Then both of you, find a TV camera," he began.

His heart pounded. How could he explain his idea quickly enough? How could they all do what they needed to before everyone was looking back at the TV?

Before all the people here—even the doubles—were trapped?

"Oh, right," Lana said as Other-Lana added, "And then we'll figure out how to hook up the feed from our cameras to this screen. We'll meet you over there—"

"Right beside the Mayor," Finn agreed.

Chess didn't have to explain his idea, even to Finn. Everyone with him understood.

"Because we're going to get the Mayor to tell the truth," Chess said. "To the whole world."

FIFTY-SEVEN

EMMA, BACK AT THE ALTERNATE WORLD'S CUCKOO CLOCK BUILDING

"You might as well take Kona and me over to the stadium and arrest us alongside everyone else," Emma said to the guard who was starting to snap handcuffs around her wrists.

Kona flashed her a puzzled look, and tilted her head to indicate the alternate-world Cuckoo Clock building behind them, with its open tunnel back to the better world. Emma could tell Kona was asking, *Don't we want to stay close to the tunnel? Close to at least the chance to escape? And a chance to get back to your mom and my dad?*

"You know, there's this story," Emma said, pretending she was still speaking only to the guard, not Kona. "It's called 'The Emperor's New Clothes.' Have you ever heard of it? It's about how kids are better than anyone at giving compliments to political leaders."

Kona gave a snort of laughter that she quickly turned into a cough. Emma could tell that the other girl understood: Emma wanted to stay close to the Mayor in case they got the chance to expose his lies.

What Emma didn't expect was the guard's reaction. He met her gaze, his eyebrows arched.

And then he took off the handcuffs.

"Hurry along," he said, giving her a little shove. "Catch up with the Mayor then."

Wait—does *the guard know the "Emperor's New Clothes" story?* she wondered. She'd just assumed it was something that wouldn't have been allowed in this world. She'd thought she was safe using it as a code with Kona. *But is that why he let me go? Because he* wants *the Mayor to be unmasked as a fraud?*

She looked around, paying closer attention to all the guards streaming out of the alternate world's Cuckoo Clock building. Or maybe they were police or soldiers—she couldn't quite make sense of the varying navy blue uniforms, all trimmed in orange. All the people in uniforms clearly worked for the Mayor or this world's other leaders. Just the sight of the blue uniforms brought her terrifying flashbacks from her mother's trial at the Public Hall, and from the fund-raising party at Other-Natalie's house, which had ended in gunfire.

But the guards swarming around her and Kona now seemed more . . . independent . . . than the guards and police and soldiers she'd seen in this world before. They weren't rushing to obey the Mayor's every command with a snappy salute. They weren't moving in lockstep, keeping their eyes trained directly ahead. They were sneaking furtive glances here and there. Some of them were even whispering, though they fell silent when Emma edged closer.

Have they stopped being so loyal? Emma wondered. *Have they stopped being so brainwashed and afraid?*

But they were still marching toward the stadium. They were still carrying weapons: nightsticks and handcuffs and holstered guns.

Emma linked arms with Kona again and followed along with the guards and the police and the soldiers.

She and Kona reached the stadium just as the Mayor approached the stairs up to the stage right beneath the giant screen. An attendant handed him an official-looking navy blue coat, which he slipped on and buttoned up to his chin before mounting the stairs. Emma expected the guards to hold her and Kona back from the stage and the Mayor. But, oddly, the guards all stepped aside.

Emma and Kona raced up the stairs. They reached the stage only a few steps behind the Mayor.

"I think I preferred the catwalk," Kona groaned.

It was dizzying to be on the stage in front of the giant screen—to see the Mayor striding relentlessly ahead of them while a seven-story-tall version of the same man calmly smiled and waved from the screen.

This is like at Mom's trial, Emma thought, her heart sinking. *The crowd's seeing an entirely different version of what's really happening.*

But the crowd wasn't reacting the way the crowd had at Mom's trial. They weren't even reacting the way everyone had in this stadium before the coins dropped. People were leaning their heads together and mumbling, frowning and squinting doubtfully.

It gave Emma hope.

She and Kona caught up to the Mayor just as another group of people rushed toward him from the other side of the stage. Emma's heart clutched: It was Chess and Finn and Kafi; Rocky and Gus and another man who looked almost exactly like Gus—could it possibly be Mr. Gustano? And with them were two identical mother-daughter pairs: Natalie and her mom; Other-Natalie and the Judge.

But we left Natalie and her mom behind in the better world, Emma thought, desperately trying to figure out what had happened. *Mr. Gustano should still be back there, too. . . .*

The Mayor turned to glare at Emma and Kona just as Emma began tallying up who was missing.

He probably meant his glare to be fierce and forbidding, enough to silence any kid.

But Emma was done with being silent.

"What did you do to my mom and Kona's dad?" she shouted at the Mayor. "What did you do with the rest of the Gustanos?"

Her words seemed to echo, to boom out much louder than Emma was normally capable of speaking.

Just past Chess and Finn and the others, Emma saw Lana and another girl who could have been her twin—Other-Lana, perhaps?—both shouldering professional-looking video cameras. Emma turned her head—and saw her own face. Only, it was multiple stories high, taking up a vast section of the giant screen.

Lana—both Lanas, maybe—had just made sure that everyone in the stadium heard Emma's question. They were making sure that everyone in the stadium would see and hear the Mayor's answer.

Or were they broadcasting even farther than that?

What if all the people of both worlds were listening and watching?

FIFTY-EIGHT

FINN

Finn ran over and hugged Emma.

"You're safe!" he cried. "I was afraid the Mayor had gotten you!"

Emma absent-mindedly wrapped an arm around his shoulder. But her face said, *Uh, Finn? Don't you get it? We're not exactly safe right now. Not when we're standing in front of the Mayor and all his guards and police and soldiers.*

Out in the stadium, though, a collective sigh rose from the crowd, an adoring, "Awww . . ."

From the corner of his eye, Finn could see how he and Emma looked on the giant screen: an eight-year-old boy still wearing his Lego Batman pajamas, hugging his older sister in her math club T-shirt and gym shorts. Both of them still had coins masking-taped to their wrists. His hair stuck up at the back and hers stuck up at the front—*Well, sorry,* he thought, *we've been a little too busy this morning for either one of us to hunt down a comb.*

But people thought they were cute.

Finn was used to that. What he wasn't used to was thinking, *So we use that. "Cute" is our weapon.*

He turned back toward the Mayor.

"Could you answer my sister's question?" he asked. He held his eyes wide and hoped his face looked the same as it did when he was begging his mom for ice cream. "We just want to know where our mom is. And Kona's dad and Rocky's mom and brother and sister. Because . . . you attacked them. It was so scary."

Finn wasn't acting now. The Mayor and his stink grenades *had* been scary. It was still nightmarish, standing before this horrible man who had so much power.

If it weren't for Emma's arm around Finn's shoulder, he wasn't even sure he could keep from crying.

Maybe it would be okay to cry.

"I feel so sorry for these little children," the Mayor said. He gazed out toward the crowd as if he actually wanted all their sympathy for himself. As if he wanted to use Finn's cuteness weapon for his own cause. "I hate to break it to you, little boy, but your mother—these other children's parents, too—they're all criminals. Rebels. Outlaws. Enemies of the people." He seemed to be trying out insults, trying to see which would make the crowd hate Finn's mother the most. "Kate Greystone and Joe Deweese have been conspiring with our enemies for years, spreading lies and fomenting revolution. They're the ones who enlisted the warmongers from the other world to attack us. Warmongers like the entire Gustano family. So of course we had to arrest them. Of course we will need to punish them, to sentence them once and for all. That's how we keep our world safe."

"But that's not true!" Finn exploded. He heard Emma and Kona protest along with him; across the stage, he could see Chess, Rocky, and Natalie objecting, too.

"Isn't it?" the Mayor sneered. "Weren't your mother and Joe trying to overthrow the government? Didn't they criticize everything we did?"

Wait a minute—that part was true. How had the Mayor managed to twist everything around so completely?

"You're making it sound bad that they wanted your world to be a better place!" Emma complained.

"They weren't trying to hurt anyone," Kona added. "They were trying to help!"

"Yeah!" Finn agreed. But the word came out too weakly.

The Mayor patted Finn, Emma, and Kona on their heads.

"You're too young to understand now," he said, in the smarmiest voice ever. "But when you're older, I'm sure you'll want to make up for your parents' crimes by swearing your allegiance and undying loyalty to our government. And serving the cause faithfully, every day for the rest of your lives."

Finn had never felt so much like punching anybody. But that wouldn't help.

Desperately, he gazed across the stage toward Gus and Mr. Gustano, the Judge and Ms. Morales. They were grown-ups. Why weren't *they* helping?

Gus looked as sweaty and panicked as he had practically since Finn had met him. Mr. Gustano and Rocky were bent over him, as though they were trying to calm him down.

Okay, no help there, Finn thought.

The Judge and Ms. Morales had matching stony expressions, staring daggers into the Mayor's back.

"Judge Morales!" Finn cried. "You tell the crowd! You know the Mayor's a liar!"

The Judge clenched her jaw. Lana and Other-Lana turned their cameras toward her, and her beautiful, magnified face appeared on the screen behind the Mayor.

"Judges . . . must be impartial," the Judge said. "I might be asked to preside over the trial of one of these . . . defendants.

So I can't comment publicly on this matter."

Now Finn wanted to stare daggers at her.

But you hate the Mayor! he wanted to protest. *You want the government to change, too! You've been secretly working with my mom for years! The Mayor tried to kill you!*

"She must not think we can win," Emma whispered in Finn's ear. "She must think she still has to keep her true views secret. So she can continue to have power to keep working for good behind the scenes."

Ms. Morales put her arm around the Judge, as if she, like Mr. Gustano, thought she needed to comfort her double. But she also hitched her head slightly to the right, as if she was trying to tell the Lanas to put Finn and Emma back up on the screen.

This was ridiculous. The grown-ups were useless.

Or . . . was Ms. Morales just saying that the crowd would listen better to Finn and Emma than they would to the Judge?

The audience fell completely silent. Everyone seemed to be waiting for what came next.

This reminded him of the moment when Mom and Mrs. Gustano were staring each other down back at the Greystones' house. Each of them had seemed completely stuck, until Finn suggested going to the Cuckoo Clock.

So what's the Cuckoo Clock solution now? he wondered.

It really shouldn't all be up to him.

The coins were supposed to work, he thought. *Me talking on TV was supposed to work. Having the doubles come back was supposed to work.*

But everything had failed.

Or, no—everything had seemed to help . . . but only for a moment or two.

Finn thought about Mom and Gus saying it had taken all sorts of little, bad decisions to ruin this world.

Maybe it also took a lot of little, good decisions to make everything better.

What's the next thing that can help? Finn wondered. *After the coins, after the levers, after the coin-wands, after the doubles . . . the doubles of the people who wanted their double here, anyway . . .*

And then he knew.

"You know," he said to the Mayor, "you have a double in the other world, too." He peered out at the crowd—past all the guards, soldiers, and police officers to the rows and rows of people who had sought help from their doubles, and the doubles who had answered their pleas. "You all know how a double can understand a person. Can see what they're really like. *I* don't have an exact double myself, but I have other people around me who love me and understand me really, really well." He darted a glance at Emma, at Chess, at Natalie. Somehow the glance included Kona, Rocky, and Kafi, too—all the other kids who had been through so much with him. "Don't you think it would help to bring Mayor Mayhew's double up here on stage? Don't you think *he* would be able to tell us if the Mayor is lying or not? Don't you want to hear what he has to say?"

For an instant, the entire stadium remained silent. Then a whisper began at the back of the stadium. Quickly, it built into a roaring chant: "Bring! The Mayor's! Double! Bring! The Mayor's! Double!"

The Mayor's face went pale. He turned to the Judge, as if he expected her to tell him what to do. As if he thought she'd prop him up, as she'd always done.

But the Judge shouted out toward the guards and soldiers and police at the front of the crowd. "Didn't you see the Mayor give the order?" she called, even though he hadn't. "Go!"

"Yes, ma'am! Yes, sir!" someone yelled back. "We'll go and get your double from the other world immediately!"

They were lying, too—pretending to follow an imaginary order. Or . . . were they siding with the Judge instead of the Mayor?

A huge clump of people in blue uniforms broke off and began running back toward the Cuckoo Clock building.

Maybe this wasn't so much like lying, anymore.

Maybe they were just doing exactly what they wanted.

FIFTY-NINE

CHESS

Natalie reached over and clutched Chess's hand.

"My dad's weak," she whispered. "He doesn't like doing things that are . . . unpopular. What if having him here doesn't help at all? What if it just puts him in danger, too?"

Chess's heart beat so fast it felt like it might explode.

Natalie's holding my hand up here on this stage in front of hundreds of people! he wanted to scream. Oh, who cared about all the other people. Just the fact that Natalie was holding his hand was enough to make his heart do somersaults.

In another world, this would have been the moment when Chess said, "Do you want to be my girlfriend?" This would have been the moment when he thought of nothing but how good it felt to hold Natalie's hand; how wonderful it was to peer into her beautiful brown eyes.

But Chess was in the disastrous world he'd been born into, the world he'd vowed to help. It *did* feel amazing to hold Natalie's hand and peer into her eyes. But he couldn't forget about all the people around him.

He couldn't forget what he'd promised.

"We'll . . . figure out something," he whispered back to Natalie. "Isn't it a good sign that nobody's throwing stink grenades right now? And nobody's changing what the two Lanas are filming and putting up on the giant screen."

Natalie's eyes widened.

"I think the Mayor's afraid that if he gave orders about any of that, none of his guards would obey," she said.

Just then a cheer went up at the back of the crowd. Natalie's father, Mr. Mayhew, had arrived.

The crowd went silent as the guards walked him up to the stage. Mr. Mayhew was wearing a neon yellow polo shirt that could have been the twin of the one the Mayor had worn to impersonate him. And Mr. Mayhew was grumbling, "If you've done anything to harm my daughter or my ex-wife, I'll, I'll—"

Natalie let go of Chess's hand and flew to her father's side, assuring him, "We're fine. We're both fine." The Mayor gazed toward his daughter, Other-Natalie, as if he expected her to hug him, too. But she lifted her chin and said loudly enough for everyone to hear, "I'm not a political prop, Dad."

The crowd gasped.

"My daughter likes to make jokes," the Mayor said, sounding desperate. He looked toward Mr. Mayhew. "You understand what it's like, raising a teenager."

"I understand that I was playing a good round of golf this morning until I was interrupted," Mr. Mayhew complained. "Then guards rounded up everyone there, and we were all held hostage at some children's restaurant, along with my daughter and ex-wife and a lot of other innocent people. The Cuckoo Clock—is that what it was called? And then suddenly my daughter and my ex-wife were clutching a bunch of those coins from your world and saying, 'Oh, we have to leave now'—and then they just vanished. And then I was hustled over here, through that strange tunnel. I understand that—" His eyes met the Mayor's, and he fell silent for an instant. Then he said, in a marveling tone, "Oh. I do understand. I understand completely."

The weird doubles mind-meld was kicking in. Chess had seen it happen before with Natalie and Other-Natalie, with Mom and Mrs. Gustano, with the two Lanas. And, indirectly, with the entire stadium full of doubles. But he'd never seen it happen with doubles who were as different as the Mayor and Mr. Mayhew.

"What, Dad?" Natalie cried. "What do you understand?"

But Mr. Mayhew shook his head.

"What I heard was . . . in private," he mumbled, his gaze still locked on the Mayor. "I couldn't violate another man's confidence."

"Violate another man's confidence . . . ," Chess thought. *What's he talking about? He's never even met the Mayor before. Has he?*

And then Chess understood.

"He means he can't reveal what the Mayor told him through the coins!" Chess exploded. "Even as he was arresting people for sending coins to the other world, the Mayor was doing the same thing! If that's collaborating with the other world, then the Mayor's guilty, too!"

SIXTY

EMMA

The entire stadium erupted into shrieks and gasps. And boos.

The entire stadium—even the guards and police and soldiers—were booing the Mayor.

"We won!" Finn cried. "They don't like the Mayor anymore!"

"That's just how the crowd feels right now," Emma said. "Feelings can change. The crowd needs proof. Facts. Evidence."

Emma saw both Mr. Mayhew and the Mayor plunge their hands into their pockets at the same time. Both men hunched into identically defensive stances.

They're both carrying coins they're trying to protect, she thought. *Mr. Mayhew has the ones the Mayor sent. The Mayor probably has ones he's recorded but not sent anywhere.*

If only Emma could force either of the men to let the entire stadium hear their coins.

I'm still not going to be able to overpower the Mayor, she thought. *I'm still just a ten-year-old, and he's stronger and more in control.*

But what if she could trick him?

Suddenly she knew how to do it.

With trembling fingers, she picked off the coin taped to her own wrist. It was the undeciphered one she and Chess and Finn had found by pressing the angel wing back at the Cuckoo Clock. She still didn't understand who it belonged to, and she didn't want to let it go. But it was the only thing she could think of to use against the Mayor.

"Is this one of yours?" she asked, trying to sound innocent even as she flipped the coin toward the Mayor.

Panicked, the Mayor pulled his hands out of his pockets to catch Emma's coin.

At the same time, two coins fell from his own pocket. The Mayor scrambled so desperately to catch them that he missed reaching Emma's coin, too.

Emma darted quickly to his side. She snatched up all three coins.

"Those are mine!" the Mayor screamed. "Give them back!" He suddenly seemed to realize what he'd said, and jerked his attention straight out to the crowd. "I mean . . ."

"Of course I'll give them back," Emma said, smiling sweetly. She pocketed her own coin, but held out the other two. She pretended to trip in her eagerness to do the Mayor's bidding.

That meant that the top coin brushed the Mayor's thumb twice in a row.

Just like when Gus activated his own coins for us to hear, Emma thought. *Oh, please, let me be right about how this works. . . .*

The Mayor's voice came rolling out of the coin: "I get so tired of telling lies all the time. Just once, I would like to confess everything I am guilty of. . . ."

Quickly, the Mayor pressed the coin again, silencing it.

The entire stadium went starkly quiet.

It would have been fun to gloat, "Aha! I outsmarted you! I proved that you've been lying all along! And that you're guilty! And, look, I'm still only a ten-year-old girl. How stupid do you feel now?"

But Emma just leaned toward the microphone between the Mayor and Mr. Mayhew, and said, "So, confess. Tell everyone what you've been lying about all along."

"Oh no—I promise you, I only ever lied for good reasons," the Mayor said frantically, his eyes darting back and forth between Mr. Mayhew and the crowd. "My people, the citizens of this great city—any time I lied, it was always for your own good. And it's only ever been white lies, only in support of the government. Only to keep everyone safe."

"Safe?" Natalie sneered, stepping forward as well. "How can you call it 'safe' when you yourself arranged to have gunmen at the political fund-raiser at your house a week ago? Were you trying to kill your mother-in-law, your wife, *and* your daughter?"

"No, no—I didn't want anyone to die!" the Mayor said, gazing around, as if he expected Mr. Mayhew or the crowd to back him up. "What you're describing, that was just . . . political theater! I was just trying to hold on to power! Because the people need me as a leader!"

The crowd's silence felt different now. Emma saw people putting arms around each other's shoulders. Many of the pairs clinging to one another seemed identical. Emma squinted at them in amazement, and looked back and forth between the crowd full of doubles and the pair of Natalies, the pair of Lanas, the pairs of Ms. Morales and the Judge, and Gus and Mr. Gustano.

"The coins brought those doubles back," Finn whispered in her ear. "When the doubles got a full set—at least one of every kind of coin, I mean—the coins became, like, magic lever-wands. Emma, you would have loved seeing that!"

"I bet it was science, not magic," Emma whispered back. "Somehow."

Then she noticed that it wasn't just the doubled pairs hugging each other, out in the crowd. All the doubles were moving into clumps of four or six or eight, ten or twelve or twenty.

People were uniting all over the place, bracing themselves for what the Mayor might say next.

"But you did arrange for *my* grandmother to be killed, didn't you?" Natalie asked, staring fiercely at the Mayor. "In the other world."

"That was just . . . an accident!" the Mayor said. "We were figuring out links between the doubles in this world and that one. We didn't mean for it to happen like that! She was . . . collateral damage! Because we knew the other world was going to attack us—guards, soldiers—tell them!"

Mr. Mayhew, Other-Natalie, and both versions of Ms. Morales rushed forward to hug Natalie. But in the stadium beyond, a mumbling flowed through the crowd. Emma heard the same words rise up again and again: "Which guard . . ." "Which soldier . . ." "Who will tell the truth?"

And then a solitary voice spoke up, from a row Emma couldn't see: "The other world didn't attack us. We attacked them."

And then another voice that sounded almost exactly the same came after it: "I can guarantee she's telling the truth. I'm her double."

That's what the doubles are here to do, Emma thought. *"Help us tell our stories." Because they're the ones who know the truth.*

Emma turned to Mr. Mayhew.

"Can *you* vouch for the Mayor?" she asked. "Is anything he's told us true?"

"I can say . . . it's what he *wants* to believe," Mr. Mayhew said. "I can say . . . he's told so many lies, it gets harder and harder for him to know what's true and what isn't."

"You're going to bring up the kidnapping of the Gustano children next, aren't you?" the Mayor asked. "*That* was justified! It was just a slight mistake that we got the wrong kids. . . ."

"How dare you!" Mr. Gustano exploded. "How can you make that seem like an inconsequential thing—as if my children weren't harmed, my family wasn't harmed. . . ."

"You think it would have been all right to kidnap Finn and Chess and me?" Emma asked incredulously.

"Because your mother was such a threat to this world," the Mayor said. "She encouraged such insubordination, she spread so many lies. . . ."

"She just wanted people to be allowed to tell the truth!"

Finn cried. "It sounds like you wanted to be able to tell the truth, too, when you made all those coins and sent them to Mr. Mayhew."

"No, no, I just made them because . . . because . . ." The Mayor winced and clenched his fists. Then he opened his eyes wide and waved his arms as if he could make all the accusations disappear. "As a test! Yes, that's it—I only pretended to sound lonely. Only pretended I had any regrets. And I didn't send out any coins until today. That was just a . . . test, too. *My* coins didn't threaten the government. I never sent enough to change anything."

Except, he did, Emma thought. *Even if he only sent one or two, that was enough for Mr. Mayhew to know some of his story.*

Chess stumbled forward. As soon as she saw his face, Emma knew what he was going to ask.

"What about our father?" His voice came out clotted with agony. "Did you kill Andrew Greystone? Did you order his death? His and Gina's . . . Gina the physicist . . . Gina . . ."

"Chiukov," Gus said quietly from behind them. "Gina Chiukov."

The Mayor glanced around frantically, like he was looking for someone else to speak for him. His eyes lit on Mr. Mayhew's face.

"You tell them!" he appealed to Mr. Mayhew. "You understand, if you're like me. I'm not good—I mean, *we're* not good—at standing up to people. We don't like making hard decisions. Everything I did, I was just following orders. Doing what the people higher up in the party told me to do! The governor. The president. The people who were *really* in charge!"

"You—you—" Chess choked on his own words. He swung his arms like he wanted to hit the Mayor.

Emma and Finn rushed over and clung to Chess, anchoring him in place. It felt like Emma and Finn were taking care of Chess for once, not the other way around.

"So you *did* kill our dad and Gina?" Emma asked. Her voice came out sounding just as strangled as Chess's. "And Natalie's grandmother? You're guilty of all three of those murders?"

"No!" the Mayor exploded. His eyes darted about, as if he was trying to find a friendly expression to gaze at, someone to explain for him once again. But Mr. Mayhew stood as silent and stony-faced as everyone else in the stadium. Nobody moved. The Mayor wiped a trembling hand across his forehead and went on. "The rest of it—yes, I did those things. I made those mistakes. But I never killed anyone on purpose. I never *intentionally* ordered any deaths. That was the line in the sand that I promised myself I would never cross."

"You just made people wish they were dead," Lana said from behind her camera.

The Mayor grimaced, but he didn't deny it. He went back to staring directly at Chess, Emma, and Finn.

"You have to believe me," he begged. "Andrew Greystone was my *friend*. I liked him. I trusted him. I knew he—and your mom—would always tell the truth. And that was so rare, even eight years ago. I knew other people hated that about him—about them. But I was so low-level in the party back then, I didn't know about the plot to kill him. Or Gina Chiukov. And that's the absolute truth."

"But you benefited from his death," a voice rang out from behind them. "You used it."

It was the Judge. The Judge was weighing in now, too.

Does that mean she thinks our side is winning? Emma wondered.

But the crowd in the stadium started to boo the Judge, too.

"Don't do that!" Finn shouted into the microphone. "She's secretly good! She was just pretending to be a bad guy so she could smuggle endangered people out without anyone knowing!"

"If I had any doubts about revealing my secret, I guess it's out now," the Judge said with a wry smile at Finn.

One of the guards near the front of the crowd shouted, "It's true! I worked with her!" And then others shouted that as well. The crowd might have even worked their shouts into another chant, but the Judge motioned for silence.

"I made mistakes, too," she admitted. "What if I'd spoken up right away back then, instead of waiting until it was too dangerous to speak out publicly? It was so much easier to see the mistakes my husband made. The mistakes that turned into horrific crimes." She drilled her gaze into him. "People respected you back then. You had a choice. You could have called for an investigation into Andrew Greystone's death. People would have listened. You could have helped Kate Greystone reveal the rot and corruption at the top of the party. You could have helped put the *right* people in prison. But you chose to lie and cover up other people's crimes. And then your own career began to rise. . . ."

"I didn't have a choice!" the Mayor cried. "I didn't!"

"You did," Mr. Mayhew said, stepping up beside the Judge. "You had a choice. You were just too afraid to see it. And you still have choices now."

It's almost like Mr. Mayhew is the Mayor's conscience, Emma thought. *Because he understands him so well, because they're so much alike . . .*

The Mayor collapsed to the stage. He was weeping.

"I'm sorry!" he cried. "I'm sorry!"

Chess's face stayed rock-hard and angry.

"That doesn't fix—" Chess began. Emma couldn't tell if Chess was going to say "everything" or "anything."

But there was a stirring at the edge of the stadium just then, the crowd shifting around the same entryway Mr. Mayhew and the guards had come through. And then the crowd divided, people stepping aside for a small group of newcomers.

It was Mom. Mom and Joe and Mrs. Gustano and Other-Emma and Other-Finn.

At first they moved furtively, as if they were ready to dash off and hide if they needed to. But then, as the crowd parted for them, they began to walk more confidently, their backs straight, their posture proud.

"Kate Greystone! Joe Deweese! Kate! Joe! Kate! Joe!" the crowd began to chant. And then, throughout the stadium, the doubles who had come from the other world held up their coin-wands. The sunlight gleamed off one fused stack of coins after another—it looked as if everyone was holding up a torch to honor Mom and Joe and everything they'd done.

And maybe to honor Gina Chiukov and Dad, too.

As soon as they got to the stage, Mom and Joe took off running: Mom to embrace Chess, Emma, and Finn; Joe to wrap his arms around Kona. He pulled Kafi from Chess's arms and hugged her, too. And Kate Gustano and her two youngest kids were only a few steps behind, rushing toward

Rocky and Mr. Gustano.

The crowd's chant turned into "Thank! You! Thank! You!"

The guards and the soldiers and the police officers were chanting, too. They were showing their true loyalties, just as much as all the people who'd been arrested, just as much as the doubles who'd come from the other world to help.

And everyone was siding with Mom and Joe and truth, not with the Mayor, who'd wanted to control both worlds with his lies.

Laughing, Mom leaned toward the microphone.

"We don't need thanks," she said.

Emma scanned her mother's face, and for the first time in weeks—maybe the first time in Emma's life—Mom looked completely overjoyed and delighted, without the slightest hint of fear. And then Emma understood that she had nothing left to fear either. Between Mom's expression, the crowd's chanting, and the coin-wands still gleaming in the sunlight, Emma felt like she'd solved the easiest-ever code, read the least-hidden message, discovered the most apparent truth.

"None of us need any thanks," Emma said, leaning into the microphone beside her mother. "We've got each other again, now. We're safe, and you are, too. We know the truth. Nobody's lying to us anymore."

And then Finn leaned toward the microphone, too. He was Finn; how could he *not* want the last word? But Chess leaned with him.

In that instant, Emma realized what Chess had been about to say a moment earlier: *That doesn't fix the past.* It didn't. But everything they'd done had cleared the way for a better future. Chess—and everyone else—could move on. They'd fixed as much as they could.

For both worlds.

And so all four of the Greystones said the same thing, all of them together: "Now we've got everything we need."

SIXTY-ONE

EVERYONE, THAT EVENING

The Greystones were finally home. Again.

But this time they had lots of company with them.

The house where Natalie and her mother lived had been so badly damaged in the Mayor's attack that Mom had offered them a place to stay for the night.

"Oh, I couldn't—" Ms. Morales had protested, even as Mom countered, "Are you kidding? After everything you've done for us?"

Of course, Natalie and Ms. Morales could have just stayed in a hotel. But after being separated for so long, Natalie and the Greystone kids had a lot to catch up on.

Especially Natalie and Chess.

With Gus's help, the Gustanos—including Mr. Gustano—had managed to straighten out everything with the local cops in the better world. Nobody was accusing Mr. Gustano of anything anymore; the cops were just glad to see the family reunited.

But it had taken so long that the Gustanos were going to stay with the Greystones, too, before flying back to Arizona the next morning.

And Kona and Kafi and Joe were staying, too, along with Kona's mom, who'd rushed to join the rest of the family as soon as she'd heard that her daughters were in danger.

Even Mr. Mayhew had stopped by to join in the festivities—and to bring back the Greystones' cat, Rocket.

Now all the grown-ups were planning pizza orders.

"Which toppings do you all want?" Mom asked, her fingers hovering over the laptop keyboard. "Oh, never mind—this is a celebration! We'll get one of everything!"

"Seriously?" Finn asked. "Ask them to make up new flavors, too. Let's get pickle pizza! Succotash pizza!"

Just then, all the cell phones in the room made the same dinging sound.

"News alert," Joe read from his screen. "Peace delegations

between the two worlds sign agreement to end all hostilities."

Kona read over his shoulder.

"And the representatives from this world agreed to help the other world in arresting and prosecuting their corrupt leaders," she said. "And holding new elections." She looked up from the phone and grinned. "With more than one political party!"

All the adults began cheering and hugging.

"And the video of Emma tricking the Mayor into playing his own coin has now officially gone viral in both worlds!" Natalie reported, looking up from her own phone.

"Wait—was that in the official news report?" Ms. Morales asked.

"No, Other-Natalie and the two Lanas and I just made that happen," Natalie said. "We've been comparing numbers all afternoon."

"You got your cell phones to connect between the worlds?" Joe asked incredulously.

"Well, yeah," Natalie said with a shrug. "We're all friends now. We've got to have some way to communicate!"

While Natalie showed Joe her phone and explained what the four girls had figured out, Chess went straight to Mom.

"We don't have to hide anymore," he said. "So can I have

my own cell phone now? I'll pay for it myself. I'll do whatever chores you ask me to do. I'll put it away when it's time for homework. I'll—"

"Yes," Mom said, laughing. "Yes, Chess, you can have your own cell phone now."

"Now he'll just text Natalie all the time!" Finn complained. "He'll be all, 'Natalie, will you be my girlfriend? Y or N?'"

Chess froze, an embarrassed flush creeping over his face. But then Natalie's eyes met his over the top of her phone.

She was actually blushing, too.

"No, Finn," Chess said. "It'd be rude to ask a question like that by text. I'd do it out loud."

"So ask already!" Emma said.

"In private, I mean!" Chess said. "Just between the two of us!"

But Natalie was already nodding.

Everybody laughed and cheered all over again.

The pizza arrived, along with salad and breadsticks and chicken wings and chocolate-chip cookies and ice cream. Mom really had bought out the entire menu. Everyone ate their fill. Finn started out at the kids' table set up in the living room—where he and Other-Finn discovered they were great at sharing Hawaiian pizza, since Finn liked the ham but gave away the pineapple, while Other-Finn liked the pineapple but gave away the ham. Natalie and the younger two Greystone kids told about how awful it'd been when they were trapped at the Cuckoo Clock, unable to do anything but watch the mind-control TV for hours on end. The Greystones, Rocky, and Kona told about their adventures in the other world.

But before very long, Finn drifted back into the kitchen where all the grown-ups were eating in the midst of all the pizza boxes.

Mom and Joe were talking about the trials that would happen in the other world for all the leaders who'd lied and cheated and manipulated people in so many awful ways.

"The judges and juries will have to take their time and make sure everything is done fairly," Mom was saying as Finn sidled up beside her to give her a hug.

"They'll need good journalists covering those trials, too," Joe said. "So people *know* that everything is done fairly. I'm signing up to help—I can commute from this world every day. Are you in, Kate?"

"I'd love to, but . . ." Mom looked down at Finn, who still had his arms wrapped around her waist. "It's a little harder for me."

"You mean, because of Chess and Emma and me?" Finn asked. He gulped. Then he made himself push away from her, just a little. "Mom, that's crazy! You can go back and forth through the Cuckoo Clock's tunnel, and commute, too. If Chess is old enough to have a cell phone and a girlfriend, he's old enough to babysit Emma and me after school every day!"

"I can swing by and help if they need anything," Ms. Morales offered.

"I can, too," Mr. Mayhew said. "I really miss having your kids around every afternoon after school. Finn and me, we still need to work on our baseball skills!"

Mom threw up her hands.

"I guess I'm outnumbered!" she said. "So it's settled!"

But she was grinning, too.

When Finn went back into the living room, he saw all the other kids rushing toward the basement stairs.

"What happened?" he asked.

"Natalie and the Gustanos, they said . . . Oh, come on! You'll see!" Emma told him.

"This is how it felt when I started getting all the coins from the other world!" Natalie explained as she opened the basement door. "From Other-Natalie. But this time . . ."

"This time, wouldn't it be easier for her to text you than to use a coin?" Finn asked.

"We don't think it's from her!" Emma told him, pulling him along.

When they got down to the basement, Kona put Kafi down

on the carpet, and the little girl immediately crawled through Mom's Boring Room and into the secret room beyond.

"More," Kafi said, plopping down onto her diaper beside a little carving on the doorframe that none of the Greystone kids had ever noticed before.

It was an angel with impressive wings. Just like under Judge Morales's desk. Just like at the Cuckoo Clock—in both worlds.

"Why didn't you tell us you had a carving like this, too?" Kona asked.

"Because we *didn't*," Emma said. "I swear, that was never there before."

But suddenly she wasn't so sure. Could they have just overlooked it, again and again?

"I feel like I'm supposed to hit it first," Natalie said.

She did, and a coin rolled out into her palm.

"Now us," Rocky whispered as all three Gustano kids pressed their fingers on the angel's wing together.

They were rewarded with a coin, too.

Both coins contained the same type of code as the one the Greystones had found at the Cuckoo Clock, and the one Kona and Kafi had found in Kentucky or Tennessee.

"Oooh," Kona breathed. "Kafi, when you found our coin, did you press an angel wing, too? At that rest stop in wherever-it-was?"

Kafi nodded solemnly, as if she actually understood.

"But none of these coins change, right?" Natalie asked as she pressed hers again and again, and the Gustanos took turns doing the same with theirs. Natalie sent a quick, one-handed text, and then reported, "Other-Natalie says she didn't send me any more coins. In fact . . ." She waited for the next text to pop up. She squinted and shook her head. "She wants to know if *I* just sent *her* a coin. And Lana and Other-Lana are asking each other the same question."

Why would this all be happening at once? Emma wondered.

And then she knew.

"What if we all press the coins we got at the exact same time?" Emma asked.

Rocky shrugged.

"Worth a try," he said.

Natalie sent instructions to Other-Natalie and the two Lanas for a thirty-second countdown. And then all the kids announced the last few seconds together: "Five . . . four . . . three . . . two . . . one . . ."

They all pressed their coins. And as soon as they all pulled their fingers back, they all gasped at the same time.

The strange code had melted away on every single one of their coins to almost identical messages: either INTER-WORLD RESCUE SQUAD or PLEASE JOIN THE

INTER-WORLD RESCUE SQUAD.

"Press them again!" Finn shouted. But then, so did everyone else. Maybe even Kafi. He was just the loudest.

They all touched the coins again, all at once, and waited to find out whose voice they would hear.

At first, nothing happened.

And then the air before them seemed to shimmer and move to the side. It wasn't like when Kona and Emma had seen the tunnel between the worlds appear. This was more like suddenly facing a mirror they hadn't known was there—except that it was an infinity mirror. They all suddenly saw hundreds of Chesses and Emmas and Finns stretching before them in endless rows; hundreds of Natalies and Lanas and Konas and Kafis; hundreds of the Gustano kids as well. Or maybe it was thousands of all of them.

Maybe it was too many to count.

"Ohhh . . . ," Emma breathed. "We're not seeing just the other world now—we're seeing *all* the other worlds! Of course there are more than just two worlds! Of course! We should have thought of that all along!"

The words JOIN US fluttered across the mirror, followed by the words BECAUSE SOMETIMES SOMEONE NEEDS HELP ONLY YOU CAN PROVIDE, and then SOMETIMES IT'S ENTIRE WORLDS IN NEED. And

WE KNOW YOU CAN DO IT.

And finally, WE MAY CALL ON YOU AGAIN AND AGAIN.

And then the mirror image faded away.

Later, the kids would debate about exactly what they'd seen. Chess was convinced that in some of the images, Dad had been beaming proudly out at him—only it was actually other versions of Dad, alive and well alongside his children in some other world. And it didn't hurt Chess to see this. It only made him think, *I'm glad there's a happy ending somewhere.*

It was the same thing he thought every time he saw Rocky with Mr. Gustano.

Emma was convinced that Gina Chiukov—a *version* of Gina Chiukov, anyway—was the one who launched the words JOIN US across the mirror. And she thought that that Gina Chiukov had held a small penknife—exactly the kind that someone might use to carve an angel into a flat wood surface, possibly across multiple worlds. This wasn't quite proof, but Emma saw it as a great theory for who had made all the angel carvings.

And Finn? Finn maintained that a different tuft of hair stuck up in every single image of him, and that would give him a way to tell the different versions of himself apart if he ever got to visit more of the worlds.

"Let's watch that again!" Kona exclaimed.

But no matter how many times they tried to bring the images back, they were left with nothing but the coins saying INTER-WORLD RESCUE SQUAD.

"I guess it's a 'Don't call us; we'll call you' situation," Natalie said.

"It must be adults in charge of all of this," Finn said disgustedly. "The kind of adults who say, 'Rest up, because you've got a big day tomorrow.' And 'Don't get overexcited.' And 'You'll be able to do that when you get a little older. Just be patient.'"

"Isn't it great just to know that there *are* other worlds?" Other-Emma asked. "Where anything is possible?"

"And that we'll probably get to see a lot more of them?" Kona agreed. "And our adventures aren't over?"

"I'm going to get ready," Emma said. "I can't wait. I'm going to read everything I can about alternate worlds. And maybe about psychology and politics and anything else that could go wrong with any other world, that we could help fix . . ."

"Emma, didn't you *already* want to know everything?" Finn laughed.

"I—oh, right," Emma said. "Wonder if that's the same about me in every world?"

Somewhere, Chess thought, *there's a Chess who's just as excited as Emma and Finn about the possibility of going to other worlds again and again. Somewhere there's a Chess who doesn't wonder if he still needs to ask Natalie in private if she wants to be his girlfriend, or if that's already settled. Somewhere there's a Chess who's not always scared of anything new.*

And somehow, just thinking about those other Chesses made him feel better. He felt better about his place in this world, too. He'd work out things with Natalie. It wasn't like he was the old Chess, the one who was terrified of speaking to any girl besides Emma. Or the old Chess who'd been pretty much terrified of everything.

If we need to go help any of those other worlds, we'll be fine, he thought. *We all make a great team. And if there are more of us helping—even better.*

More worlds just meant more possibilities.

And right now, Chess could see only good possibilities ahead of them all.

ACKNOWLEDGMENTS

Writing a book is always a journey. Writing an entire series feels more like an odyssey, and that makes me even more grateful for all the help I've received along the way with Greystone Secrets.

From the very first book, I have greatly appreciated the way my editor, Katherine Tegen, and everyone else at Harper-Collins welcomed the Greystones and their friends into the world. (Er . . . this world. The real one.) This book in particular is so much better because of the questions Katherine asked me during the editing process. I appreciated her tact, consideration, and thoughtfulness throughout the process. Thank you also to Suzanne Murphy, Mark Rifkin, Kathryn Silsand, Sara Schonfeld, Nellie Kurtzman, Ann Dye, Audrey Diestelkamp, Robby Imfeld, Maggie Searcy, Audrey Steuerwald, Aubrey Churchward, Barbara Fitzsimmons, Aurora Parlagreco, Joel Tippie, Molly Fehr, Patty Rosati, Allison Brown, Andrea Pappenheimer, Kathy Faber, and Kerry Moynagh. And I am supremely grateful for the beautiful artwork Anne Lambelet created for the book covers, endpapers, and chapter headings.

When I decided the Gustano family would need to come back in this book, I wanted help thinking about what they would and wouldn't know about the kidnapping that set the whole series in motion. That also meant thinking about how the police would handle everything. So I decided to lay out the facts the police had—the limited facts without the very necessary detail that an alternate world was involved—to my cousin Karima Tahir, who is a sergeant II with the Los Angeles Police Department. It is a testament to her professionalism that she did not laugh at any of the outlandish details I gave her and went straight into telling me how the police would approach the case. (Maybe it is also a testament to her years of experience dealing with sometimes outlandish reality?) I was so grateful for her patience, her insight, and her perfectly logical questions, even if some of her questions made *me* laugh. The only cops who ended up in this book were alternate-world ones—and, in the background, ones who just did not know enough to draw the right conclusions. But Karima's help still played a huge part in setting the groundwork for me, and inspiring certain plot twists.

My sister and her husband and kids—Janet, Robert, Will, Jenna, and Meg Terrell—very helpfully served as consultants on certain kid expressions for the book. They graciously claimed that comparing the sarcasm levels of a kid saying, for example, "Seriously?" versus "*Obviously*" provided entertainment for them during the spring 2020 coronavirus lockdown—I mean, that kind of thing is always hugely entertaining for *me*, but I think they were just being kind.

I am always grateful to my entire family, especially my husband, Doug, for their support and encouragement. And I am always grateful as well for my overlapping set of Columbus writer group friends—Jody Casella, Julia DeVillers, Linda Gerber, Lisa Klein, Erin McCahan, Jenny Patton, Edith Pattou, Nancy Roe Pimm, Natalie D. Richards, and Linda Stanek—who feel like fellow travelers on every book journey I make.

This time I have saved my agent, Tracey Adams, to thank almost at the very last, because a journey's end always makes me think back to the journey's beginning. That is even more true when a journey becomes an odyssey. Greystone Secrets is the seventh series I've worked on, and *The Strangers, The Deceivers,* and *The Messengers* were/are my forty-third, forty-fifth, and forty-sixth books. But in many ways this series marked a new beginning for me. I remember sending Tracey a list of possible ideas for what I might write next, back in the fall of 2016. I am so grateful to her for zeroing in on my sketchy, incomplete description of something about a kidnapping and two sibling trios who have way too much in common—something that I described as only a "half idea."

But she confidently assured me, "That's the One."

She was right. And her confidence made me confident, too.

My wish for all my readers is that they have as many wonderful family, friends, and helpers around them on all their journeys and odysseys as I do. And as the Greystone kids do.

And thank YOU for reading this book!